MURDER
most
MAINE

MURDER

most

MAINE

—— *A* ——
Gray Whale Inn
Mystery

Karen MacInerney

MIDNIGHT INK
WOODBURY, MINNESOTA

First Edition
First Printing, 2008

Book design by Donna Burch
Cover design by Ellen Dahl
Cover illustration © 2008 Bob Dombrowski/Artworks
Editing by Connie Hill

Midnight Ink, an imprint of Llewellyn Publications

Library of Congress Cataloging-in-Publication Data

MacInerney, Karen.
  Murder most Maine : a Gray Whale Inn mystery / Karen MacInerney. —
1st ed.
      p. cm.
ISBN: 978-0-7387-1300-7
  1. Bed and breakfast accommodations—Maine—Fiction. 2. Murder—
Investigation—Fiction. 3. Cranberry Isles (Me. : Islands)—Fiction.
4. Maine—Fiction. I. Title.
  PS3613.A27254M85   2008
  813'.6—dc22

Midnight Ink
Llewellyn Publications
2143 Wooddale Drive, Dept. 978-0-7387-1300-7
Woodbury, MN 55125-2989, U.S.A.
www.midnightinkbooks.com

Printed in the United States of America

To Abby and Ian, the lights of my life.
I love you!

ONE

As I SIPPED MY first coffee of the day—a mug of steaming French Roast, topped off with hot milk and a dash of sugar—I pulled open the kitchen curtains of the Gray Whale Inn and watched a robin belting out a love song in a nearby maple tree. After several months of nothing but the sound of the wind whipping past the eaves, his lilting call was a delightful change of pace.

It was my second May in Maine, and although the bluebonnets had carpeted the hillsides in my former hometown of Austin two months ago, flower buds were just starting to appear on the hillsides of Cranberry Island. It was already in the 90s in Texas, but here, the last of the snow had just recently melted.

I gazed out the window at the big blue van I had transported to the island over the winter for hauling guests and luggage, and my outlook darkened a bit. The first birds might be returning to the island, ready to get spring underway, but the van was still hibernating. Despite a full tank of gas, I couldn't get it started, which was not good news, because it was the first day of the Lose-It-All

Weight Loss retreat, and ten people were due at the Gray Whale Inn that afternoon. It was a big booking for me, and the last thing I needed was for something to go wrong.

Of course, as it turned out, the van was the least of my troubles. But I didn't know that then.

I picked up the phone and dialed, turning to stare out the back window at the green spruce trees, the white-capped blue waves, and the fresh green field below the inn, which I knew would soon be awash in the blues and pinks of lupines. It was fresh, serene—and deceptively peaceful.

"Cranberry Island Store," my best friend trilled. Charlene was the owner of the little store that was often called the island's living room; it was also the island's pantry, post office, and gossip hub. Which came in very handy: kind of one-stop shopping.

"It's me," I said.

"Nat! The big retreat starts today, doesn't it? How are you holding up?"

"A little stressed," I admitted. "If the food order doesn't come in right, I don't know what I'll do." Hosting a weight-loss retreat was a new thing for me, and I had high hopes for it. If it went well, there was a good chance the Gray Whale Inn would be a regular location for it. After a lean winter at my fledgling inn, I was hungry for business. Ironically, though I was relieved the retreat would fatten my business's rather anemic balance sheet, I was also hoping it would force me to start trimming my own calorie intake. At my annual checkup a few weeks ago, both my cholesterol levels and the number on the scale had come up on the high side, and my doctor had issued a rather stern warning to cut back on the cupcakes. Since I was the owner of a bed and breakfast, and surrounded daily by tempting treats, this proclamation was not welcome news.

"Relax, Nat. I'm sure everything will be fine," Charlene said. "And if you need anything, you know I've got staples at the store."

"Thanks," I said.

"I'm glad you called; I tried getting in touch with you last night, but the phone lines went out for a few hours." Which was normal on Cranberry Island—along with regular power outages. "There's some big news."

"What happened?" I asked, my heart in my throat.

"Nobody got hurt," Charlene said quickly; she must have heard the dread in my voice. "At least not recently."

"What do you mean?"

"You know how they started the lighthouse renovation?"

"Yeah," I said. "I couldn't believe they started in February. In that brutal weather!"

"They're trying to get it done before tourist season," she reminded me.

After years of discussion, the island had recently decided to renovate its historic lighthouse, which had been boarded up for years. I was all in favor of the project, of course—not only are lighthouses a big attraction for visitors (and potential guests), but there was something magical about the round white building that graced Cranberry Point.

"Anyway, I guess you haven't heard the big news. They found a skeleton hidden inside it."

"You're kidding me," I said, my eyes drawn to the window and the innocent-looking lighthouse in the distance. I'd gone by that lighthouse a zillion times—as had everyone else on the island—

3

and had never imagined that there was a body inside it. The hairs on my arms stood up just thinking about it.

"Nope. Apparently it's an adult, but that's all they know at this point. They're taking it to a lab on the mainland for testing."

A shudder passed through me. "So that's two historic murders on the island." I'd recently discovered that a young woman had been murdered almost 150 years ago in the Gray Whale Inn, and although it had never been solved, I'd found a diary that implicated one of the island's most prominent citizens. How many other secrets were hidden on the island? I wondered. Biscuit, my ginger-colored and slightly obese tabby, brushed against my legs, and I jumped.

"They don't know if it was historic," Charlene said. "And no one said it was murder."

"Why else would you board someone up in a building?" I asked. Biscuit had started a plaintive meowing; to quiet her, I grabbed the bag of cat food and filled her bowl.

"I know a few of your guests would have benefited from a little time in solitary confinement."

"True," I said, thinking of some of the colorful characters I'd hosted since opening the inn a year earlier.

"Anyway, I'll keep you posted on the skeleton," she said. "Do you need any help getting everyone to the inn?"

At the mention of my guests—and my groceries—I glanced out the window at the van. Unless I could magically get it to start, I was in a bit of a pickle. Most of the time I relished the quaintness of living on an island where all of your supplies were delivered by mail boat. That was until I had ten people with very strict dietary requirements scheduled to stay for a week.

"I can't get the van to work."

"What's wrong with it?"

"I don't know—it just won't start. The problem is, how am I going to get my groceries from the dock to the inn?" I asked. "And the guests?"

"Hmmm," she said. "Why don't you take the guests over in the skiffs? It's supposed to be a gorgeous day—and that's sure to make an impression."

"I don't know…"

"If it doesn't start, just bring over the *Little Marian*. Get John to bring *Mooncatcher*, too. Between you, John, and Eleazer, we can manage."

I glanced out the window at the water, which was a bit choppy today. Unless a storm came up and turned the sea into Italian meringue, getting my handsome neighbor and the island's shipwright to help out just might work. I glanced out at the van. "If I can't get it started, I just may do that. Will you ask Eleazer when he stops by for coffee?" I knew the boat builder would be at Charlene's store today, not just for the sweets, but for a respite from his goodhearted but rather stern wife.

"Sure." She paused for a moment, then asked, "Any word on the personal trainer?" Charlene was between men at the moment, and actively looking for a new romantic interest. Which she could easily have found among any number of smitten lobstermen on the island—her curvy, padded figure and caramel-colored locks had been the subject of many local yearnings. Unfortunately for the lobstermen, though, none had passed muster.

"You're in luck," I said. "From what I hear, he's male, blond, and very handsome,"

"Straight?"

"You'll have to ask him that yourself," I said, grinning. In a place the size of Cranberry Island, which boasted a population of approximately 100 year-round residents, the arrival of handsome male visitors were quite an event. Charlene's last love interest had died unexpectedly, and since then, she hadn't shown much enthusiasm for dating. I took her renewed interest as a sign that the mourning period might be coming to a close.

"God, I hope he's not gay," she said. "Have you seen a picture of him?"

"No, I haven't. But he'll be on the three o'clock mail boat, so you can see for yourself."

"I'll be there with bells on," she said.

"I'd recommend a bit more than bells. It's still pretty darned chilly out there. Isn't it supposed to be spring?"

"Welcome to Maine, my dear," she said. "Oops ... got a customer. See you later!"

As I hung up the phone, I glanced out the window and said a brief prayer that the van would start. I had no idea exactly how many pounds my guests had to lose, but if they were extra-hefty, that would limit the number of people I could load on a skiff. Which meant it might take more than one trip to get everyone to the inn.

Maybe I should give the van one last try after all.

I grabbed my windbreaker, slipped on a pair of clogs, and flung open the kitchen door.

The scene was breathtaking—and not just because a brisk wind whipped most of the air out of my lungs the moment I opened the door.

The field stretched out below the inn like a soft green comforter, just coming to life after months buried under the snow. Across the dark blue water, the mountains of Mount Desert Island hulked, their granite shoulders cloaked in pale green. Despite the sparkling sunshine, the morning air was still brisk, and laced with the lingering scent of wood smoke from the carriage house just down the hill.

The sound of a boat motor floated to my ears, and as a skiff eased into view, I smiled. The panorama had just gotten a whole lot better.

"John!" I called, and my handsome neighbor docked the skiff and waved. He was wearing a green jacket that I knew matched his eyes, and the morning sun glinted on his sandy blond hair.

"Good morning, sunshine!" he called back as I paused on the path. "I decided to head out, see if I could catch us a couple of fish." He raised a hand, showing me a string of plump, gleaming fish as I stepped onto the dock.

I rewarded him with a long, lingering kiss that drove away any remaining chill. "You are the best neighbor *ever*," I said. More than just a neighbor, actually. We had been dating for some months, and although we hadn't officially spelled it out, we were slipping into comfortable couplehood. "I may have to ask another favor, too," I said.

"What?"

"If I can't get the van started, I'm going to have to get the guests here via the water. Can you and *Mooncatcher* give me a hand?" I asked.

"My pleasure," he said, grinning.

"My knight in shining armor," I said. "However can I repay you?"

"I wouldn't object to a plate of your blueberry pancakes."

"Done," I said. As he headed back to the dock to clean the fish, I climbed back up the path to the van in the driveway, which again refused to start. After the sixth try, which resulted only in a strong and worrying smell of gasoline, I retreated to my kitchen and pulled a bag of frozen local berries from the freezer. The van might not be working, but all was not lost. Not only would I have fresh fish for lunch, but I'd get to have breakfast with John to boot.

After a moment's hesitation, I grabbed a package of bacon from the fridge. Might as well have a last huzzah; from this afternoon on, it would be turkey bacon and melba toast all the way.

Things couldn't get much better, I thought a few minutes later as I folded frozen berries into the thick creamy batter.

Perhaps not. But they were about to get a whole lot worse.

———

When John knocked at the kitchen door twenty minutes later, carrying a Ziploc bag of fresh fillets, a pot of coffee was brewing, the table was set, and I had a big stack of wild blueberry pancakes waiting, accompanied by bacon and warm maple syrup. I'd laid two plates; since we didn't have guests yet, and I didn't expect my niece—and helper—Gwen to be up anytime before noon, we had the kitchen to ourselves.

"Coffee?" I asked as he peeled off his jacket. Even under his blue plaid flannel shirt, his well-muscled torso and trim waist were visible. I tugged at my sweater over my rather less-defined waist self-consciously, but he didn't seem to notice. Instead, he crossed the kitchen, swept me into his arms, and kissed me. His bristly cheeks were chilled from the wind, but I felt warm tingles anyway.

"Smells delicious," he murmured into my ear when I came up for air some time later.

"The last batch of pancakes just came off the griddle," I said.

"That's not what I meant," he said, nibbling my earlobe.

"I thought you were hungry."

"I am," he said. "Can't you tell?"

He kissed me one more time before releasing me reluctantly. "To be continued later," he said. A moment later, I poured two mugs of coffee and joined him at the table, where he shoveled half a dozen pancakes onto his plate.

I watched as he smeared a knob of butter on them and followed it up with about a cup of maple syrup. "It's just not fair," I said.

He looked up with a pancake-laden fork halfway to his mouth. "What?"

"You and Gwen can eat mountains of food, and you never gain an ounce." It was true; like John, my curvy niece had not an ounce of spare flesh on her slender frame. Yet she could—and frequently did—eat more chocolate chip cookies in one sitting than anyone else I'd ever met.

"It's all genes, I guess. Anyway, I think you look great," he said, pushing the pancake plate toward me. "Go ahead. With the celery-crunchers coming, it may be the only food you'll get all week."

I laughed. "Also true." My eyes drifted to the window, and the lighthouse framed in the distance. "Did you hear about the skeleton?" I asked.

His green eyes glinted. "The one they found in the lighthouse?"

"How did you know?"

"I talked with Eleazer last night."

"And you didn't tell me?"

"I guess I forgot," he said, taking a sip of coffee. "I wonder if they've finally found Old Harry?"

"Who's Old Harry?"

"Old Harry was one of the first keepers, back in the 1800s," John said, selecting a piece of bacon from the platter. "He was at the lighthouse for about ten years ... lived all by himself, and only came down to the store once in awhile." John took another bite of pancake and swallowed it down before continuing. "There was a big storm one January night. The winds were fierce—ripped the roof right off a couple of houses. But the light never went out at the lighthouse—the story is that it kept at least two ships from running up on the rocks out at the point."

"What happened to Harry?" I asked.

"That's the thing," John said, spearing another bite of pancake and mopping up a puddle of syrup with it. "No one knows. The light stayed lit, but Harry just disappeared."

The skin on my arms prickled. "Vanished?"

"Everyone figured the storm swept him away," John said, "even though the body was never found."

"Well, if it was boarded up in the lighthouse somewhere, that would explain a lot," I said.

"Whatever happened to old Harry that night, he was dedicated to his job; he never let the light go out."

"How sad." I glanced out the window in the direction of the lighthouse, and the keeper's house huddled beside it. "Did he have family?"

"I don't know," John said. "Of course, there's a legend that the original light still flashes," he said, "even though that lantern hasn't been lit in more than fifty years. The oldtimers consider it an omen of death."

I shivered, suddenly cold despite the toasty yellow kitchen. John reached for another piece of bacon.

As I levered a forkful of maple syrup-drenched pancake to my mouth, I thought of the graceful building that had stood out on the point for centuries, guiding ships away from rocks like dark teeth. Lighthouses had a natural mystique, of course, but the story of the disappearing keeper made Cranberry Island's sole lighthouse even more haunting.

I washed down a bite of pancake with some coffee, thinking of the skeleton and the legend of the flashing light. I'd had a brush with the supernatural at the Gray Whale Inn last fall, and now there was this story of the mysterious lighthouse. I loved living in a place where the buildings were steeped in history, but why did so many of the stories have to be tragedies?

———

When the mail boat chugged into view at 2 p.m., I was at the dock, waiting for the retreat participants to arrive. The *Little Marian* was tied up nearby, next to *Mooncatcher* and Eleazer's skiff *Windward*. The van hadn't shown any sign of moving, and I couldn't get a mechanic out to look at it in time, so I'd wrangled John and Eleazer into helping transport my guests over to the inn.

"Thanks so much for coming to help," I told John as the wind buffeted us at the town pier, blowing my brown hair into my eyes.

The *Island Princess* was chugging slowly over the water, pitching to and fro on the choppy waves.

"No problem," he said, eyeing the sky, which had turned ominously gray. "Hope we get everyone to the inn before it starts raining." A strong wind buffeted the dock. "It'll be a rough ride there, looks like."

"I just hope the power doesn't go out. Hard to cook with no oven." I glanced at the sky nervously; I'd been meaning to install a generator to deal with the island's frequent outages, but after spending so much money on the van, it would be awhile before I could scrape up enough cash for a generator.

"That's all right. They're here to lose weight, right? Just feed them salads."

I laughed.

"Why did they pick Cranberry Island for the retreat, anyway?" John asked.

"Apparently the woman who runs it used to summer here," I said.

"What's her name?"

"Vanessa something." John's eyebrow twitched up a little. "I can't remember her last name," I continued. "It was unusual, though."

"And don't forget that hunky trainer you were telling me about," said Charlene, who had just trotted up to the dock wearing a fresh coat of lipstick and a green jacket that hugged her generous curves. Her dark blond hair gleamed in the watery light.

John flashed her a smile. "Hi there, Charlene. Here to check out the offerings?"

She smiled fondly at my neighbor. "There's supposed to be a cute physical fitness expert on board, and I thought I might just need a bit of personal training."

I rolled my eyes at John, but Charlene didn't notice; she was squinting at the boat.

"Ooh," she said a moment later, pointing to a burly man on the boat's stern. "Would you look at that." She bit her lip. "Let's hope he doesn't have a girlfriend."

"Or a boyfriend," I said.

"He can't be gay," Charlene said, raising her field glasses for a better look. "He just can't."

"We'll find out soon enough," I said as the *Island Princess* docked, pitching heavily in the waves. I was happy to see boxes of groceries strapped to the top; it might take a few runs over in Charlene's truck, but at least I'd have something to feed my guests.

"Welcome to Cranberry Island!" I said as the retreat participants stepped off the boat a minute later, looking cheerful despite the rough weather. I hoped they remained that way after the skiff ride to the inn. I needn't have worried about the average tonnage; more than a few of them, I was chagrined to notice, were actually thinner than I was. Maybe my doctor was right about me dropping a few pounds after all.

It wasn't hard to spot Vanessa, a slender super-model type with a high-wattage smile and shiny black hair cut in a pert wedge. My own slightly gray-streaked bob didn't hold a candle to it, I knew. "You must be Natalie," she said as she stepped gracefully off the heaving boat. With her sleek black coat and matching hair, she looked out of place on the weather-beaten dock.

"And you must be Vanessa," I said, smiling. "It's so nice to finally meet you."

From behind me, John said, "Vanessa?"

"John?" Vanessa's dark eyes darted past me and lit up. "I can't believe it! I had no idea you were still here!"

I glanced from John to Vanessa, both of whom were inspecting each other with intense interest. Charlene was looking on with raised eyebrows, the hunky trainer temporarily forgotten.

"You two know each other?" I asked.

"Of course," Vanessa said. "We spent summers here together. But it's been so long…" She beamed at my neighbor. "Remember those nights, out by the lighthouse?"

I glanced at John. Summer nights out by the lighthouse? I'd heard all about John's sailing trips with his grandfather, but somehow enchanted lighthouse evenings with Vanessa had never made it into our conversations. Evidently John recalled them quite well, though, because he smiled back warmly and said, "How could I forget?"

As the two of them basked in the glow of shared memories and Charlene sidled over to the hunky blond guy, who was looking very manly in a leather bomber jacket, I shifted from foot to foot and pulled my jacket tight against the brisk wind. I was getting the feeling that hosting the weight-loss retreat might not be such a great idea after all.

TWO

"WELL, WE'LL HAVE TO catch up on old times later," Vanessa said as a big gust just about knocked her over. She gave John's arm a squeeze and flashed him one of her mega-watt smiles. I couldn't be sure—it could have been the wind—but it looked like a faint flush was creeping up his cheeks. Then Vanessa turned to face the women huddling on the dock. "Welcome to Cranberry Island. I'm sure you'll love it every bit as much as I do. Now, Natalie," Vanessa said, turning toward me, "how do we get to your wonderful inn?"

"We thought it might be a nice change for the guests to arrive at the inn by boat," I announced, pointing to the three skiffs bobbing in the waves. They say it's all in the marketing, and it sure sounded better than, "The van broke, so we're taking dinghies."

"How fun!" she said. Five minutes later, she had expertly directed most of the group onto the skiffs and escorted the remaining few into the pier restaurant to wait. Charlene, I noticed, had cut the trainer from the herd and was sparkling at him as they headed for the door of Spurrell's Lobster Pound. Although her restaurant was usually closed until June, Evie Spurrell had kindly volunteered to provide my guests a place to wait for the boats—along with mugs of steaming hot coffee.

By the time the first group reached the inn, fat droplets of rain had started falling, and the wind had picked up even more. From the quiet emanating from my huddled guests, I worried that the retreat was off to a bad start. But their faces lightened as they took in the gray-shingled Cape-style inn, windows glowing warmly, perched atop a green, rock-studded hill. When my niece greeted them with mugs of (sugar-free) hot chocolate, they cheered up immediately, chatting excitedly as John, Eleazer, and I headed back for the rest of the group.

When we reached the pier, Vanessa divided the remaining group among the three boats. Charlene stood on the dock, looking remarkably chipper, as the trainer—she introduced him to me as Dirk—leaped into Eleazer's skiff, just about swamping the little boat in the process.

"He helped me load the groceries into the truck," she murmured to me. "He's just gorgeous—and sweet, too!" As she mooned over Dirk, Eleazer helped a young woman into the *Little Marian*. In the meantime, John helped Vanessa, with whom he appeared to be in deep reminiscence mode, into *Mooncatcher*. As I smiled up at the single, dark-haired woman in my skiff, Vanessa's tinkly laugh reached me over the thrum of the engines. I glanced back to see John and Vanessa all cozied up in the back of *Mooncatcher*. I was beginning to understand how John felt when my former fiancé paid me a visit the previous fall.

"Sorry about the weather," I called to my passenger.

"It's not your fault," she replied, hugging herself against the wind. "Cold rain comes with the territory this time of year."

"Are you kidding me? I'm a Texas girl. I don't think I'll ever adjust."

My passenger smiled back at me, and her serious face suddenly lightened. She had high cheekbones and piercing eyes, and like mine, her dark hair had a few strands of gray.

"I'm Natalie," I said. "The innkeeper."

"I'm Elizabeth," she said, extending a chilly hand.

"Ever been to Maine before?" I asked.

"Actually, yes," she called back over the thrum of the little boat. "I live in Portland. I'm a reporter for *Maine Monthly Magazine*."

"So this isn't a big change for you then, I imagine."

She grinned and shook her head.

As we headed toward the inn, I glanced back at John's skiff. Vanessa was still right next to John.

"What made you decide to host the retreat?" Elizabeth asked, tearing my attention away from the happy couple.

"It seemed like a good opportunity, so I jumped on it," I said. "It's the first one I've hosted, and I'm hoping it will be the first of many." I was about to ask her what kind of article she was writing, but the wake of a passing lobster boat threatened to swamp us, and I had to adjust my course. It was bad enough having to transport my guests to the inn on borrowed skiffs; the last thing I needed was to drown them along the way.

My hands felt frozen on the rudder by the time we tied up at the Gray Whale Inn's dock. While Elizabeth and I clambered onto the dock, Eleazer bounded onto it like a mountain goat, despite the fact that the few hairs he had left under his tam were white.

John, too, was remarkably limber, and paid special attention (or at least it seemed so to me) to Vanessa as she daintily stepped off onto the dock.

As the women—except for Vanessa, who lingered with her old lighthouse buddy John—hurried up to the inn, I turned to the spry, gray-haired captain of the little wooden boat. "I can't thank you enough, Eleazer; you and John really saved the day. Will you stay for some hot chocolate? No cookies, I'm afraid; this group is here to lose weight, not gain it."

"Hot chocolate?" he asked, eyes glinting.

I laughed. "Even your wife would approve. It's sugar-free." Eleazer's wife, Claudette, though far from slight herself, was perpetually lecturing her comparatively lean husband on the perils of sugar. And baking him her legendary sugarless cranberry pies. My mouth puckered just thinking about them.

"Thank you kindly, but I think I'd better motor on home now. We've got the grandkids coming up tomorrow, and Claudie wants me to get the place ship-shape for them."

I smiled. Claudette had recently reconnected with the son she'd given up for adoption almost forty years earlier, and she was enjoying her new role as grandma to two young children. And since her son and his wife were renovating a house down by the island's bog, the young family had been frequent visitors lately.

"I owe you one," I told him. "Tell Claudette and the kids hi— and I'll take an extra batch of brownies down to the shop this week, just for you," I said.

"That's more than payment enough," he said as he hopped back into his skiff and revved the engine. "Thank you kindly!"

"Thank *you,* Eli!" I called, and as he untied the skiff and headed toward home, I grabbed the one box of groceries I'd tossed into the skiff and turned to follow Vanessa and John, who were walking shoulder-to-shoulder up the path to the inn. John's chivalrous instincts seemed to have evaporated when Vanessa appeared, I thought sourly as I trudged up the path behind them, my arms loaded with groceries.

Charlene was waiting in the driveway with the rest of the groceries; it took us several trips to get everything to the inn while Gwen got the guests checked in and served hot chocolate. Charlene offered to help me put the groceries up, but when I saw her look longingly at the kitchen door, I took the eggs out of her hand.

"Go talk to him," I said.

"Are you sure?"

"Absolutely," I said. A moment later, the kitchen door swung shut behind her, leaving me alone.

As I peeled off my jacket and started to put away the cartons of low-fat ingredients—skim milk, fat-free yogurt, whole-wheat flour, and about twelve bushels of fresh fruits and veggies—I realized the flaw in my brownie plan.

How was I going to bake a batch of brownies when I was hosting an inn full of half-starved, chocolate-deprived dieters?

———

By the time I got the last celery stalk tucked into the crisper, the warmth of my buttery yellow kitchen—and a mug of coffee—had dispelled most of the chill, but the absence of John in my kitchen had not done anything to thaw my rather frosty-feeling heart.

Evidently Dirk was taking his time unpacking, because after twenty minutes of loitering in the living room, Charlene had given up and headed back to the store to take over for her niece, Tania.

"No luck?" I asked when she returned to the kitchen.

"We didn't get to talk much—but he did agree to go to dinner with me," she said, eyes shining.

"Quick work," I said. Charlene practically danced to the door.

As her ancient truck—which, like most vehicles on the island, was missing major parts, like windows, bumpers, and a passenger-side door—growled up the driveway, I checked my menu plan for the evening and poured another cup of coffee. I'd chosen an easy dinner of broiled citrus chicken and steamed veggies, for which I'd already thawed and prepped the chicken breasts. My hand strayed to the cookie jar, which I knew was stuffed with gingersnaps, and paused. I couldn't eat them in the dining room, but surely there would be no harm in snagging one and munching it now?

With great effort, I replaced the lid and pulled my hand back. If I was going to take advantage of the health benefits of hosting a weight-loss retreat, I'd have to stay on the same regimen as my guests. Besides, Vanessa probably wouldn't give in to temptation, I told myself. With one last, longing look at the ceramic jar, I pushed through the swinging door of the kitchen into the dining room.

The retreat was already in full swing; while the guests sat at my antique maple tables sipping hot chocolate and munching the carrot and celery sticks Gwen had put out—the crunching reminded me of a field full of crickets—Vanessa stood at the front of the room, smiling brightly and revving the participants up for a week of weight-loss excitement. The tall windows looked out over the water toward the mainland, and for a moment, the sun peeked through a cloud to touch on the gray back of Cadillac Mountain. It glowed briefly, then disappeared, giving the mountain almost a brooding look.

I turned from the window and scanned the room, my eyes seeking Elizabeth, whose angular frame didn't look like it needed to lose an ounce. I couldn't help wondering why *Maine Monthly* had chosen to send a skinny person to review a weight-loss retreat.

"We're going to give you a jump start over the next seven days," Vanessa said, "and teach you some lifestyle habits you can practice at home." Vanessa's teeth were blindingly white, contrasting attractively with her dusky skin and shiny black hair. The look was exotic, and I wondered what her heritage was. Part Asian?

She was dressed in formfitting jeans and an Aran sweater that somehow managed to accentuate her curvy figure. I loved my own Aran sweater, but was only too aware that it made my silhouette look rather like that of a sheep with an overgrazing problem. If following the Lose-It-All plan could make me look like that even under four pounds of wool, I decided—it might be worth paying attention. John certainly was. His eyes were trained on Vanessa like he was on the *Titanic* and she was showing him how to operate the lifeboats. I knew he wasn't here for the slimming tips—my neighbor was plenty trim already—and since he wouldn't touch sugar-free anything, it wasn't the hot chocolate, either.

I tore my eyes from the back of my neighbor's sandy head and scanned the rest of the room. Vanessa had given me a quick rundown on the participants, and I was placing names with faces. I spotted the mother-daughter duo, Megan and Carissa, in the corner; they shared the same pale blond hair and rounded bodies. The three well-dressed and slightly plump women by the window must be the sorority sisters, Boots, Sarah, and Caterina, who had chosen to prepare for their thirty-year reunion by attempting to return to their college weight. Elizabeth had pulled out a notebook, doubtless to take notes for the article she was writing. Up at the front, near Dirk, was another woman, pale and chubby, with curly brown hair. She must be Bethany. The sole man at the retreat sat by himself in a corner. Like John, he was paying rapt attention to Vanessa, but since he was taking copious notes in a little spiral-bound notebook, I was guessing at least part of his interest was in her list of "lifestyle tips." He was an attractive man, with reddish-brown hair and a physique you could tell used to be muscular, but had collected a little padding around the middle over the years.

In contrast, Dirk, the trainer, was looking bored and chiseled, but—based on the fact that his eyes kept straying toward the generous bosom of one of the sorority sisters—*not* gay. Which was good news for Charlene.

As my eyes drifted back to John, who hadn't yet noticed my presence, Vanessa said, "Ah, there you are, Natalie." Several pairs of eyes turned to look at me, and I smiled welcomingly as Vanessa continued. "Natalie is our innkeeper this week. Not only is she the owner of this gorgeous place, but she'll be cooking lots of delicious healthy meals that can help you stay on-plan." Which, from what I had seen of the program, involved controlled portions of protein and vegetables, a few whole grains, virtually no fat, and enough exercise to fell an Olympic athlete. Vanessa looked at me with a big smile. "Dinner's at six, right?"

"Right," I said. "Tonight's menu is tangy citrus chicken and crisp-steamed Asian vegetables." I'd read somewhere that lots of adjectives help 'sell' a dish. And with the paucity of butter and other delicious, sinful substances in this week's menu, the dishes I'd be preparing needed all the help they could get.

"Sounds scrumptious," Vanessa said. "Especially those veggies. But before we eat, Dirk's going to introduce you all to the weight-training component of the program. Then we'll have some free time to unpack and get to know each other before dinner. So, if you'll finish up your hot chocolate, we'll get started, okay? No need for workout clothes … yet," she said with a twinkle.

The women hurriedly slurped down the rest of their drinks and trotted after Dirk and Vanessa into my living room, which was doing double-duty as a weight-lifting and yoga room. The over-stuffed sofas were still in place, but I knew they'd be pushed back against the walls for an evening exercise session later. In fact, all the furniture in the living room would be moving around a lot this week; I just hoped it didn't scratch the floors.

John joined me as I carried the empty mugs and plates to the kitchen and stowed them in the dishwasher.

"So," I said as he brought in the last mug. "You and Vanessa seemed pretty cozy."

"It's been a long time," he said with a shrug. "Lots to catch up on."

"How many summers did you spend together?" I asked.

"I don't know. Three or four, I guess. We were just kids."

"Funny; you've never mentioned her."

"I guess it just never came up," he said, looking out the window at the darkening sky. "I'm going to head back to my place; let me know if you need anything."

A moment later, he was gone, leaving me alone with my thoughts —and a pack of hungry dieters.

THREE

At FIVE-FORTY-FIVE, I WAS pulling a tray full of chicken breasts out of the oven as my niece Gwen plated the steamed veggies. "How much sesame dressing should I use?" she asked.

"It's on the recipe," I said, pointing to a stack of papers on the counter. Every meal I'd designed had been vetted and measured by Vanessa, and I was under strict orders not to "fudge" anything.

"Two teaspoons," Gwen read. "I'll just eyeball it."

"Use the measuring spoons," I said.

"Are you serious?"

I sighed. "Just because you can eat two pounds of chocolate and not gain an ounce doesn't mean everyone can."

"Thank God," she said. "I'd hate to have to measure my salad dressing. Geez."

Ten minutes later we transported the plates into the dining room, where they were met with great enthusiasm by our guests. Cooking for dieters had a definite benefit, I decided, in that they were so hungry that just about anything you served them was a treat. Although it was only the first day, I was already jonesing for some chocolate. Maybe it was because I'd spent so much time hustling to get dinner ready that I hadn't eaten anything myself.

"Ooh, that looks delicious," Bethany said as I deposited a plate in front of her. "A nice buttered roll would make it just perfect."

"Oh, I don't know," Vanessa said. "I just love the freshness of steamed veggies. So much lighter than starchy bread."

Bethany shot her a look that was pure venom, then masked it with a smile. "You're right, Vanessa. After all, as Dirk always says, veggies are much better than starches!"

To each her own, I thought as I retreated to the kitchen to pick up the rest of the plates. I'd take a fresh-baked cloverleaf roll over steamed broccoli any day.

So far, I was pleased at how the retreat was going. This was the first time I'd done full meal service—usually I limited the inn's culinary offerings to breakfast and the occasional batch of afternoon cookies—and I was still getting the hang of planning for three meals daily. With the amount of cooking on my plate this week, I thought, odds were good I'd drop a few pounds even without restricting my calorie intake.

When I pushed through the swinging door with two more dinner plates, Dirk was distributing little capsules to the guests.

"What are these?" asked Elizabeth, who still had her notebook with her.

"They're special herbal supplements," Dirk said. "They boost lipolytic action and help reduce hunger pangs."

"What's lipo … What was it you called it?"

"Lipolytic action? It's the ability of the body to burn fat," he said. "The supplement is a combination of green tea catechins and

Rhodiola rosea, a Siberian herb that's been used for centuries to improve metabolic processes. I've also included a couple of special ingredients that I've developed to assist the weight-loss process."

"Are they safe?" she asked, cocking a sculpted eyebrow.

"Of course," he said glibly. "I've used them for years."

I didn't know about Elizabeth, but the whole 'mystery ingredient' thing didn't inspire much confidence in me. My impression of the Lose-It-All program had been that it focused on (admittedly rather extreme, at least in my case) lifestyle changes; I hadn't realized that supplements would be part of the retreat. And to be honest, I wasn't too excited about it. What if something went wrong? Could I be held liable if a guest had a reaction?

I deposited another plate, watching Elizabeth turn the capsule around in her fingers. As Dirk turned his back to hand one to another participant, she slipped the capsule into her pocket—which is probably exactly what I would have done under the circumstances.

Greg was at the next table, along with Megan and Carissa, the mother-daughter duo who shared blond hair, blue eyes—and a passion for jelly doughnuts, from the look of them, although Carissa appeared to be outpacing her mother in the weight-gain department. "Doesn't that look delicious, dear?" Megan asked her daughter, patting Carissa's pale hand and glancing at Greg, whose chambray shirt was so tight that gaps appeared between the buttons, exposing flashes of the white T-shirt he wore under it. Megan adjusted the plunging neckline of her own tight-fitting blouse, which clung to the spare tire around her middle like Saran Wrap. "Aren't you glad we came here?"

Her daughter, who had donned a shapeless blue sweater that had been worn so much its sleeves were covered with pills, shrugged, looking miserable. I felt a stab of pity; earlier that afternoon, during the introductions, the poor girl's mother had regaled the group with tales of Carissa's chocolate debauchery. After detailing how Carissa had consumed an entire tub of frosting with her fingers—which I could totally understand, to be honest, although I preferred home-made to the prefab stuff you get at the store—Carissa's mother had announced, "She could be so beautiful if she just lost fifty pounds. And at the rate she's going, she'll be single forever. She's already eighteen, you know. It's time she dropped the baby fat." My heart had gone out to Carissa, who had said nothing, only wrapped her faded gray cardigan tighter around herself and stared at a spot on the floor.

Greg was eyeing the little mother-daughter drama with inter-est, and Megan was certainly aware of him. Despite the presence of her daughter, I saw her give him an appraising look as he inspected Dirk's proffered capsule and downed it with a swig of water. Me-gan's wedding band glinted on her left hand as she reached for her own water glass. Charlene always said that just because you were dating someone, it didn't mean you were dead; I guess that trans-lated to marriage, too.

The next table was the rowdiest of the bunch—the three middle-aged sorority sisters who looked on hungrily as I laid out the plates. "Looks great," said Boots. Her nails were expertly polished, and al-though she had a few extra pounds to lose, her khaki pants and cream sweater were perfectly cut. She tucked a strand of her gleaming page boy behind one ear. One delicate, well-dressed ear—she was wearing diamond earrings that looked to be at least three carats each.

"Would look better with mashed potatoes on the side," said one of her sorority sisters gloomily. Sarah, I told myself mentally; I was trying to keep everyone straight. Unlike Boots, whose hair was cut to precision, Sarah's hair was faded blond streaked with gray, and she wore a green velour sweat suit that made her pale skin look sallow. Although Sarah and Boots must have been the same age, Sarah looked ten years older.

Just think how fabulous we'll look," Boots said, nudging the third woman in the party. "Right, Cat?"

The third sorority sister, a pretty woman with large brown eyes and a mane of long hair, looked up, startled. "What?"

"Oh, stop ogling the trainer," Sarah said.

"I wasn't," Cat said, blushing slightly. Like Carissa, she was dressed in a formless blue sweater and jeans, although I was guessing they were much more expensive. Her long hair had been swept up into a clip; the effect accentuated her large, slightly uptilted eyes. If Cat had a slender figure as a sorority girl, it had changed significantly over the years. She was carrying about fifty extra pounds, and fell firmly into the "pear-shaped" category.

"Yes you were," Sarah teased, her tired face lighting up with an evil grin. "You've hardly taken your eyes off him since we got here."

"Oh. Really? I didn't realize," Cat said, her eyes dropping to her plate.

"If you're going to stare, though, at least he's worth looking at." Boots crossed her long, khaki-clad legs and ran a critical eye over the handsome trainer. Although Dirk wasn't my type—he seemed kind of full of himself, and his conversation, as it was limited to low-fat eating and exercise regimens, was less than riveting—he was a handsome man, and many of the women kept darting glances at him. "Do you think he and Vanessa are an item?" Boots murmured, narrowing her long-lashed eyes.

"Somebody told me they were," Sarah replied. "But they don't act like it. I haven't seen them together at all today."

"Maybe they're just being professional," Boots replied, brushing a piece of lint from her sweater. "I know they have separate rooms."

"Which one is Dirk in?" Cat asked, blinking her huge eyes.

Boots arched a tweezed eyebrow. "Upstairs, last one on the right. But I thought you said you weren't interested," she said with a wicked grin.

"Do you need anything else for now?" I asked, interrupting their musings over Dirk's availability.

"Not right now, but the food looks great," Cat said. "Thank you."

"I hope you enjoy it," I said, and returned to the kitchen for another round.

When everyone had their plates—and their pills from Dirk—I made my way from table to table, making sure everyone had what they needed. When I was satisfied that all the guests were taken care of, I retreated to the kitchen to help Gwen put the finishing touches on dessert—my "Sweet Nothing" chocolate meringue cookies with a garnish of fresh raspberries. I was helping her plate the last two dishes when the doorbell rang.

"Go ahead and get it, Aunt Nat," Gwen said, smiling up at me. "I'll take care of the rest of the berries."

"Thanks," I said, hurrying to the front door.

To my surprise, Tom Lockhart stood there.

"I didn't hear you drive down," I said. "Come on in!"

"I took the boat instead," he said, stepping through the door-way after me. "I just stopped in for a couple of minutes." Tom was always welcome at the inn—the tall, rangy man with bright blue eyes was one of my favorite people—and not just because he'd helped save the inn from developers last year. Tom was one of the pillars of Cranberry Island; he had grown up on the island, and was now president of the lobster co-op, in large part because of his friendly nature and even temper. He grinned at me, and I could see why his wife, Lorraine, had fallen in love with him ten years ago. His two boys, Tommy Jr. and Logan, shared the same win-ning smile. "I wanted to drop a bunch of lobsters by," Tom said. "I left them in a pot off the dock—they'll be good all week. I figured they're low calorie, so you could serve them to your guests."

I blinked in surprise—he'd never brought fresh lobster to the inn before—but I wasn't about to argue.

"Gosh. Thanks. Won't you come in, and have something warm to drink?"

"Thank you," he said.

Vanessa was deep in conversation with Dirk when Tom and I walked into the dining room. "I told you, it's nothing," she was saying urgently to Dirk as we passed. Then she looked up, and her eyes widened suddenly. "Tom."

"Vanessa!" His blue eyes lit up like a beacon. "I didn't realize you were here!"

I resisted the urge to snort. On this island? *Please.*

She hesitated for a moment, then stood up to greet him, hold-ing out a hand for him to shake. "Gosh. It's been years," she said.

Tom ignored the proffered hand and pulled her slender frame into a bear hug, his eyes sliding to Dirk, who was looking on with impatience. After a hug that lasted an uncomfortably long time, he released her, running his eyes up and down her. "How are you? What have you been up to?"

"Oh, keeping busy," she said, glancing over at Dirk, who was glaring at Tom.

"We'll have to get together, talk about old times," Tom said. Before Vanessa could answer, Bethany appeared at the doorway.

"Dirk?" she asked, her pale, moon-shaped face glowing with desire. "I have a few questions about my protein-carbohydrate mix. Can you come talk with me for a moment?"

Dirk hesitated, glowering at Tom; then he rearranged his chiseled face into a more pleasant expression. He reminded me of one of those guys you see in toothpaste commercials, I realized—all tanned skin, ripped biceps, and blindingly white toothy smiles. "Sure," he said, still sounding a tad surly as he walked over to her.

"Isn't it wonderful that we have a whole week together?" Bethany cooed, putting a plump hand on Dirk's arm. A flash of irritation passed over his features before he masked it with a thin smile.

"Dirk is just the most wonderful trainer," Bethany gushed to us. "He's been training me for years, but with the business taking off the way it has, he had to cut down on his hours, so we don't get to see each other as often."

"The price of success," I quipped.

"That's why when I found out he was co-hosting this retreat, I just had to sign up." She blinked up at Dirk. "It's such a romantic setting, isn't it?" She squeezed his arm, and he flinched. "And I'm so glad he's here. I always do everything he tells me to—without his help, I'd be a blimp!"

Based on the extra thirty pounds she was carrying, I suspected she wasn't being entirely honest about following Dirk's instructions to the letter, but I didn't volunteer the thought. "Thanks for the lobsters, Tom," I said, turning to the rangy lobsterman. "I've got to get back to the kitchen and get dessert ready. You're welcome to a chocolate meringue if you're interested."

"Oooh, chocolate meringues? How divine," Bethany said, evidently oblivious to the tension between Dirk, Vanessa—and Tom, who looked like he couldn't wait for all of us to clear out. "Sounds like they're to die for." Bethany gave Dirk a predatory look. "I'd kill for something sweet about now."

"I'll go get them ready then," I said, heading for the kitchen as Bethany led Dirk to her table.

As I moved away from Vanessa and Tom, I heard his low voice say something about the lighthouse, but I didn't catch the rest. I doubted the conversation involved the skeleton they'd found in the hidden chamber, though. How many men *had* Vanessa seduced out on Cranberry Point? I wondered.

And what would Tom's wife say if she knew what was going on in my living room?

I passed Dirk and his admirer on my way to the kitchen, where Gwen stood with one hand on her slim hip, counting plates of my "Sweet Nothing" meringues. She looked glamorous as always in a cashmere sweater and designer jeans, and I reflected once more that her boyfriend, a local named Adam Thrackton, was one lucky lobsterman. Gwen had come up the previous summer to study art with Fernand LaChaise, Cranberry Island's artist-in-residence—and to help me out with some of the housekeeping.

Fortunately for me, she'd fallen in love, not just with the island, but with a local lobsterman, and had managed to convince her mother to let her take a sabbatical from UCLA and stay on with me. My sister had agreed grudgingly, perhaps in part because she was under the impression that her daughter was dating a shipping magnate on the island. Neither Gwen nor I had informed her that the magnate's fleet consisted of one small lobster boat named *Carpe Diem*, but it was only a matter of time before my sister descended on us for a visit and the truth came out. (I was hoping Adam's Princeton degree would help—even if he *had* tossed it into the drink when he bought the *Diem*.) For now, though, Gwen and I were both happy that her mother lived two thousand miles away—and that she wasn't a fan of cold weather.

"Who was at the door?"

"Tom Lockhart," I said. "He left a pot full of lobsters down by the dock. For free."

"I didn't know it was on the menu."

"It wasn't," I said. "Until now. He just dropped a bunch of them by."

Gwen cocked an eyebrow. "That doesn't sound like Tom," she said. "Why did he do that?"

"Who knows?" I said, shrugging. I didn't want to think about it right now, to be honest. "I'll save them for the last night—it will make the last meal special." I glanced at the Tupperware container of meringues. "I'll go clear the dinner plates. Do you have dessert under control?"

"We need ten plates, right?" Gwen asked.

"Yup."

My niece pushed a lock of her dark, curly hair behind one ear and looked up at me. "You know, this retreat is turning out to be a lot of work. Are you sure you'll be okay if I go up to Fernand's in the morning?"

"It'll be fine. Marge is coming to help me out, remember?"

Gwen cocked a dark eyebrow at me.

"She's doing a great job," I said. "Honest." Gwen's reticence was understandable, if unwarranted. For years, Marge O'Leary had had a reputation as one of the island's nastiest—and least fastidious—residents. She'd worked as a part-time cleaner for the island's summer population, but based on the feedback from her clients, I had once sworn I would never let her wield a feather duster in my inn.

Since last fall, though, when I'd helped Marge escape the hellish life she was secretly living—trapped with an abusive, homicidal husband who had almost murdered both of us—she had been working hard to turn her life around. As much as I supported her efforts to change, when she'd asked me for a job in December, I'd had serious misgivings. Marge had surprised me, though; with a little bit of training, she had transformed into a reliable, conscientious—and even pleasant—employee.

I was about to head out and clear plates when Gwen asked, "What's up with John and the retreat leader woman? Vanessa-what's-her-name?"

"Tagliacozzi," I supplied. "What do you mean?"

"I was doing a sketch of the mountains from my window earlier this afternoon, while you were prepping for dinner, and I saw her go down to the carriage house," she said. "John answered the door, and she must have been in there for like twenty minutes."

"Oh," I said, feeling my stomach sink.

"Do they know each other or something?"

"She spent a few summers here on the island. They appear to have been friends." And perhaps a bit more, I thought but didn't add.

Gwen raised an eyebrow again and said nothing.

"Do you want to clean the kitchen or do turndown tonight?" I asked, hoping to change the subject.

"How about I clean tonight and we switch tomorrow?"

"Sounds good to me," I said. "I'll start picking up plates in the next room."

When I pushed through the swinging door into the dining room, everyone was standing at the windows, peering at something in the distance.

"What is it?"

"The lighthouse," Vanessa said; evidently she'd managed to send Tom on his way at some point. "I didn't know it was working!"

"It's not," I said. "Maybe it's someone with a flashlight."

"It's awfully big for a flashlight," Bethany said.

I stepped up to the window and peered over her shoulder. Bethany was right. If it was a flashlight, it was a pretty massive one; the bright white light made a sweeping arc through the dark night.

The hairs stood up on my arms, and I turned away from the window. "I know they're renovating it," I said lightly, thinking of the skeleton they'd turned up yesterday—and the story John had told me about the ghost light. "I didn't realize they'd fixed the light so soon."

"It's eerie, isn't it?" said Cat, in a low voice that sent a cold finger of ice down my spine.

"We were planning to jog out there in the morning," said Vanessa. "We'll have to check it out!"

"Is everybody ready for dessert?" I asked, turning away from the light.

"What is it?" asked Sarah, with a hungry look in her pale eyes.

"'Sweet Nothing' chocolate meringues with fresh raspberries!" I announced, and the mysterious light was instantly forgotten. Except by me. As the guests smacked their lips over the diminutive cookies, my eyes followed the arc of the light. It flashed three more times. Then it went dark.

FOUR

IT WAS ALMOST HALF an hour before the tables were clear and I
had a moment to eat my own dinner. My stomach rumbled loudly
as I fixed myself a plate of chicken and veggies; I hadn't had time
to fix the fish that John had caught. The dinner was delicious—the
marinade on the chicken was tangy and the sesame-flavored veggies were tender, but still crisp—but the portions were woefully
insufficient. As I scraped the last bit of sauce from the plate, my
eyes strayed to the cookie jar.

No, Natalie.

I turned my back on it and slid my plate into the dishwasher.

"How was it?" Gwen asked from her station at the sink.

"Good, but kind of small," I said. "I'm still starving."

She shook her head as she rinsed the steamer. "I just don't understand the diet mentality."

"That's because you eat whatever you want and don't gain an
ounce," I said.

"I watch what I eat!" she protested.

"I know you do," I said. Gwen *did* watch what she ate—that is, if you counted observing the food as it moved from the plate to her fork to her mouth—but there was no use arguing with her. "I'm going to go take care of turn-down service while everybody's exercising," I said.

"See you in a few," she said as I grabbed a basket of sugar-free mints and headed out of the kitchen. I sidled past the guests, who had changed into spandex and baggy T-shirts and were flailing their arms to Dirk's count in the living room, and grabbed the skeleton key from the front desk. Normally I wouldn't provide the service—it required either Gwen or me to be around at eight every night—but since I was hoping the Lose-It-All retreat would pick the Gray Whale Inn as its regular location, I'd decided to pull out all the stops. On the other hand, I thought darkly as I let myself into the first room, if that meant having Vanessa on the premises regularly, maybe winning the business permanently wasn't such a good idea. What *had* she been doing in John's carriage house for twenty minutes today? I wasn't sure I wanted to know.

I was about to let myself into the first room when the phone rang again. I hurried back to the front desk and grabbed the phone just before it went to the answering machine. "Good evening, Gray Whale Inn."

"So, do you think he's gay?" It was Charlene, of course.

"No, I don't," I said, thinking of his interest in a few of the retreat participants' feminine charms.

"Thank God," she said. "I was going to come over tonight, but I couldn't get away from the store."

"Dirk's leading a jog out to the lighthouse in the morning," I said.

"Really?" she said brightly. "I'll definitely be there, then. Maybe we'll even see a bone or something!"

"Did they hear anything back from the lab on that skeleton yet?"

"Not that I heard," she said. "I'll keep you posted, though."

I hung up a moment later and returned to my duties. The ladies were still huffing in the living room by the time I finished with the first floor and headed upstairs. Most of the rooms had been relatively neat, with clothes tucked tidily into dresser drawers and toiletries arrayed on the countertops. I did spot a few boxes of illicit treats (either Megan or Carissa had a stash of mini Snickers bars), but for the most part, everything looked neat and orderly. Which was nice to see, as it meant less housekeeping work for Gwen, Marge, and me.

The second floor was a bit more interesting than the first. Although I make it a rule not to pry into my guests' belongings, it's hard to miss things when they're spread out all over the dresser. And in Bethany's room, it quickly became apparent that weight loss was more than likely a secondary motivation for attending the retreat.

The top of the maple dresser had been turned into a monument to Dirk. It was covered with carefully arranged articles featuring the handsome trainer, and there were a few candid shots—Dirk getting into his car, Dirk through a window, helping someone with a weight machine—that looked like they'd been taken by someone doing surveillance. Bethany? I wondered.

I yanked my eyes away from the disturbing montage and focused on turning down the sheets. After placing a sugar-free mint on Bethany's pillow, I took a step back, knocking a book from the nightstand. It was a journal, and it landed open—and face-up—on the hardwood floor.

"Dirk said hello to me today," read the entry on the open page. It was dated the previous November. "I know he loves me. He just doesn't realize it yet." I stooped to pick up the journal, and couldn't help flipping through a couple more pages. As I suspected, the little book was littered with similar entries. "January 12. Saw Dirk this morning. He says he won't be working with me anymore; I know it's because he's afraid of his attraction to me. Soon he'll figure out that we're destined to be together." And later, in February, just before Valentine's Day: "He says he's involved with Vanessa, but I know that's a lie. He likes women with a little bit of padding, not skinny skeletons. I sent him a dozen roses with a note that I'll do anything in my power to help him overcome his fear of commitment."

My skin crawled as I put the journal back onto the nightstand and backed away. Bethany might look normal, but she was anything but. A moment later I closed the door on Bethany's photo montage, feeling very uneasy. And thankful that I wasn't the object of her obsession.

As I relocked the door, one of the doors farther down the hall opened, and a woman stepped out. It was Elizabeth.

"Hi," I said.

The slim woman jumped, startled. "Oh. I didn't know anyone was up here."

"I'm just doing turn-down service," I said. "Do you need anything?"

"No, no, I'm fine," she said, and hurried past me down the hall.

She was starting down the staircase when I realized why she'd looked furtive. The room she'd come from didn't belong to her.

It had been assigned to Dirk.

My eyebrows rose as Elizabeth hurried down the stairs to the living room, where I could hear Dirk dishing out words of encouragement in a rich, baritone voice. I knew Elizabeth was a reporter, and reporters are nosy by nature, but how much undercover work would you need to do to write a destination article on a Maine weight-loss retreat? At least that's what Vanessa told me she was writing when I'd asked her earlier.

With a quick glance behind me, I closed the short distance to Dirk's room and tried the knob. Maybe Dirk had left it unlocked earlier, but it was certainly locked now. Which was disconcerting. Had Elizabeth managed to get a key?

And should I confront her about it—or tell Dirk what I'd seen?

I could hear thumping from downstairs—jumping jacks?—as I unlocked Dirk's door with the skeleton key and slipped through the door.

Dirk's suitcase lay open on the bed, its contents spread out on every available surface. In addition to a big can of Aveda hairspray, a box of tooth-bleaching trays, and an expensive-looking vial of pore minimizer, two giant Ziploc bags of capsules lay on the dresser: the supplements Dirk had been handing out at dinner, presumably. The desk was stacked high with paperwork, including several manila folders. Client files, I realized as I got closer. Starting weights, goals, dietary habits, medications, allergies—pretty personal stuff. Had Elizabeth been looking for these?

Tucked under the client files was a folder stuffed with my original meal plans, with a few scribbles here and there where changes had been made. And a shipping notice from Nature's Path supplement company. The latest order was for 2,000 units of capsules: underneath was a list of ingredients. I ran my eyes down the page, curious what Dirk was handing out to my guests. The list was pretty short, actually: *Rhodiola rosea*, Green Tea Extract, Creatine, and something called EPH. I didn't remember Dirk listing Creatine or EPH among the ingredients he'd recited earlier. Were they safe? And what were they supposed to do to help weight loss?

Whatever was in the capsules, Dirk appeared to be an avid user of the stuff himself; as I turned down the sheets and laid a sugar-free mint on his pillow, I noticed a bottle of the capsules on his nightstand. At least he practiced what he preached.

After a brief check of the rest of the room, I closed and relocked the door, unsure what to do about the Elizabeth situation—and uncomfortable with the fact that Dirk was handing out supplements to my guests. Vanessa and Dirk hadn't mentioned them to me when they were scheduling the retreat. On the other hand, since the company had recently been featured in a national women's magazine—and evidently had hundreds, if not thousands, of satisfied clients—maybe I was worrying about nothing.

The faint aroma of spicy perfume hit me as I opened the next door. Vanessa's door.

I closed it behind me and did a quick visual survey. Like most of the other rooms, Vanessa's was neat. Unlike the others, though, and in distinct contrast to Dirk's, it was so neat that it looked uninhabited. The dresser and bathroom counters were completely free of the personal care items—hairbrushes, bottles of lotion, shampoo—that usually accumulated there, and her suitcase was tucked neatly in the corner of the closet.

Despite my more-than-cursory glance at Dirk's room, as an innkeeper I generally try to take a minimalist approach to my guests' room—kind of a get-in, get-out, notice-as-little-as-possible way of doing things. But I must confess that it's hard to resist snooping in your boyfriend's ex's room.

Particularly when you're wondering whether she has designs on your beau.

So even though I was probably breaking the innkeeper's code of ethics (if such a thing exists), I couldn't help opening one or two drawers.

Within a matter of minutes I learned many things about Vanessa. One, that her Donna Karan Jeans were a size zero. Two, that she didn't take Dirk's supplements to maintain her previously mentioned disgustingly skinny status. And three, that she had received a lot of recent correspondence from attorneys. I didn't open the envelopes—you have to draw the line somewhere—but I found a stack of them in the top drawer of the desk. Why would a weight-loss program need attorneys? Were there problems with the supplements? Or was it a personal issue? I was about to go ahead and peek into one of the envelopes, just to find out, but then a stab of conscience hit me. It wouldn't be ethical to go through the envelopes. Heck, it might not even be legal. Reluctantly, I stepped away from the desk and picked up my basket of mints. A minute later I let myself out of the retreat leader's perfume-scented room.

By the time I'd made it back downstairs to the first floor, the group had finished their evening calisthenics, and Dirk's baritone had been replaced by the murmur of primarily female voices. Before heading into the fray, I stopped at the front desk to return the skeleton key to its hook in a cabinet behind the desk—and to see if the spare key to Dirk's room was in place. To my relief, the little gold key was hanging on its hook, right where it belonged. Unfortunately, there was no way to know if it had been earlier; when I'd picked up the skeleton key, I didn't remember seeing any missing keys, but I hadn't been paying much attention. How had she gotten in, I wondered.

"What's on the agenda for tomorrow?" Caterina was asking Vanessa as I walked into the living room a few minutes later. Dirk was gathering up exercise mats and stowing them under the window, and most of the guests had moved to the dining room, helping themselves to the thermos of hot water and the herbal tea bags I'd laid out on the sideboard. I glanced at Elizabeth; her dark eyes flickered to mine, then away.

"Breakfast at eight," Vanessa responded with a smile so white it made me wonder if she sprayed her mouth with Clorox every night. "You'll want to wear your workout clothes, because Dirk has an excursion planned for everyone."

"Where? A restaurant?" Boots asked, a touch of sarcasm in her voice.

Vanessa smiled. "We're going to jog out to the historic Cranberry Point Lighthouse," she said.

"The one that was flashing tonight," Sarah said.

"Exactly."

"Let's hope the weather clears up," I said, glancing at the window, where fat drops of rain were splattering against the glass.

"I'm sure everyone has rain gear," Vanessa said cheerfully.

"Can we bring snacks?" asked Carissa meekly. Her mother reached over and squeezed her arm, giving her a stern look.

"We'll have a little pick-me-up when we get there," Vanessa said. "Don't worry. We want you to lose weight, but we don't want you to starve!"

"Too late," someone muttered, and I stifled a laugh. I had to agree with her; I'd been following the program along with the participants, and even though we were only hours into it, my stomach was protesting loudly.

As the women drifted back to their rooms, I headed to the kitchen to check on Gwen—and maybe snag a gingersnap to get me through the rest of the evening. My niece was elbow-deep in suds, scrubbing a skillet.

"How's it going in here?" I asked.

"Almost done," she said. "Need any help prepping for breakfast?"

"It's Pumpkin Pie Oatmeal or soft-boiled eggs and toast, so I think I've got it under control."

Gwen made a face.

"The pumpkin oatmeal's yummy," I said. "Trust me."

"I think I'll nuke one of your cinnamon rolls instead," Gwen said, and my stomach rumbled just at the mention of something sweet. There were cinnamon rolls and blueberry muffins in the freezer, I knew. It would take only a moment to heat one up …

No, Natalie. I forced myself not to stare at the freezer.

Gwen rinsed the skillet and set it on the counter, then drained the sink. "Did you know that Dirk guy was just handing out pills in there, by the way?"

"Again? He just gave them some at dinner."

"I wonder what's in them?" she asked, drying her hands on a dish towel.

"I saw the ingredient list in his room," I said. "Green tea, some Siberian herb, and two things I've never heard of. One of them was something called EPH, and the other was crea-something. Creatine, I think."

"Creatine," Gwen confirmed. "Bodybuilders use it a lot," she said. "I dated a guy who was into that stuff for a couple of months. He popped those pills all the time; it made me kind of nervous."

"Me too," I admitted. "By the way, we need to make sure the key cabinet is locked."

Gwen slung the dishtowel over a hook and looked at me. "Why?"

When I told her about Elizabeth, she sucked in her breath and said, "Are you going to tell Dirk someone was in his room?"

"I'm tempted to let it go," I said. "I don't want to upset anyone, and it didn't look like she did any damage."

"But wouldn't you want to know if someone had been going through your things?"

I thought guiltily of the drawers I'd opened in Vanessa's room. Did that qualify as "going through someone things"? "If it happens again, I'll mention it," I said.

Gwen planted one hand on her slender hip. "I still think you should say something."

"We'll see." I grabbed a dishtowel and started wiping down the counters.

"What do you want me to do about the tables for tomorrow?" Gwen asked as we put the last dish away a few minutes later.

"I have to measure and plate everything, so don't worry about dishes, but if you could set out the silverware and the cups, that would be great. I'll get everything set up in the kitchen."

"Will do," she said, and headed into the dining room to get the tables ready for the morning. When the door swung shut behind her, I reached for the cookie jar. The lid was off and I was breathing in the aroma of ginger and cinnamon, fingers about to close around a cookie, when my sagging willpower kicked in. I pulled my hand out and thrust the lid back down.

"Oatmeal," I told myself sternly. "You're in here to prep the oatmeal."

I had just opened the pantry and pulled out a can of pureed pumpkin when Gwen pushed back through the kitchen door. "Done already?" I asked.

She sucked in her breath. "Not yet. But John's here."

"Really?" I said, wondering why he hadn't come to the kitchen door. "Why don't you tell him to come join me in the kitchen?"

Gwen bit her lip and said nothing.

"What is it?" I asked, although something told me I didn't want to know.

"I'll go tell him," she said, "but right now he's on the couch in the other room. With Vanessa."

I put the can of pumpkin down and leaned against the counter, feeling a little light-headed. And not just because of the near-starvation diet.

"Why don't I take care of the kitchen while you go talk to him?" Gwen offered.

"No," I said. No way I was going to hover around like a jealous girlfriend. When I was done in the kitchen, I'd consider heading into the living room, but I wasn't going to go scurrying off to keep John from talking with another woman. Even if that woman *was* gorgeous—and an ex-girlfriend to boot. "I think I'll finish up in here. If he wants to see me, he knows where to find me."

"Are you sure?" she said softly.

I nodded and reached blindly for the pumpkin pie spice as the door swung shut behind Gwen. *Stay cool*, I told myself. *They're old friends, that's all. And besides, you need the business.*

After measuring out the oatmeal and spices and setting up the coffee pot (I'd recently invested in one with a timer, which had made dark winter mornings much more bearable), I checked my reflection in the window over the sink and prepared to face John. And Vanessa.

FIVE

VANESSA'S THROATY LAUGH GREETED me as I pushed through the kitchen door. I ignored the pang of jealousy that clutched at my chest as I arranged my face in a pleasant expression and headed past Gwen into the living room.

Just as Gwen said, they were on my overstuffed blue sofa, in front of the fire I had lit earlier that afternoon. On opposite ends, at least, but their body language was anything but distant; Vanessa was semi-stretched out on the couch, her delicate sock-clad toes just inches from John's knee, and John was leaning toward her, green eyes glued to her heart-shaped face.

"Hi," I said.

"Natalie!" Vanessa said, turning to look at me. The glow of the fire deepened the hollows under her cheekbones and made her dark eyes and glossy hair shine. "We were just reminiscing about old times. Won't you join us?"

John's gaze flickered to me—a little guiltily, perhaps?—and I could see what a handsome couple the two of them made. They

looked like those pictures you see in *House Beautiful* magazine—
the happy couple relaxing in their gorgeous period home, enjoying
a few hours by the fire. Only this was my inn, not theirs—and besides, they weren't a couple. *But they used to be*, a little voice whispered in my head.

"Actually, I think I'll just turn in early," I said, determined to be
nonchalant about the whole gorgeous ex-girlfriend thing.

"Are you sure?" John asked.

"I have to get up early tomorrow to get breakfast going," I said.

Vanessa stretched like a cat and checked her watch. "You know,
it *is* getting late. I should probably head up, too." Her eyes slid to
John. "We're jogging out to the lighthouse in the morning, if you
want to come. It'll be just like old times."

"Only with a lot more company," I joked stiffly.

John gave me a tight smile, but before I could pursue the lighthouse issue further, Dirk appeared in the doorway. His blue eyes
took in the scene on the couch, and Vanessa stiffened slightly. At
that moment, Cat came down the stairs and headed past us to join
her friends in the dining room, evidently oblivious to the tense
scene that was playing out before her.

"What's up?" Vanessa asked.

Whatever charm Dirk had must have been used up on the women
who were paying for the retreat, because his voice was brusque.
"I need to talk to you," he said to Vanessa, ignoring John and me.
"Now."

"Of course," she said, with an apologetic glance at John. She
got up and hurried toward the glowering trainer, then turned back
to John. "I hope you'll join us tomorrow morning."

"Sure," he said, unfolding himself from my sofa and stretching his lean torso.

"Oh, that would be wonderful!" Vanessa said, beaming at him. Dirk didn't look like he agreed; he put a proprietary arm around her, glancing over his shoulder at John, who was eyeing him with frank dislike. A movement at the other end of the room caught my attention. It was Bethany, standing at the dining room door, her face half in shadow. When she saw me looking at her, she stepped back out of sight.

After Dirk and Vanessa left, I turned to John. "You and Vanessa are awfully chummy."

He shrugged. "It's been years; there's a lot to catch up on." He glanced toward the doorway that she and Dirk had just disappeared through. "I get a bad feeling about that guy. The trainer—Dirk."

"Why?" I asked.

"I don't know. Something about how Vanessa reacted when his name came up. They're supposedly partners in this business, but she didn't want to talk about him at all."

That made perfect sense to me, assuming the rumors were true and Vanessa and Dirk *were* an item. After all, if you're angling for your ex-boyfriend, you don't generally want to talk about your current flame.

"Do you know how long they've known each other?" I asked.

"I don't know," he said. "But from what I've seen, I don't like the guy. There's something shady about him." He stretched again and glanced at his watch. "I'd better let you get some sleep."

"What about the 'to-be-continued-later'?" I asked, remembering this morning's kiss in the kitchen. It had only been hours ago, but right now it felt like years.

"You look like you're pretty busy," he said, leaning down to kiss my forehead. Which wasn't quite what I had in mind. "How about we save it for a time when you don't have a pack of starving guests to feed?"

"Are you sure?" I asked.

"Positive." He kissed me again—this time on the lips, but so lightly I could barely feel it. "See you in the morning?"

"Sure," I said, feeling a gaping hole open up in my stomach. "Sleep well," I said, trying not to sound hurt.

"You too," he said, giving my arm a squeeze and pulling on his jacket. When I heard the outside door close behind him, I stalked off to the kitchen.

Gwen was there, nursing a cup of tea. "There is no way I'm going to Fernand's tomorrow morning," she said.

"Why not?"

She gestured toward the door John had just exited. A few raindrops gleamed on the wooden floor. "And let John revisit the lighthouse with Vanessa? Without you?"

"The rest of the group will be there."

"And so will you," she said.

I bit my lip and stared at the carriage house. "Do you think I need to be?"

"If I were you, I wouldn't miss it," she said.

I closed my eyes and massaged my temples. Only six more days, I told myself. She couldn't win him over in six days.

Or could she?

———

The combination of my rumbling stomach, my worries about keeping an inn full of dieting guests happy for a week, and my nagging concerns about John and Vanessa kept me tossing and turning for hours. Biscuit abandoned me at midnight, annoyed at having her beauty sleep continuously interrupted, and at 1 a.m. I headed to the kitchen to make another cup of chamomile tea. I was just dunking a tea bag into the mug when I caught a flash of light in the darkness. I glanced out the front window; there, at the top of the hill, shone a pair of headlights. As I watched, they turned and disappeared back down the road. Who would be driving by the inn at one in the morning? I wondered. I waited for the lights to return, but they didn't. I'd ask at the store tomorrow, I decided; someone there would know.

My stomach rumbled audibly, and I was about to give in to temptation and grab a handful of gingersnaps when I heard the squeak of the front door. I closed the lid on the jar and pushed through the kitchen door, adrenaline pumping through me.

Who was coming in—or out—in the middle of the night?

I crept through the dining room and peered around the corner into the front hall. It was Vanessa, her black hair damp with rain. "Vanessa?"

She looked up, startled. Her cheeks were flushed, and her dark eyes shone. "Oh my gosh. You scared me!"

"You scared me, too," I said. "What were you doing out there? Is everything okay?"

Her eyes darted to the door, then back to me. "I had a hard time sleeping," she said, "so I went for a walk."

"In this rain?" I asked.

"It's kind of a nice change from California," she said. "I just spent a few weeks there."

"Did you see the car outside?"

Vanessa blinked at me with doe eyes. "Car? No, I didn't."

Yeah, right. "It was up at the top of the hill, just a moment ago."

She shook her head slowly, then shrugged. "I must have missed it. Anyway, I'm off to sleep now. See you in the morning. Eight o'clock, right?"

"Right," I said as she disappeared up the stairs. Who had she just met with? I wondered. Tom Lockhart again? Or another man she'd seduced and left, years ago?

I glanced out the window at the falling rain and retreated to the kitchen, where I retrieved my cup of tea and headed back upstairs. Biscuit had returned to the bed in my absence. She snuggled in at my feet as I pulled the covers around me once more, struggling to get to sleep—and hoping it wasn't John that Vanessa had come in from seeing.

———

Seven o'clock the next morning found me standing in my kitchen, clutching a mug of coffee in one hand and feeding eggs into a pot of cold water with the other. Sleep had not come until well after two the previous night, and even though I was on my second cup of coffee, I wanted nothing more than to crawl back under the covers with Biscuit.

When the last egg was nestled in the water, I turned on the burner and took another swig of coffee before retrieving the can of pumpkin. The oatmeal wouldn't take long to cook, so I had a few minutes of peace—and time to get something into my empty stomach—before tackling the next steps. I tossed a piece of wheat bread into the toaster—it wasn't a cinnamon roll, but at least it would get me through to breakfast—and sat down at the kitchen table, staring through the window at the green world outside.

The sky had dumped a few more inches of rain onto the already soaked earth, but the plants didn't seem to mind a bit; I swear the grass had doubled in height overnight. I hoped the group planned to take the road, and not the cliff path, down to the lighthouse this morning. If they didn't, they were at risk of being mired in the mud.

The rumble of a car interrupted my reverie; it grew steadily louder, and then stopped outside the inn. A moment later, Charlene appeared at my kitchen doorstep, stamping mud from her boots and trying to rearrange her hair under the hood of her green jacket.

"You're here early," I said as she peeled off her boots at the kitchen door.

"Wouldn't want to miss the jog," she said. "Although how they're going to get to the lighthouse in this, I have no idea." She eyed the mug in my hand. "Got any coffee? I'm still half asleep."

"Coming right up," I said, pouring her a mug as she hung her slicker on the hook by the door. Under her jacket she was dressed in a form-fitting pink sweater and designer jeans. "You're jogging in that?" I asked.

"Beauty before practicality," she said, pulling up a chair at my big farm table.

"Maybe you'll just have to stay in by the fire," I suggested.

"That would be lovely," Charlene sighed. "I wouldn't mind a little one-on-one time with Dirk. As long as we could get rid of all those other people."

I laughed. "Better watch out. Rumor is that he and Vanessa are a couple."

She pushed out her lower lip. "Really?"

"I can't tell," I confessed. "They don't seem very close if they are."

"Speaking of close, what's up between Vanessa and John?"

"I don't know. But they've been doing a bit more 'catching up' than I'm comfortable with. And Tom Lockhart was here last night, with fifteen pounds of free lobster."

"Uh-oh," she said.

"Exactly. He seemed absolutely smitten. Does Lorraine know?"

"I don't know, but you'd better watch out for that one," Charlene said, cradling the mug of coffee between her hands as she slid into a kitchen chair. "Eleazer told me last night that she broke a lot of hearts on the island."

"Was John's one of them?"

"One of many, from what I've heard." She took a sip of coffee and plunked the mug down on the table. "That woman," she said, "is a menace."

"I'm positive she met with someone in the middle of the night. There was a car at the top of the hill, and she came in a few minutes later."

Charlene arched an eyebrow. "Sounds to me like Dirk's a single man, then. Which is good news for you, too," she added. "John doesn't have a car on the island, so she must have been out with someone else."

"You're right," I said, feeling a bit more chipper all of a sudden. "How come I didn't think of that?"

"That's what friends are for," she replied, glancing at the clock. "By the way, shouldn't you be cooking something? It's almost seven thirty."

"Already?" I glanced at the clock; she was right. I grabbed my now-cold toast from the toaster and tore off a bite before opening the pumpkin. I was scraping orange goo out of a measuring cup when Gwen trundled downstairs.

"You're up early," I said.

"You're jogging up to the lighthouse along with John and Vanessa," she reminded me.

"Good plan," Charlene said. "I wouldn't leave him with that woman for a moment. It's not that I don't trust John. It's just ..."

"Exactly," said Gwen.

I glanced out the window and shuddered, thinking of my last attempt to jog. I added a teaspoon of pumpkin pie spice to the oatmeal, suffusing the kitchen with the warm scents of allspice and nutmeg. After stirring it a few times, then stepped away from the stove. "The things we do for love," I grumbled as I headed upstairs to find a decent pair of shoes.

SIX

When I walked into the dining room in my sneakers a little while later, Bethany, who had donned a rather tight black sweat suit for this morning's outing, was standing beside Vanessa, who had hardly touched her oatmeal.

"Where's Dirk?" Bethany asked. "Isn't he going to be leading the hike?"

"I'm sure he'll be down at any moment," said Vanessa, who didn't seem to be showing any signs of sleep deprivation despite her late-night sortie. "We don't leave until nine, so why don't you go ahead and enjoy this delicious breakfast!"

Bethany reluctantly returned to her table, and after one more bite of the fragrant oatmeal, Vanessa headed for the stairs, leaving her charges to grumble over the small portions.

"This oatmeal is delicious," said Cat, who had traded in her formless blue sweater for an equally formless purple sweatshirt and a pair of black cotton pants. "Just like pumpkin pie—only healthy!"

"I would have preferred an omelet," complained Sarah as she cracked a soft-boiled egg onto a piece of dry toast. She was looking smart in white-trimmed pink workout pants and a matching jacket. "I don't know how I'm going to run on this little food."

"Just think how gorgeous you'll be for the reunion," Boots reminded her, reaching down to adjust her sleek black Spandex jogging pants. She'd paired them with a tank top and a trim aqua jacket that brought out the deep blue of her eyes. I tugged at my own bulky jacket enviously; Boots, I decided, should give classes to full-figured women on dressing to flatter your shape.

"I'm not sure it's worth it," Sarah said, adjusting her waistband. "Did Vanessa say there would be snacks along the way?"

"I hope so," said Cat, "or she's going to have to carry me back."

"I don't know. Ever since we got here, I've just had so much more *energy*," said Bethany. "It must be all the clean eating."

Sarah rolled her eyes and took a bite of egg and toast as I headed back to the kitchen.

"I'll serve the rest of the guests. You'd better go get ready," my niece said.

"Thanks, Gwen. Marge should be here by nine thirty. Why don't you plan on heading over to Fernand's as soon as she gets here?"

"We'll see how it goes," she replied, tucking a stray strand of dark hair behind one ear. I couldn't help smiling to myself as I headed upstairs to change. When Gwen first arrived, her housekeeping skills had been minimal at best. Now, she was concerned that the help I'd hired wasn't up to her exacting standards.

At nine o'clock, everyone had left the dining room, Gwen was elbow-deep in soapy water again, and the rest of us were all assembled outside the inn, breathing in the cold morning air. The

59

sun had come out from behind the clouds again, and the contrast of the robin's-egg-blue sky against the green and gray of the island was breathtaking.

John showed up as we gathered in front of the inn, and after kissing me briefly on the top of the head, had been pulled into Vanessa's orbit. As Vanessa smoothed down her sleek black windbreaker, I pulled my puffy jacket around me, wishing yet again that I had invested in something a bit more stylish. I looked around at the rest of the group, who were standing on the front porch with their hands burrowed into their pockets. Things with John might not be going swimmingly, but I was happy to see that despite the size of the breakfast, everybody looked pretty chipper. There was only one thing missing: Dirk.

"I keep looking for that gorgeous man who's supposed to be leading us," my friend said, her blue eyes scouring the area for signs of the trainer. "Shouldn't he be here by now?"

Charlene wasn't the only one who had noticed his absence. "Where's our leader?" asked Bethany, looking up at what I knew to be Dirk's window. "He didn't even come down to give us our supplements this morning."

"I don't know," said Vanessa, a small furrow appearing in her otherwise flawless brow. "He said he might go for an early run this morning. I'm sure he'll be back soon, but "I'll go knock on his door again. Maybe he's in the shower. But if he's not here by ten after, I promise we'll go on our own. After all, we have an excellent guide with us." Her sleek hair shone as she nodded toward John, who was standing on the front doorstep. His shoulders straightened slightly, and he smiled.

"I told you she was trouble," Charlene murmured.

When Dirk didn't show up by 9:10, Vanessa started up the hill at a light jog, with the rest of us puffing behind her like ducklings. Although she was interminably perky, her smile was a bit dimmer than usual, and I noticed her shooting frequent glances back toward the inn.

Despite the cool breeze off the water behind us—and despite the fact that Vanessa, once resigned to her trainer's absence, stepped right back into motivational mode and kept exhorting us to "pick up the pace" and "really work those glutes," it was a beautiful morning to be out attempting to jog. (By the time we got halfway up the hill, most of us were purple, so Vanessa bowed to the inevitable and slowed to a brisk walk.) The pine trees filled the air with their fresh scent, which I got ample lungfuls of, since I was gasping for breath. As we crested the hill, another robin swooped over the road in front of us.

"First robin I've seen since the fall," Charlene said. "Spring really must be here to stay."

"It's about time," I said. As exciting as winter had been for me, with the novelties of snow and icicles, I was glad to kiss it goodbye. We started down the other side of the hill a few minutes later, panting, and got our first view of the lighthouse in the distance. A shiver ran down my back as I remembered the light I'd seen the night before.

"Did they already get the new lamp installed?" I asked, pointing at the lighthouse.

"Not that I know of," she said.

"We saw it last night," I said, finally catching my breath. "At dinnertime: it flashed about a half a dozen times."

She shrugged. "Maybe I'm wrong."

"Do you think it has anything to do with the legend?" I asked.

"Oh, the omen thing? It hasn't happened while I've been here, and lord knows we've seen more than our share of tragedies." She fell silent for a moment, and I knew she was thinking of Richard McLaughlin, the rector she had dated briefly—and who had been murdered just last fall.

"By the way," I said, hoping to get her mind off those not-so-distant memories, "any word on the skeleton?"

She sucked in her breath. "Didn't I tell you?"

"No. You were too busy mooning about Dirk."

"I wasn't mooning," she said, pushing a lock of hair out of her eyes. "I was admiring. Or bemoaning his absence."

"Whatever," I said. "What did they find out?"

"The results came back yesterday—or at least that's what Matilda said." Matilda Jenkins was the island's historian, and had spearheaded the conservation effort. "Apparently the skeleton belonged to a man, and they think he's been there for about a hundred and fifty years," Charlene continued. "They said they could estimate the time period from the buckles on his shoes."

"No wonder the population's so small on this island," I joked. "The murder rate appears to be well above average."

"Actually, they *do* think he was murdered," Charlene said.

"Why?"

"I'm not sure yet—Matilda didn't tell me the details. I'm not sure *she* knows yet."

A shiver passed through me when I thought of the bones that had lain hidden in secret for all those years. "Do they think it was the lighthouse keeper?"

She shrugged. "The timing's right, so it's a good guess, but there's no way to know. It may just be another unsolved mystery. On the other hand, it should help the tourist trade; nothing like a good ghost story to draw visitors." Vanessa's throaty laugh reached us—she was shoulder-to-shoulder with my neighbor—and Charlene nudged me. "We'd better get up there," she said.

Personally, I wasn't sure my presence was going to make any difference; for starters, in my bulky, shapeless jacket, the whole comparison thing wasn't exactly in my favor, and I didn't think my turning up was going to do much to quell John's evident attraction to Vanessa anyway. But Charlene urged me forward, and a minute later she and I were trotting along right behind the slender retreat leader and my flannel-clad boyfriend.

"Hi, Natalie," John said when he saw me, flashing me a white-toothed grin that made my heart melt. "Great morning to be out, isn't it?"

"It is," I agreed. Particularly now that we were headed downhill, and no longer jogging.

"How far is the lighthouse?" asked Cat, who was sandwiched between her sorority sisters behind me.

"Another twenty minutes," John said.

"Will there be snacks when we get there?"

"Don't worry, I've got you covered." Vanessa patted her smart little backpack, which I knew was filled with energy bars that looked and tasted like sawdust mixed with miniscule chocolate chips.

We spent much of that remaining time listening to John and Vanessa catch up on old times, with Charlene interjecting what she knew of longtime island residents.

"So Murray Selfridge made it big, I hear," Vanessa said.

"He's been trying to do the same for the island," John said, referring to Selfridge's repeated attempts to push developments through the board of selectmen.

"It looks like he hasn't been successful so far," Vanessa said. "The island hasn't changed a bit."

"Not yet—and a lot of it's due to Tom Lockhart."

"Why is that?" Vanessa asked.

"He's a pretty big deal around here," Charlene said. "He stepped into his father's shoes as head of the lobster co-op, and he's also chair of the board of selectmen."

"It doesn't surprise me," Vanessa said, smiling. "He was always charismatic. It was good to see him again …" There was an odd look in her almond-shaped eyes as she spoke. Had she seen him more than once yesterday? I wondered.

"What about you?" John asked her. "Last I heard you were engaged to some real estate mogul in New Jersey."

"Didn't work out," she said quickly. "He was already married to his business. But tell me about everybody else. What happened to Eric Hoyle?"

As John and Charlene filled Vanessa in on the rest of the gossip—some of which was interesting, but much of which I already knew—I glanced behind me to see what everyone else was up to. Bethany was looking distraught, doubtless at the absence of her love object, and the three sorority sisters appeared to be taking their own little trip down memory lane. Megan was walking stolidly alongside Greg; Carissa trailed them, looking miserable. Once I glimpsed her slipping something into her mouth—it looked like a mini Snickers bar—and again I felt that stab of pity. The reporter was at the rear of the line, alone.

Elizabeth had put away her notebook, but was snapping pictures with a little digital camera. I couldn't blame her; with the fresh green leaves springing up on the sides of the road, and the dark trees finally free of their blanket of snow, the scenery was breathtaking.

As we approached the lighthouse, I could see the construction equipment from the renovation clustered at the end of the trail. The area around the lighthouse was ringed by a construction fence, and the previously narrow, rarely traveled path had widened considerably with all the traffic. I thought again about Vanessa's late-night outing; had she and either Tom or John come back last night to revisit their old haunts?

Stop being ridiculous, I told myself. John didn't even have a car.

"Watch out for rocks!" Vanessa said in a cheery voice as she started down the path. John followed her, and I fell in behind him, Charlene trailing me.

"All this effort, and Dirk didn't even show up," Charlene muttered. "I'm sweating for nothing."

"What's that?" It was Elizabeth, from somewhere behind me. She was pointing to something that looked like a speed bump on the trail. I craned to look over John's shoulder; whatever it was was blue, with a flash of white.

"I don't know," I answered. "Maybe it's something the workers left behind."

We had only taken a few more steps when Vanessa screamed.

SEVEN

"OH MY GOD," CHARLENE breathed beside me as Vanessa stumbled up the path and dropped to her knees beside an inert form.

"What is it?" asked Boots from behind us.

I stared at the still form Vanessa was bending over. I recognized the thatch of blond hair.

"I think it's Dirk," I said, feeling sick.

"Vanessa," John called, following her up the path. He pressed two fingers to Dirk's neck, checking for a pulse. Then he turned to Vanessa, pity in his eyes. "I'm sorry, Vanessa. He's gone; there's nothing else you can do for him."

"No," she wailed. "No, no, no." Her voice was hollow with despair. "Dirk! Answer me!"

"Vanessa, please move away from him," John said quietly, in his deputy voice. "We have to call the detectives so they can find out what happened here."

"But he can't be dead!" she sobbed. "He was alive just last night!"

"I know," John said, and pulled her in to his chest. One hand cradled her dark head and the other stroked her slim back. Charlene shot me a glance.

As Vanessa wept in John's arms, I glanced at the inert form on the path. Dirk's sightless blue eyes stared at the matching sky. After a moment, my own eyes flicked to the lighthouse behind him. Had last night's light been an omen after all?

"Natalie." John's voice was calm. "Please go to the nearest house and call the police. Then take everyone back to the inn."

"Sure," I said, glancing back at the group. Bethany looked stricken; tears coursed down her pale cheeks. A stray thought flitted through my mind. What was she going to do now that the center of her universe was gone?

Boots, Sarah, and Cat were murmuring among themselves, shaking their heads at the tragedy, but watching with the avid interest of rubberneckers passing an accident. Megan had taken the opportunity to grip Greg's arm, and he was patting her hand absently while Megan's daughter, Carissa, stared slack-jawed at the dead trainer, a trace of something that looked like chocolate visible on her pale lower lip. Elizabeth quietly snapped shots of the body with her digital camera, then tucked the camera away and pulled out her notebook. To her, I realized, this was a benefit. A murder made for a much better story than a bunch of people trying to lose weight.

I turned back to where Vanessa was still clutching John and weeping.

"I'll take the group back to the inn," I said. "But what about Vanessa?"

He touched her chin gently and tilted up her tear-stained face. "Vanessa," he said. "I think you should go back with Natalie. She's going to call the police."

"But ... I can't leave him!" she wailed.

"Sweetheart, you need to. Think of the retreat. You've got to keep it together."

Sweetheart? I could feel my jaw tighten.

"You're right," she said, straightening her shoulders and taking a deep breath. A moment later she wiped the tears from her face and faced the group. "Okay, everyone. We should probably head back to the inn so we can ..." Her face crumpled, and she burst into tears again.

"Come with me," I said, more shortly than I meant to. As I held my hand out, John helped her stumble across the trail toward me. I looked at him. "I'll send Charlene to the store to call the police while I take your sweetheart back to the inn," I said.

His green eyes flickered briefly. Then he said, "Fine. I'll stay here with the body until the police arrive."

"Right." I took Vanessa's skinny arm. "Charlene, will you head down to the store and call the police?"

"Sure," she said, her blue eyes glued to the trainer's body. As were everyone else's. After the initial gasp of shock, it had been eerily silent, except for the sound of waves crashing against the rocks, and the occasional mournful call of a gull. "Let's head back to the inn," I called to the retreat participants, who shuffled back down the path, away from the lighthouse—and from Dirk.

Vanessa kept looking over her shoulder as we followed the group back to the road. "I can't believe he's dead," she whimpered. I squeezed her thin arm and said nothing.

"What do you think happened to him?" Elizabeth asked as we sat in the inn's dining room forty minutes later. Once we got back, I'd brewed Vanessa a cup of chamomile tea; she'd taken it and retreated to her room, probably in part to avoid Elizabeth, who kept peppering her with questions. Bethany had disappeared as well, after traipsing back to the inn looking like the love of her life had just died. Which, in a way, I guess, he had. Despite my anger over John's behavior toward Vanessa, I was more than a little concerned for both of them.

I took a sip of my sugarless hot chocolate, wishing I'd spiked it with brandy—I could use a little fortification right about now. I had broken down and snagged a small stack of gingersnaps, figuring since I'd just seen a dead body and heard my so-called boyfriend use a term of endearment to address his ex-girlfriend, it was completely warranted. *Sweetheart*, he'd called her. I knew I should be more upset about Dirk's untimely demise, but right now I was feeling numbed by what had passed between John and Vanessa.

"I don't know what happened," Megan said from her chair by the window. She had managed to lower the zipper of her sweatshirt so that it exposed a good inch of cleavage, I noticed. Her daughter had disappeared—probably, like me, to find solace in something sweet—but Greg hadn't; he was seated just inches away from her. "I didn't see any blood."

"Me neither," said Boots.

"I didn't look that closely," said Cat. She shuddered. "Maybe he had a heart attack or something."

"What I want to know is, what was he doing out there?" asked Sarah. "I mean, we have like six exercise sessions scheduled a day."

"He is…was…pretty fit," Cat said, swinging a heavy leg. "Maybe he was one of those exercise addicts, and it finally caught up with him."

"The big question is, what does this do for the rest of the retreat?" Sarah complained, crossing her arms over her ample stomach. The sun gleamed on her pale, gray-blond hair. "Now that the trainer's gone, do we get our money back?" And I thought *I* was crass for being upset about John and Vanessa.

"I'm more worried that there may be a murderer on the loose," Megan said, inching closer to Greg. The wedding band on her left hand glinted in the light from the window, and I found myself wondering what Carissa thought of this new coziness between her mother and the portly man in sweats.

"We don't know he was murdered," I reminded them. "Like Cat said, it could have been a heart attack or something."

"If he was murdered, that will probably change the slant of your article," Boots said to Elizabeth.

She gave us an enigmatic smile and said, "Perhaps."

There was a knock at the front door, and all of us jumped. A moment later, Charlene joined us.

"Who's manning the shop?" I asked.

"Tania's taking over for me. I wanted to come and help out."

"Marge is doing the rooms for me," I said, "but I need to start on lunch. Why don't you keep me company?" I asked.

"Sure," she said.

"If anybody needs anything," I said to the group in the dining room, "I'll be in the kitchen. Just knock."

When we were safely behind the kitchen door, I fixed Charlene a cup of hot chocolate and pulled a package of cod fillets from the refrigerator. I hadn't had the heart to cook the fish John had caught, and had ended up tucking it into the freezer. "Okay," I said, turning to my friend. "What's the scoop?"

Charlene sighed and toyed with her spoon. "I haven't heard anything yet, but I know the police are on their way. What a waste, though. Another gorgeous man, dead." She looked up at me. "Do you think I'm jinxed?"

"Of course not," I said. "You thought he was attractive, but it wasn't like you were dating or anything."

"Actually," she said, "I asked him to come over for dinner some night this week, and he agreed, so technically that may not be true."

"But you hadn't actually gone on a date yet," I pointed out as I minced some ginger and garlic.

"True."

"Did you hear anything about how he died?" I asked as I added orange juice and a touch of brown sugar to the aromatic mixture. I could already taste the teriyaki marinade in my head; it would be light on oil, but heavy on flavor.

"They're still working on that," she said. "Tania's supposed to call me if she hears anything down at the store. And I'm hoping John will tell us."

"I'm not sure I'm speaking to John," I said as I pulled a bottle of sesame oil from the pantry.

Charlene winced. "That sweetheart thing was a pretty big slip."

"Yeah," I said, my heart squeezing. "Maybe too big."

"Natalie, it may not be what you think. Maybe he was just trying to calm her down. A heat of the moment kind of thing."

"Brought on by the lighthouse where they shared all those special summer moments," I said sourly. Then I shook myself. A man had just died, and here I was worrying about a lovers' squabble. "There's nothing I can do about it now, though. I need to focus on my job." Although if we did break up, having John live next door would put a big damper on the enjoyment of my new life.

I had mixed the soy sauce and a dash of sesame oil together with the ginger mixture and was pouring everything over the fish when the phone rang. I sloshed a bit of marinade onto the counter in my haste to pick it up.

"Gray Whale Inn," I said into the receiver.

"Natalie, it's John."

My heart seized in my chest. "Oh. Hi."

"I wanted to let you know the police are on their way over to the inn."

"Why?"

I could hear him suck in his breath. "They haven't done the autopsy yet, but it looks like Dirk's death was suspicious."

"What does that mean?"

"It means we could be looking at another homicide investigation."

I closed my eyes and sank against the counter. "Wonderful."

There was silence for a moment. Then he said, in a tentative voice, "How's Vanessa?"

"I don't know," I snapped. "You can ask her yourself when you get back."

And then I hung up on him.

Charlene was staring at me. "What was that all about?"

"It looks like it was murder," I said, feeling my stomach sink.

"That's what I figured," she said, grimacing. "Do they know how he died?"

"They haven't done the autopsy yet. But I do know they're sending the cops over to the inn."

"Better toss in a few more fillets then," she said. "If I remember correctly, Sgt. Grimes looked like a pretty big eater."

I groaned. "Thanks for reminding me."

EIGHT

THE DOORBELL RANG JUST as I slid the bowl of cod into the fridge. I rinsed my hands at the sink and ran to answer it.

To my surprise, it wasn't Grimes; it was a stout woman with a Brillo pad of hair and a shiny badge glinting from beneath her blue coat. Her eyes were icy gray under a wide, oily-looking forehead. "Miss Natalie Barnes?" she asked.

"That's me," I said.

"Detective Rose," she said. "You and your group found the body, is that right?"

"Yes," I said. "I heard you'd be stopping by. Won't you come in?"

"Thank you," she said brusquely, not bothering to wipe her shoes before stepping into my entry hall.

"I understand you're running a retreat of some kind here," she said.

"That's right. A weight-loss retreat."

"Are the participants still on the premises?"

"As far as I know, yes," I said.

"I'll need to question them, then."

I stifled a sigh. This week was looking like it might be a total disaster. Still, there *had* been a death, and the police needed to do what they could to find out what happened. I was glad it wasn't Grimes here to do the questioning; otherwise, there was a good chance I'd already be the prime suspect for a murder nobody was sure had even been committed. "Can I take your coat?" I asked.

"Thank you." She shucked the blue coat off, and as she handed it to me, I got a strong whiff of Ivory soap. Which was a definite improvement over the cigarette aroma of Sgt. Grimes.

"Where are the individuals who were with you when you discovered the body?" Detective Rose asked, looking past me to the living room, where several of the guests were already staring at the police officer.

"Some are in the living room," I said, "and the rest are in their rooms."

"I need them all to stay in their rooms until I've had a chance to speak with them individually," she said.

"Some of them have roommates," I pointed out.

"Even so, they are not to discuss the case."

That horse was already out of the barn, but I decided not to mention it. Instead, I led her to the living room and allowed her to share the unpleasant news that everyone was to be quarantined to their rooms. The guests filed out of the living room with wide eyes when she informed them it was a murder investigation. I tried to keep a smile on my face as she told everyone they were confined to the premises while she conducted the questioning. House arrest, essentially. Just what my guests were looking for out of a high-priced luxury weight-loss retreat.

"I'm getting things ready in the kitchen," I said to the detective. "Would you like a cup of coffee to warm you up while you're waiting for the other officer to arrive?"

"It'll just be me today," she said, following me toward the kitchen, where Charlene sat perched on one of the kitchen chairs. "But thanks, coffee would be good."

"This is my friend, Charlene Kean," I said as we pushed through the swinging door. "She runs the Cranberry Island Store; she was with us when we found the body."

"Detective Rose," the police officer said, extending a hand abruptly to shake Charlene's hand before sitting down at the opposite end of the table. She pulled out a notebook as I poured her a mug of coffee from a carafe and fixed a plate of gingersnaps to go along with it. Like Grimes, Detective Rose looked like an officer who enjoyed her food. Speaking of Grimes, where was he? As I set the mug of steaming coffee in front of the detective, I inquired after him.

"Sgt. Grimes took a leave of absence," Detective Rose said shortly, adding a spoonful of sugar and a glug of milk to her coffee. I breathed a sigh of relief at the news. But the relief was short-lived. "I understand you've been mixed up in a number of investigations over the past year," she said, her hawk-like eyes focusing on me in a way that made me distinctly uncomfortable.

"Unfortunately, there have been a number of tragedies on the island in the past year," I admitted, pulling a bag of snow peas from the refrigerator.

"Ever since you arrived, from what I hear."

Perhaps she wasn't such an improvement over Grimes after all. "Apparently it's a longstanding island tradition," I said, thinking of the skeleton the contractors had recently found at the lighthouse.

"How did you know Mr. DeLeon?"

"I'd just met him, actually. He handled the personal training portion of the retreat."

"I understand he distributed supplements as well," she said.

"Yes," I said.

"Any idea what was in those supplements?"

"No," I said, not entirely truthfully. "I'm sure there are some in his room, though; I saw a bag of them while I was doing turndown service last night."

"I'll have to be sure to send some to the lab," the detective said, making a note in her notebook. The warm light shone on her steel-wool-colored hair.

"Why are you asking about the supplements?" Charlene asked. "Do they have something to do with Dirk's death?"

"I cannot discuss the details of the case," Detective Rose said, focusing on Charlene and sniffing slightly. For a moment, I almost found myself wishing for Grimes again. The devil you know, I guess... "Were you acquainted with Mr. DeLeon?" she asked.

"We just met yesterday," Charlene said, running a finger under her right eye to check for smudged mascara. There wasn't any, of course—Charlene applied her Mary Kay makeup with expert precision. "We'd talked about having dinner, but things... well, he died before we could do it, obviously."

"So neither of you met the deceased before yesterday afternoon," she said. "Is that correct?"

"That's correct," I confirmed.

"When did you last see Mr. DeLeon?"

"Last night," I said. "He came in and told Vanessa—Vanessa Tagliacozzi, the other retreat leader—that he needed to talk to her."

"What time was that?"

"Around seven, I think."

"And what time did he leave the inn?"

I shook my head. "No idea. I didn't know he was gone until this morning, when no one could find him."

She wiped her wide forehead with the back of her hand and made a note on her pad. "Did anyone else leave the inn last night?"

"Not that I know of ... except Vanessa."

"The other retreat leader?"

"Yes. I was in the kitchen making myself tea at around one—I was having a hard time sleeping—and I heard the front door open and close. I went out to see who it was, and it turned out to be Vanessa. She said she'd gone out for a walk."

"So she went out for a walk sometime last night and returned at approximately 1 a.m.," Detective Rose repeated.

"Only I'm not sure she was walking. There was a car outside at about the same time, just before she came in."

"Do you know whose car it was?"

I shook my head. "No; it was too dark."

"If you'd like," Charlene offered, "I can ask around and see who was out."

Detective Rose gave her a sharp look. "Please leave the interrogation to the police, Miss ..."

"Kean," she reminded her, giving the officer a chilly look in return. "Charlene Kean."

In my opinion, Detective Rose was making a huge mistake. If anyone could find out who was driving that car, it was Charlene, who could probably tell you what half the island had for dinner last night if you wanted to know.

"Where were you last night, Miss—it is Miss, right?"

"Ms.," Charlene said frostily. "I was here for dinner, and then I went home."

"On foot?" Detective Rose asked.

"In my truck."

The policewoman's left eyebrow shot up, and she jotted something down in her little notebook.

She asked us a couple more logistical questions, which we answered easily, before draining her coffee and standing up. She tugged her polyester trousers up over her ample middle—based on the two police officers I'd gotten to know so far, there must have been a whole lot of donut-eating going on back at the station—and said, "I'm going to begin questioning the guests now."

"Is it all right if I head back to the store?" Charlene asked.

The detective nodded shortly. "You can go back to the store," she said. "But please don't leave the island for a couple of days. Either of you." Her piercing gaze flitted from Charlene's face to mine.

Lovely, I thought, as the swinging door shut behind her.

"So, do you think you can find out who was out and about last night?" I asked Charlene once I was sure Detective Rose was out of earshot.

"I don't know," she said, looking sourly at the door the officer had just exited through, "but you can bet I'm going to try."

Lunch was a quiet affair. It had to be, really, since Detective Rose hadn't finished questioning everyone, and nobody was allowed to talk. But the hush that fell over the dining room wasn't entirely due to police procedure. Dirk's death had put a pall over the retreat—not just of sadness, but of fear.

I had invited the officer to join us for lunch—after all, with the trainer out of commission, I had an extra fillet on hand—and she pulled up a chair at a table by the window, next to Megan and Greg, who were seated across from each other like an old married couple. Which they weren't, I had to remind myself. Carissa and Bethany hadn't emerged from their rooms, but everyone else was present, including Vanessa, whose oval face was ashen. Boots, Sarah, and Cat, who shared a table with the retreat leader, looked stricken as well, and as I served plates of fragrant teriyaki codfish with sautéed snow peas, everyone eyed their plates with reluctance. Which seemed strange to me until I heard Megan ask the detective something in a low voice.

"Poison?" Detective Rose answered loudly. "Let's hope not. But even if it is, I doubt anyone would try it with officers on the premises." She hacked off a slab of codfish and started shoveling it in; a moment later, everyone else reluctantly followed suit. It was a shame they were so worried about the food. The teriyaki fish was a killer recipe, even if it was low-cal, and it was frustrating to see it wasted on an unappreciative audience.

I retreated to the kitchen, hoping the cause of death turned out to be something other than lethal chemicals. A dead guest was bad enough. The last thing I needed was a detective suggesting my food might be poisoned. Gertrude Pickens of the *Daily Mail* would be on my doorstep in five minutes flat. And if they shut down my kitchen, the inn was finished.

Speaking of Gertrude, I was surprised I hadn't heard from her yet. Usually she was one of the quickest off the mark when there was bad news to be spread.

As if on cue, the phone rang. I hurried to pick it up, hoping I hadn't jinxed myself. But it wasn't Gertrude. It was Charlene.

"What did you find out?" I asked quietly as I scooted behind the desk.

"I think I know who came by the inn last night," she said.

"Who?" I asked.

"Don't you want to guess?"

"No!"

"Tom Lockhart," she said. "Ernie lives two doors down from him. He has a hard time sleeping, so he's up nights a lot."

"How does he know it was Tom?"

"He heard Tom's truck go by at around one, headed up the road, in the direction of the inn. When he heard it on its way back, he peeked out the window—said he saw it pull into Tom's driveway."

"Did he see Tom?" I asked.

"No. But who else would it have been?"

"I don't know. His wife, maybe?"

Charlene snorted. "Do you really think Vanessa would turn up in the middle of the night all rosy-cheeked because she'd spent an hour with Lorraine Lockhart?"

I sighed. "Should I tell Detective Rose?"

"You could, but I don't know what it will accomplish. Besides, since I didn't see it myself, I hate to get Tom involved just because Ernie thought he saw him."

"True," I said.

"Do you think they might have set something up while he was over at the inn yesterday?"

"Probably. They had a few minutes on their own, in the living room."

"That must have been it, then. I know Tom had a crush on Vanessa when she used to spend summers here. Apparently he pined for her for years—Lorraine still gets upset if you talk about her. And he was pretty quick to show up with free lobsters."

A pit opened up in the bottom of my stomach. Even-tempered, happily married Tom Lockhart, who was chair of the board of selectmen, president of the Cranberry Island Lobster Co-op, and one of my favorite people on the island. I could picture his blue eyes, twinkling merrily. I couldn't imagine him as a murderer. "Are you saying you think Tom might have killed Dirk?" I asked.

"I don't know," she said. "I've known Tom a long time, and I just can't see it."

"Me neither," I said, relieved that Charlene agreed with me. "Then again, Vanessa does seem to have an effect on men."

"We're jumping to conclusions here, Nat," Charlene said. "We don't even know when he died. Or how. Or if it was homicide, even."

I looked out the window at the lush spring grass, the dark blue water. It looked the same as it had that morning. But for me, everything had changed. "You're right. But there is a detective here, asking questions," I reminded her, "and suggesting it might have been poison. So the police must be thinking in that direction."

"Let's hope they're at least slightly more competent than Grimes. Although I don't get a great read off that Rose woman." I hadn't either, but I didn't voice the opinion. "Do you think you can find out details from John?" she asked.

"Maybe," I said. "But then again, maybe not. With Vanessa around, things are a little chilly."

"Maybe you could invite him over for a candlelight dinner."

"Yeah," I said sourly, looking out the window at the craggy mountains of the mainland. The peaceful scene was deceptive; in the last twenty-four hours, my life had been stirred into a maelstrom. "Fat-free chicken breast and steamed vegetables. How romantic."

"Which reminds me—any chance of getting some of your mint bars down here? I've been getting a lot of requests."

"I'll see what I can do," I said, wondering how I was going to be able to bake something as sinful as my Midnight Mint Bars with a starving horde of dieters on the other side of the kitchen door.

"I've got to go—half the island just walked through the door. Word must be out about Dirk."

"Let me know what you find out," I said, hanging up and walking into the dining room. The guests had been eating so quietly I had almost forgotten I still had lunch to clean up after. I was beginning to see the downside of running a full-service inn; you never finished cooking or cleaning.

I cleared the empty plates and began washing up the dishes in the kitchen, and an hour later, when everything was back in shape, I thought about the mint chocolate bars Charlene had requested.

Did I dare make a pan of such sinful treats in an innful of hungry guests?

I debated briefly—and headed for the pantry. Diet or no diet, baking made me feel better—and delivering a pan of mint chocolate bars would give me an excuse to get out of the inn for an hour or two. And maybe steal a couple of tastes of chocolate while I was at it.

I grabbed the flour and sugar from the middle shelf, then retrieved a bottle of peppermint extract from the rack on the door. But when I reached for the baking chocolate, the box was empty.

Empty?

It had been full yesterday, when I'd made the meringues. How could it possibly be empty?

Unless I was mistaken, someone had been pilfering my pantry. I did a quick inventory, and discovered that a big bag of chocolate chips was gone, as well. The chocolate chips I could understand. But who the heck would eat a box of unsweetened baking chocolate?

My thoughts turned to Carissa, who had been surreptitiously sneaking squares of something brown into her mouth that morning. I had thought they were candy bars, but they could have been baking chocolate. I cringed just thinking about the taste of straight, unsweetened chocolate—but if she was that desperate, she was welcome to it. With a mother like that around, telling me every five minutes how gorgeous I would be if I lost my 'baby fat,' I might be reduced to similar measures myself. I'd just have to do a better job of hiding my calorie-laden loot in the future. Or maybe invest in a padlock.

I replaced the box on the shelf and dug around for a can of cocoa and some vegetable oil. It wasn't perfect, but it would do in a pinch.

Twenty minutes later, the baking had done its magic yet again. Working with the warm, dark chocolate had soothed me, and combined with the view of the sparkling blue water outside—thankfully, the kitchen island didn't offer a direct view of the lighthouse—had helped relieve some of the tension I was feeling. The batter was just about ready to go into the pan, and I'd only stolen two or three—okay, maybe four or five—spoonfuls when Marge, my new helper, came into the kitchen, carrying a stack of dirty towels.

"Hi, Marge!" I said brightly as I greased a baking pan. "Thanks for taking care of the rooms."

She nodded at me over the stack of terrycloth and then shook her head, making her jowls wobble a little bit. As usual, she wore cotton pants and an oversized T-shirt that did little to disguise her ample middle. "I heard about the trainer. Dead guests—ain't good for business."

No kidding. "At least it didn't happen on the premises," I said, trying to look on the bright side of things. At the mention of the death, my mind flashed back to the awful experience we'd shared in the fall, when we'd almost both been killed by her abusive husband. He was currently in jail on the mainland, and divorce proceedings were almost complete—and Marge, after years of living in a private hell, had been transformed by her liberation.

"I heard it might be poison," Marge said.

Uh-oh. "As far as I know," I said, trying not to sound strained, "they're still waiting for the autopsy results."

"You'd better make sure Gertrude Pickens over at the *Daily Mail* don't get wind of it," Marge said sagely. "Although how you're going to keep that nosy parker out of it, I'm sure I don't know." She clumped into the laundry room and filled the washer as I slid the mint bars into the oven and set the timer. *Please, please, please let Dirk have died of natural causes*, I thought. *Or at least not of poison.*

When she had loaded the towels into the washer, I invited Marge to join me for a cup of coffee.

"Still got two rooms to do," she said.

"You can do them in a minute," I said, anxious to ask her a few questions about Vanessa's island visits. "Why don't you take a break and keep me company while I make the frosting?"

Marge plumped down on one of the kitchen chairs; a moment later, she was munching through gingersnaps as I poured her a fresh mug of coffee. "Were you here when Vanessa used to spend her summers here?" I asked as I slid the mug across the table to her.

"Ayuh," she said. "She's trouble, is that one. Broke the hearts of half the menfolk here—turned their heads, then disappeared for the rest of the year. Left them all pining for her."

As I dug in the refrigerator for cream, I said, "I hear she and John were an item one summer." I was glad my back was to Marge, so she couldn't see my face.

"She was here a few summers," she answered. "But John wasn't the only one she got her hooks into. Your neighbor and Tom Lockhart almost came to blows over her one night, out at the dock."

"Really?" I asked lightly, measuring out sugar and trying to keep a smile fixed on my face. Although I suspect it was more of a grimace.

"Ayuh," she repeated. "It never came to nothing—Eleazer broke it up, told 'em it wasn't worth fighting over a woman, and they both went home. But there was bad feeling there for a long time." She paused to eat another gingersnap. "And Lorraine is still jealous of the woman, even though it's been near fifteen years. When she heard Vanessa was back, she threatened to make him sleep out in the shed."

"Huh," I said, wondering what it was about Vanessa that brought out such strong feelings in people.

And whether John's feelings for me would be enough to overcome them.

"Well," Marge said, shoveling the last two gingersnaps in and washing them down with a swig of coffee. "I'd better get back to it."

"Thanks for the help," I said, stirring peppermint extract into the frosting and wondering whether my midnight raider had found my peppermint starlites, or if I'd have to dig up some leftover candy canes to crush and sprinkle on top. As Marge lumbered toward the kitchen door, I said, "If you see anything strange while you're cleaning, let me know, okay?"

Marge gave me a funny look. Then she nodded once and disappeared through the door.

———

The chocolate mint bars were frosted, glistening with the crushed starlight mints I'd found hidden behind the cornstarch, and kept beckoning to me from their pan as I started in on dinner preparations an hour later. It seemed like I'd just finished serving lunch, and already it was time to think about dinner! I still hadn't heard anything from Detective Rose, but I figured I'd make enough to feed her if she needed to stay. Anything I could do to stay on good terms with the police force was worth it.

I pulled a big package of pork tenderloins from the fridge and grabbed a head of fresh garlic; within minutes, I had whipped up a low-fat, no-carb dijon vinaigrette marinade for them. As delicious as the marinade smelled, though, I must admit I had eyes only for the mint bars. If I didn't find time to head down to the store soon, I'd end up eating the entire pan by myself.

I had just slid the meat into a bowl and poured the savory liquid over it when the phone rang. After rinsing my hands, I grabbed the phone. "Gray Whale Inn, how can I help you?"

"Is this Natalie Barnes?"

My heart sank. "Speaking," I said.

And then she told me what I already knew. "This is Gertrude Pickens of the *Daily Mail*. I understand there's been a poisoning at your inn."

NINE

I SHOULD HAVE KNOWN it would only be a matter of hours before Gertrude got wind of Dirk's death. I sighed and gripped the phone, looking out the window at the dark expanse of water and the foam where the waves licked the rocks, trying to regain the serenity I'd found briefly while making the brownies. "One of my guests did pass away," I said carefully, "but nobody has told me the details."

"Dirk DeLeon," she said in an insistent tone of voice. "I understand he was a personal trainer. You're hosting a weight-loss retreat there, correct?"

"Yes," I said.

"So who do you think killed him?"

"I don't know that anybody killed him," I said. "He may have died of natural causes." Although since Detective Rose was currently questioning all of my guests, I was 99-percent sure that wasn't the case.

"But they're questioning your guests," Gertrude said in a whiny voice, echoing my thoughts. "Certainly there must be some cause for suspicion."

"I think you'd have to talk to the police about that," I said.

"May I speak to one of the detectives?"

"You'll have to get in touch with the station, I'm afraid. Now, if you'll excuse me, I have guests to feed."

"They're letting you cook?" she asked.

"Why wouldn't they? They're guests at the inn."

"Well, I understand there was a question of poison," she said. "Frankly, I'm surprised they haven't closed your operation down."

I took a deep breath and tried to keep my voice even. "As far as I know, nobody has said anything about poison," I said, choosing to forget Megan's question in the dining room a few hours ago. "And since I just fed one of the detectives lunch, it seems to me that the police must feel quite confident in my cooking."

"So there *is* a detective at the inn," Gertrude said. I could hear the keyboard clicking in the background as she typed.

"I'm afraid this isn't a good time for me, Gertrude," I said as politely as I could. "I have to cook dinner for my guests. I'm sure the police will be happy to answer any further questions."

"But…"

"Thanks for calling, Gertrude," I said, cutting her off. "Good bye."

I hung up the phone and said a few choice words, startling Biscuit, who was napping on the radiator. Then I looked out the window at the water again, trying to bring my heart rate down into a normal range. Unfortunately, the scenic view was becoming less effective the longer I looked at it. Or perhaps it was just that my day kept getting worse.

I focused on the tenderloins again, making sure they were all covered with marinade, then fitted a lid onto the bowl. If Gertrude printed a single *word* indicating that my cooking might be responsible for Dirk's death, I'd sue her for libel, I thought as I shoved the bowl of pork tenderloins into the fridge and grabbed a bag of salad greens.

Of course, if the papers started printing the words "poison" and "Gray Whale Inn" in the same article, there might not *be* a Gray Whale Inn for very long.

But there was nothing I could do about it now, I told myself as I whipped up a second vinaigrette for the greens and started to chop up a cucumber. My thoughts kept straying to Dirk's blue eyes, so cold and fixed, and to the image of John, his arms around Vanessa, the morning light playing on her gleaming hair as she sobbed. *Sweetheart*, he'd called her.

I pushed those thoughts out of my mind. If John could be this affected by the arrival of an ex-girlfriend, maybe we didn't have much of a future together anyway. I thought instead of Dirk, and how ironic it was that someone so dedicated to fitness and health should die so young. I hoped that the cause of death would be determined as something nice and simple. Like a heart attack, brought on by doing too many wind sprints.

Or maybe seeing the ghost of Harry, the missing lighthouse keeper.

———

Detective Rose, as it turned out, did not stay for dinner, returning to the mainland late in the afternoon. As I finished arranging the napkins on the tables—with one less place set, which was a tangible reminder of this morning's awful events—I glanced down at the carriage house where John lived. The last rays of sunset were fading from the panes of the lower windows, but the lights weren't on. I hadn't seen my neighbor since the discovery this morning, I realized. Where had he been?

I returned to the kitchen to plate the salads and drizzle them with miniscule amounts of dressing; when I walked in to the dining room with a tray to serve, the room was almost full. Even Bethany had made it down from her room, her eyes swollen with crying, and so had Carissa, who was pale as a sheet.

Dinner passed in a subdued manner—the detective's presence had rattled everyone. Bethany ate almost nothing, and Carissa toyed with her salad and barely touched her tenderloin; when her mother chided her to eat her protein, the girl shot her a venomous look that startled me.

"Do you really think he was murdered?" Boots asked her tablemates as I walked by to refill their water glasses. Eight glasses a day was the recommended intake of the program, and despite the events of the day, the participants had certainly been trying to follow the rules; I'd had to run the dishwasher twice just filled with glasses.

"Probably overdosed on his supplements," Cat said, spearing a piece of tenderloin. "God, this is good. Maybe it's because I'm hungry, but I can't remember having a tastier tenderloin."

I allowed myself a small, satisfied grin.

"I almost forgot about the supplements," Sarah said. "Vanessa didn't give us any tonight. Do you think it's because they might be poisoned?" she asked, her watery blue eyes wide.

"I don't know," Cat said. "It could just be that she's upset. I think they may have been more than just business partners, if you know what I mean." She cut her eyes at the retreat leader. "Who knows? Maybe *she* did him in—to get a bigger cut of the business. But I'll bet if anything, he just took one too many pills."

"Or they were poisoned," Sarah said dramatically.

Cat rolled her eyes. "Sarah, that's ridiculous. If they were poisoned, don't you think we'd all be dead by now?"

I was *so* not happy that my guests were having this conversation, but I kept my mouth shut.

"She has a point," said Boots, draining her water glass and forking up a mouthful of barely dressed salad.

On that slightly more optimistic note, I moved on to the next table, where Megan and Greg were dissecting the events of the morning with the kind of morbid excitement people often have after a close call. I felt awful for Bethany, who was looking miserable—and for Vanessa, who for all her efforts to remain perky, was obviously struggling to keep things together. Elizabeth, who was sitting next to her, wasn't making things any easier; as I passed, she was asking how long Vanessa and Dirk had been working together.

"About two years," Vanessa answered, staring at her plate.

"Now that he's gone, will the business revert to you?" she asked.

Vanessa pressed her lips into a thin line. "That's for the attorneys to work out," she said, looking irritated for the first time. I didn't hear the rest of the questions—I had to return to the kitchen to prepare dessert—but when I returned with a tray of fruit salads a few minutes later, Elizabeth was still asking questions and Vanessa was still looking like a trapped animal.

Once everyone had finished their strawberries and peaches topped with faux whipped cream (whipped nonfat evaporated milk—not quite Chantilly Cream, but not bad with a dash of vanilla and sweetener), Vanessa stood up and addressed the crowd.

"Okay, everyone. I know we've had ... well, a bit of a shock," Vanessa said, which was putting it mildly, in my opinion. "And I know we missed our nutrition conferences this afternoon—we'll make that up later, if we can. But we're still here to lose weight, so in a half an hour, please join me in the living room for a weight-lifting session."

There were a few groans, but mostly silence. "You snooze, you don't lose!" Vanessa quipped feebly. "I'll see you in a half an hour, everyone. That will give you time to digest your dinners and change into appropriate clothing."

With that, she fled the room.

As the group trickled off to their rooms to prepare for some heavy lifting, I cleared the dining room tables and stacked the dishes on the counter. I was about to fill the dishwasher for the fifth time that day when Gwen burst through the door, breathless.

"Aunt Nat!" she said. "I'm sorry I wasn't here ... are you okay?"

"I'm fine, Gwen," I said as she ran up to me and wrapped her arms around me. She smelled like shampoo and salt air.

"All I heard was that there was a death on the island, and that it had something to do with the inn—I was terrified it was you!"

"It was Dirk," I said. "He died sometime last night or this morning, out near the lighthouse."

"I know," Gwen said as she released me. "Fernand and I headed over to the mainland, to do some sketches in Northeast Harbor. He went back early, and I stayed to visit with a couple of friends," she said, her words tumbling out in a rush. "I just found out when I was down at the dock. George on the mail boat told me about it on the way over—he said some of the locals think Harry, the lighthouse ghost, killed him. That maybe he's mad because someone disturbed his skeleton."

I seriously doubted that was the case, but I'd had a few brushes with the supernatural since moving to Cranberry Island, so I wasn't about to rule anything out completely. Still, I was sure Dirk's death was the result of a more mundane event. "They haven't even determined who the skeleton belonged to," I reminded her. "And whatever happened to Dirk, I seriously doubt it was due to a ghost."

"I don't know," she said. "There was that weird light last night, and then this . . ." She shivered. "And the police have been here all day," she went on, "and I haven't been here to help."

"Marge was here," I reminded her.

"I guess that's something," Gwen said, pulling a face. "But she's not family. So what happened? You found him near the lighthouse? What was he doing out there?"

"Why don't you hang up your coat and sit down?" I suggested. "I'll make you some hot chocolate." As she hung up her jacket, I grabbed a mug and filled it with milk, then popped it into the microwave. Gwen sat down at the table, picking at the leftover fruit, while I heated the milk, added sugar and cocoa, and filled her in on the details of the day.

"So she questioned all the guests?" she asked, wrapping her slender hands around the mug and breathing the warm chocolate scent in.

"Every one of them," I said. "And we're not supposed to leave the island."

"At least it wasn't that Grimes guy." Gwen took a sip from the mug, then her dark eyes flitted to me. "They don't think *you* did it, do they?"

"I hope not. I can't imagine what possible motive I could have, so I'm probably clear. It was just a precaution, I think."

"So who do you think *did* do it?"

"We don't even know if he was murdered yet. He could have died of natural causes."

"Yeah, right," she said, rolling her eyes. "That's why the police are involved and everyone's talking poison. What does John think?"

"I don't know." I studied my fingernails. "I haven't seen him."

"Oh," she said, and there was an awkward silence. Then Gwen took another sip of chocolate, looked at the overloaded countertops, and sighed. "Well, I guess I'd better get started. Why don't you get out of here for a while—go see if you can find John. Or Charlene."

I glanced at the Midnight Mint Bars on the counter. "I do need to take those down to the store—otherwise, I'll eat them all." Unless my mysterious chocolate thief got to them first, that was.

"Go on," she said. "I can take care of this."

"You'll do turndown, too?"

"Absolutely," she said. "Why don't you call Charlene, see if she can come pick you up?"

"Thanks, Gwen. But I think I could do with a walk, actually."

She looked at me disbelievingly. "With a murderer on the loose?"

"We don't know that," I reminded her. "And if there is a murderer, odds are good whoever it is, is already at the inn anyway," I said, feeling a chill down my spine as I spoke. *Unless it was Tom Lockhart*, my mind whispered. *Or John.*

"Well, take a flashlight," she said, still looking doubtful. "And call me when you get there."

"I will," I said, wondering when the tables had turned and Gwen started playing the mom.

———

The cool, moist air was bracing when I stepped out of the inn fifteen minutes later, a container loaded with chocolate mint bars in my hands, feeling only a little guilty about leaving Gwen with stacks of dishes. I'd called Charlene, who confirmed that the store was still open—and probably would be until midnight, with the steady stream of folks stopping by. She'd offered to find me a ride, but I told her I preferred to hoof it. After everything that had happened today, I needed to be by myself for a bit, and nothing cleared my head better than a walk.

A gust of wind brought the smell of the ocean to my nose as I headed up the steep road, glad to be outside in the fresh air. Halfway up the hill, I turned, as I always do, to look back at the inn. It looked like something out of a Currier and Ives painting; the sun setting low over the mountains framing the inn, the windows glowing warmly, the sweet peas starting their climb up the trellis alongside the tender green of the nasturtiums, which I had bravely planted early. Behind the inn, the green field sloped down to the rocks, where the waves licked the gray rocks. Across the water, the lights of the mainland twinkled merrily.

As I gazed at the inn, I reflected that I had taken a huge risk in buying the old house and starting the business, plowing my entire life savings into it with no guarantee of success. And even though mornings were sometimes a bit tougher than I had anticipated, and not all of my guests were adherents of Emily Post, and some months were so lean I wondered if I'd make it, it was still the best decision I'd ever made.

I turned, still smiling, and continued the trek up the hill. As the sun set behind me, the moon rose to my left, the soft light gilding the bunchberry flowers that had started blooming on the shoulder of the road. The island seemed enchanted, I thought—until I topped the hill and my gaze fell upon Cranberry Point Lighthouse, glowing red with the last rays of the sun.

I'd always loved looking at the majestic lighthouse in the past. But now—with the secret room and the skeleton, the eerie light of last night, and this morning's gruesome discovery—I hurried down the other side of the hill quickly, glad when the silent lighthouse finally fell from view.

TEN

THE LIGHTS OF THE Cranberry Island Store were blazing when I tramped down the main road a little while later. I picked up the pace at the sight of the little building, which I was sure would be filled with chatty islanders and a pot of fresh coffee. The Cranberry Island Store was more than just the local grocery and post office—it was also the hub of local life. Some folks called it the island's living room, which in many ways it was—complete with comfy couches that were almost always occupied. With the discovery of another dead body on the island, I was sure the store would be busy—and tongues would be wagging—until well into the night.

I passed by the empty wooden rockers on the front porch and the rosebushes, which were just beginning to send out pale, tender leaves. A moment later, I pushed through the front door, glad for the rush of warm, coffee-scented air. Coming into Charlene's shop was always like coming home, somehow—the shelves of dry goods, with their faint, spicy scent, the smell of coffee brewing, and Charlene at the register. Tonight, the floral couches in the sitting area at the front of the store were occupied, and four familiar faces turned to the door as the bell jingled. Charlene rose from her stool behind the counter, where she'd been sorting mail. "Natalie! You made it!"

"I'm frozen, but I'm here."

"And you brought your Midnight Mint Bars," she said, dropping the stack of envelopes and taking the pan from my hands. "Just what I needed. Anyone else want one?"

Emmeline, one of the island's longtime residents and a crack baker herself (her banana bread was to die for), nodded. "As soon as I've finished this skein of yarn, I'll have one. Don't want to get my wool sticky!"

Eleazer, who was perched on one of the stools at the counter with a mug of coffee, eyed the plate longingly, hitching up his suspenders. Then he darted a hopeful look at Claudette, who was seated on the couch next to Emmeline. When she raised a disapproving eyebrow, he mumbled, "I'll pass, thank you." He sighed dramatically, casting one last longing look at the mint bars, and turned to me, an expectant look on his weather-worn face.

"Any news?" he asked.

"Nothing you haven't heard," I said. "Detective Rose spent the afternoon questioning everyone, and the guests are pretty upset, but that's all I know."

"What does John say?" asked Emmeline from her spot next to Claudette. Her dark eyes were bright as currants in a bun-like face, and her pink dress, heavy stockings, and sensible shoes looked like something out of a Sears catalog, circa 1955. I was surprised to see her here so late; usually by now she'd be at home with her husband.

"Where's Henry?" I asked.

"Oh, he's in Ohio, visiting his sister. Hasn't been able to make it back because of the weather; I've been coming down here for the company." She finished a row and started another line of pink stitches. "And to get the latest on all the excitement. So," she asked again, "what does John Quinton think of all this?"

"I haven't seen him, actually," I said, feeling uncomfortable admitting it, for some reason. Both women were knitting away at fuzzy objects—Emmeline was working on something pink that looked like a tea cozy, whereas Claudette's yarn was much earthier, and appeared to be morphing into something like a sock. Which made sense, since she actually spun her own yarn from goat wool. I wondered how the goats, Muffin and Pudge, had survived the winter without any gardens to destroy.

"We've all been trying to figure out what happened out by the lighthouse," Eleazer said. "Emmeline here thinks it might be old Harry, but I'm not so sure."

"I'm telling you, Eli, it all started when those bones were disturbed," Emmeline said, needles clacking. "I knew when I saw that light flashing that something bad was about to happen."

"Weren't they just testing out the new light?" I asked.

"I don't think they've brought one over yet," Claudette said, and the hairs on the back of my neck rose. Had we seen a ghost light?

"Where are my manners?" said Charlene through a mouthful of mint bar. "Nat, can I get you something to drink?"

"Decaf coffee, please, if you have it. No sugar, though."

Charlene raised a sculpted eyebrow, looking at me in disbelief. "What? No sugar?"

"I'm trying to stay on the straight and narrow," I said. "Since I'm having to cook for dieters for a week, I might as well make the most of it. Besides, the doctor told me I need to watch it for a while." Claudette nodded approvingly from the couch, her gray braids bobbing. Despite the fact that she was well over 200 pounds, she was perpetually after Eleazer—and the rest of the island, for that matter—regarding the evils of sugar. If you asked me, if anyone could use a bit of sugar in his diet, it was Eleazer—he must have been half his wife's size.

"Any more word on the skeleton?" I asked, lowering myself onto the sofa across from the two women.

"Not yet," Charlene said, handing me a cup of coffee. I took a long sip, enjoying the warmth as the coffee slid down to my stomach and radiated out to my slightly chilled body. Even after more than a year, I still hadn't adjusted to Maine's cooler temperatures. "But we're hoping Matilda will stop by soon and let us know," Charlene continued as she walked back to the front counter. Licking a stray bit of frosting from one of her fingers, she picked up another stack of mail and said, "She's been calling them every hour since they found those bones, champing at the bit to find out what the lab comes back with."

I nodded, hoping the town historian had forgiven me for "misplacing" an antique diary I'd found last fall. I'd finally told her it had been stolen, but she still considered that no excuse. If I'd brought it to the museum as soon as I found it, she reasoned, it wouldn't have been taken.

Ah, well.

"It's still such a shame about Dirk," Charlene said. "I'm beginning to think it's me. I'm two for two on handsome men so far."

"Nonsense," I said. "What happened had nothing to do with you. You'd hardly met the man!"

She hmmed noncommittally. "Such a waste, though. He was so gorgeous…" Her blue eyes became a little misty, and I wondered if she was thinking about Dirk—or about Richard, her late boyfriend. Then she seemed to shake it off, taking a big bite of mint bar. Chocolate, after all, is the best medicine. "Anyway," she said through a mouthful of crumbs, "I've been asking around, and I've turned up one or two things."

"Like what?"

"Well," she said, "no one saw anyone out at the lighthouse last night, so there's no help there. But it looks like Ernie was right about Tom."

"That he was the one at the top of the hill?"

Charlene nodded. "Apparently when he got back, Lorraine was waiting for him, and showed him to the door."

I cringed. "Where did he go?"

"Spent the night in one of the shacks down by the pier," she said.

"With all the fishing tackle?" I asked.

"He's got an old foam mattress in there, so he just bunked down with all the buoys."

"God, he must have been freezing."

"I imagine Lorraine thinks it served him right."

"Why did she kick him out?"

Charlene glanced at Emmeline. "I'll let you hear it from the horse's mouth," she said.

Emmeline nodded, and then gave me the scoop. "Well, from what I hear," she said, forgetting about her knitting for a moment, "when that woman Vanessa showed up on the *Island Princess*, Lorraine got suspicious. She's always been the jealous type, you know, so it's no surprise."

"Always has been," Claudette said sagely. "Even at the wedding, ten years ago, she was worried he might like the maid of honor better. I'm telling you, those were the ugliest bridesmaid's dresses you ever saw—poor things looked like a row of eggplants in a garden!"

"Anyway," Emmeline continued, "when Tom left in the middle of the night in the truck—said he had to check on something down at the fish house—she didn't believe him, which *I* wouldn't either, come to that. I mean, if *Henry* headed off in the middle of the night to check on a shack, I'd wonder what he was up to, too! It's only natural..."

"And?" I prompted her.

"Anyway, while he was gone, his wife got up and started digging around in his computer. She just *knew* something wasn't right, and with that woman in town..."

She paused for a moment, and I waited.

"Well," she said, "I don't know for sure—I heard it from Ingrid, who talked with Betty, who's Lorraine's best friend, and you *know* how I feel about gossip—but it seems she found a whole passel of e-mails. And it turns out that Vanessa and Tom had started chatting again."

"Were they having an affair?"

"I don't know about that, but Lorraine was in a tizzy by the time he got back. Locked the door on him, deadbolt and all, and wouldn't let him past the front doorstep."

"Ouch," I said. To be locked out is bad enough, but at two in the morning? Then again, if *my* husband had left for a late-night rendezvous with a gorgeous ex-girlfriend, I might have done the same. I thought of John, with his arms around Vanessa this morning. *Sweetheart.*

"He says there's nothing to it, but I says, where there's smoke..." Emmeline broke off mid-sentence and took a sip of tea, eyeing me knowingly over the rim of the cup. I swallowed hard.

"I just can't believe it," Charlene said. "Tom doesn't seem the type. And the kids..." She shook her head. "It's such a shame. I hope they get it all cleared up, and that there's nothing to it."

"We'll see," Emmeline said doubtfully. Then she glanced at me. "I heard this morning that Tom and your boyfriend were arguing about her."

My stomach clenched. "What? Who told you that?"

"I heard it from Addie, who talked with Madeline, who says she heard them when she was taking her evening constitutional. That woman has walked the island every night for years, rain or snow or shine. Amazing, isn't it?"

"Amazing," I echoed weakly, still thinking about John arguing with Tom over the gorgeous retreat leader.

Emmeline shook her head. "But that Vanessa woman is stirring up all kinds of trouble. You'll want to watch your man around that one."

I felt myself flushing, unable to come up with a response. What had John and Tom been arguing about? Had it really been Vanessa? And if so, why?

Charlene finished her mint bar and picked up another envelope. The little store was silent but for the clacking of needles, and I shifted uncomfortably on the couch.

After a few moments, Charlene broke the silence. "Gertrude Pickens called earlier, by the way."

Gertrude. I'd almost forgotten. "What did she want?" I asked, although I already knew the answer. Nothing good.

Charlene arched a tweezed eyebrow. "The skinny on the body, of course. Who was it? Was he murdered? If so, was it poison?"

My stomach clenched. "She asked me about that, too. And if she prints one word suggesting he died because of something he ate at the inn …"

"That woman is working for the wrong paper," Eleazer complained. "Turning the *Daily Mail* into the *Enquirer*!"

Claudette and Emmeline nodded vigorously in agreement. Despite my fear over what might turn up in the pages of the local paper tomorrow, their quick support gave me a warm feeling that was better than the richest hot chocolate. Which this coffee definitely wasn't, I thought, taking another sip of the rather weak brew. Maybe I'd have to get Charlene a new coffeemaker for her birthday.

I was basking in the warm glow of community acceptance when the door banged open, jingling wildly.

It was Matilda, the local historian. Her cropped white hair stood out around her head, and her long nose was red from the chilly air, but behind her glasses, her eyes were bright.

"Matilda!" Charlene called. "Come join the fun. Can I get you a cup of coffee?"

"Absolutely," she said, smiling at everyone, including me. She must have learned *something* interesting to be in such high spirits, I thought.

"Any news?" I asked.

"I got in touch with the lab just this afternoon," she said. "And you're not going to believe what they said."

"What?"

"It's a terrible tragedy," she said, eyes gleaming. "The body belonged to a man, about thirty-five years old, they think—they're getting a second opinion on that, because it's hard to tell—people were smaller back then, you know, and apparently there are a few unusual things about these bones—but according to the lab, he didn't die of natural causes."

"We heard that yesterday," Emmeline observed. "Makes sense, since he was locked in."

Matilda ignored Emmeline. "It was a secret room on the bottom floor; that's where he was found. The body was stabbed to death, they think." Her eyes were alight with the excitement of a historian who has just uncovered a great story. "They found marks on his ribs that indicate a blade went through, right around the area of the heart. In the back, no less!" Despite the morbid nature of the information she was relaying, Matilda looked positively giddy.

Emmeline shook her head. "Poor Harry. What an awful way to go."

"We don't know for sure yet that it's Harry," she said. "Part of the reason they're getting a second opinion is that they don't think the bones are Caucasian."

"Well, then, what are they?" Eleazer asked.

"They think they may be African—that's why they're getting a second opinion. I've spent the last two hours poring through the records, trying to find out who else might have disappeared during that time period, or if there was any record of Africans or African-Americans on the island. It's a real mystery!"

"That makes two," I said.

"What do you mean?" Matilda asked, looking confused.

"There was another body found there this morning."

"Oh, that," Matilda said, tossing her cropped head. Evidently the only murders she found interesting were the ones that occurred more than a hundred years ago. "I heard it was just a heart attack, or something."

"Dirk was hardly a candidate for that," Charlene said. "I've never *seen* a man in better shape."

"I suppose we'll know soon enough," Emmeline said. Claudette nodded, not missing a beat in her knitting. "Still, with all those police officers asking questions, it makes me wonder."

"Do you think maybe…" Claudette started, then stopped.

Emmeline paused in her knitting. "Do I think what?"

Claudette sucked in her breath. "I heard he died last night sometime. Could it be… a crime of passion, maybe?"

"It couldn't be," I said, shaking my head. "Not if it was poison."

Four heads whipped around. "He was poisoned?" Emmeline asked. "No wonder the police were at the inn." Her dark eyes got round. "Do you think it was something in the food?"

"Of course not!" I said quickly. "Honestly, I don't know how he died—and since I fed Detective Rose lunch today, she doesn't seem too worried about anything coming from the inn." Maybe that would satisfy their concerns.

But they all kept looking at me. "But why do you think it was poison?" Claudette asked finally.

"I don't know," I said, shrugging. "I guess because we didn't see any blood when we found him. Honestly, though—just because they're being cautious doesn't mean it's murder. I mean, maybe he just had a heart attack or something!"

Claudette hmmed, and I groaned internally. Maybe I hadn't told Gertrude Pickens my poisoning suspicion—but I was afraid I might just well have announced it with a bullhorn.

ELEVEN

When I crested the hill and started down the road to the inn almost two hours later, I was feeling much better after some time at the store and a bit of exercise. But my improved mood dimmed a bit when I spotted a battered pickup truck next to my defunct van.

It was Tom Lockhart's.

I let myself into the inn's front door, half-expecting to see Tom's lanky frame stretched out on one of the living room couches, comforting Vanessa. But the downstairs was empty—after the weight-lifting session, all the guests must have gone to their rooms. Where could he be? I wondered. Was he in Vanessa's room, comforting her after her partner's death? I was tempted to head upstairs and listen for his voice at her door, but dismissed the idea. It wasn't my business what Tom did—or didn't—do, I told myself. And besides, I had to get ready for breakfast.

When I pushed through the kitchen door, hoping Gwen had found the time to clear the decks for me, I heaved a sigh of relief.

Thanks to my wonderful niece, the counters gleamed, and not a dish remained; she'd even dried and put up all the pots and pans. I made a mental note to do something special for her soon—maybe send her to the mainland for a nice dinner with her lobsterman boyfriend, Adam.

But I would worry about that later; there was still work to be done. Tomorrow was the second full day of the retreat, and although things hadn't exactly gone as planned so far, everyone still needed to eat. I grabbed my stack of retreat-approved recipes and flipped through until I found the menu for tomorrow.

Tomorrow's breakfast included egg-white omelets, fat-free swiss cheese, and a fat-free lemon-yogurt sauce, along with a side of high-fiber English muffins. Not exactly my idea of a taste sensation, but if the retreat participants were as hungry as I was, they'd probably consider it manna from heaven. I also had to make a dozen fat-free, sugar-free custards for dessert at lunch.

I preheated the oven and whipped up the custard, which was a light take on one of my favorite recipes. I'd tested it several times the previous week—it involved egg whites, fat-free milk, vanilla, and sweetener—before I'd finally gotten it right. Now, it went together in no time flat, and within fifteen minutes I was sliding a tray of ramekins into the oven and moving on to breakfast prep.

My stomach growled as I pulled a pack of mushrooms out of the fridge and grabbed some shallots from my onion basket, trying to ignore the cookie jar. The gingersnaps were probably stale anyway, I told myself. Turning my back on the seductive ginger-spiced cookies I knew lurked within the tall jar, I chopped veggies for tomorrow morning's omelets; if I got the prep done tonight, I could sleep a little longer tomorrow. Besides, with everything that had gone on today—not least Gertrude's intrusive questions about poison—I needed to do something to calm myself down.

As I peeled the shallots, I glanced out the window at John's carriage house. The windows glowed warmly, and my heart squeezed a little bit. I hadn't seen John since he had comforted Vanessa that morning, and the intimacy I'd seen still left a hollow place inside of me that hadn't gone away.

Should I go knock on his door? I wondered. Or wait for him to come to me?

I finished peeling the last shallot, inhaling its savory aroma, and reached for a chef's knife to mince the pinkish-purple bulbs. A moment later, I scraped the fragrant bits into a bowl and wet a towel to wipe off the mushrooms. I had cleaned all but two when the sound of raised voices reached my ears.

I glanced back at the kitchen door before I realized the voices weren't coming from inside the inn—they were floating up from the carriage house.

John's front door was open, the bright light cutting a swath over the dark grass, and two figures stood silhouetted in the glow. "It was a stupid thing to do," I heard. The voice was John's, and hard with anger. "You put your whole life at risk."

I couldn't make out the answer, but I recognized the voice—and the lanky frame—as belonging to Tom.

John spoke again. "What happened twenty years ago is over, Tom. You need to accept that, and mend what you can. *If* you can."

"No," Tom answered, shaking his head violently. "That's where you're wrong."

John started to answer, but Tom turned and stormed off toward the driveway. I pulled back from the window a bit so he wouldn't see me, but it didn't matter—Tom didn't turn his head. I glanced back at the door to the carriage house, and what I saw made my heart contract.

Vanessa had come to the door; I could see her slim form standing behind John, her dark hair gleaming. As I watched, she put a hand on his shoulder and drew him back inside. A moment later, the door closed behind them; at the same time, Tom's engine roared to life outside, and his tires screeched up the hill.

The ravenous hunger I'd felt a few minutes ago had vanished, replaced by a churning nausea. I finished the mushrooms mechanically, almost cutting myself twice as I sliced them, my eyes still glued on the dark door of the carriage house. What were they doing in there? I wondered. But my mind shied away from most of the potential answers. By the time I finished the prep work fifteen minutes later, Vanessa still hadn't come out of the carriage house.

I shoved the veggies into the fridge and hurried upstairs to my dark bedroom, where I continued my vigil at the window, Biscuit curled up by my side. The timer beeped downstairs; as if in a dream, I ran downstairs and retrieved the custards from the oven, shoving them into the fridge as fast as I could before hurrying back to my post at the bedroom window.

Finally, an interminable hour later, John's front door opened, and the two figures were silhouetted once again. I watched as John looked down at Vanessa, cradling her chin in his hand as he said something to her. Then he drew her into a long, lingering hug that I couldn't tear my eyes from. Just when I thought I couldn't stand it anymore, they parted, and acid burned in my stomach as he watched her climb the short hill to the inn before slowly closing the door behind him.

There was not enough coffee in the world to bring me to full consciousness the next morning, and to be honest, that was probably for the best. I wasn't sure I wanted to face the day with all my faculties intact.

My sleep last night had been fitful, filled with dreams of Vanessa, her sleek black-haired head atop a massive octopus body whose tentacles were engulfing the inn; also, there was the recurring image of Dirk, lying sightless under the blue morning sky, the lighthouse towering over him, a ghostly laugh sounding somewhere in the distance. Now, as I sprayed a pan with olive oil and waited for it to heat up, I took another sip of coffee and tried not to think about what I had seen last night.

I had turned the oven on warm and had just finished beating a bowl full of egg whites when the phone rang. It was Charlene.

"Bad news, Natalie," she said.

"No kidding," I said, eyeing the carriage house.

"What do you mean?"

"Tell me the news first," I said.

"I just got today's copy of the *Daily Mail*," she said.

I groaned. "How bad is it?"

"Here's what Gertrude wrote," Charlene said. "'Although the autopsy is pending, preliminary toxicology reports indicate that the death may have been a result of poisoning.'"

"Perfect," I said.

"There's more, though."

I closed my eyes. "Do I want to know?"

"Listen to this: 'The victim was a leader of a weight-loss retreat that was staying at the Gray Whale Inn. Police would not confirm whether the victim was poisoned at the inn, but are treating the death as suspicious. Several islanders, including Natalie Barnes, the proprietor of the inn where the victim was staying, have been asked to remain on the island as the investigation continues.'"

I felt my face turning red. "Poison? The inn? I fed Detective Rose yesterday—if she was worried about poison, she never would have eaten here," I spluttered. "I'm going to kill that ... that ..."

"Easy, Nat. I can think of a number of choice words," Charlene said. "If she's expecting a goodie basket this Christmas, I'm guessing she'll be disappointed."

"She wouldn't eat it anyway. Afraid I'd poison her."

"With an article like this, you would certainly be justified if you did," Charlene said.

"Why is she calling him a victim?" I asked. "The police haven't even said it was a homicide!" I tossed the shallots into the pan so hard half of them flew off onto the counter. Stirring angrily as the pan sizzled, I said, "If anything, I'm guessing he toked up on too many of his own supplements."

"I'll write a letter to the editor," she said. "Sorry to be the bearer of bad tidings—I figured you'd want to hear it from me first."

"Thanks," I said, opening a can of artichoke hearts and hacking them up with a knife, sending green bits flying around the kitchen. A moment later, I dumped them in the pan with the shallots, wishing I could do the same with Gertrude, who seemed to love nothing more than casting aspersions on my inn in print.

"So," Charlene said, "now that I've gone ahead and ruined your day, what's your news?"

For a moment there, in my anger at Gertrude, I'd almost forgotten about John and Vanessa, but as I relayed what I'd seen last night, all the pain came rushing back. "I think they're back together," I said. "Or at least heading in that direction."

"You're jumping to conclusions, Natalie," Charlene said softly.

"They were in there for an hour," I said through clenched teeth. "And he called her 'sweetheart' yesterday morning."

She sighed. "I wish I knew what to tell you," she said in a tone of voice that didn't make me feel any better.

"What do you think Tom was doing down there?" I asked. "He looked angry—like a spurned lover."

"Maybe he was jealous."

"Of John and Vanessa?"

"I don't know, Natalie."

My stomach churned, the smell of sautéed vegetables making me nauseous. "What I want to know is, what was John talking about with Tom? What did he mean when he said what happened twenty years ago was dead and gone?"

"I don't know," Charlene repeated. "But if I were you, I'd be more worried about John and Vanessa right now. Not to mention the poisoning scare." She paused for a moment, and I could hear voices in the background. "Hey—can I call you later? I've got six people lined up at the cash register."

"Sure," I said. "Thanks for the heads-up."

"Any time," she said, and hung up to deal with her customers. I just hoped not too many of them were buying the paper.

Should I be jealous? I wondered. Not that it really mattered; I already was. After all, John and Vanessa were spending an awful lot of time together, and the intimacy I was used to feeling with him had evaporated since she set foot on the island. And then there was the *sweetheart* slip . . .

But what had he and Tom been talking about so angrily last night? Was John accusing Tom of throwing away his life by chasing Vanessa?

Or was it possible that Tom, in a rash moment, might have done away with his perceived rival?

Nonsense, I told myself as I emptied a carton of fat-free yogurt into another bowl and grabbed a few lemons from the fridge. I couldn't see Tom committing a crime of passion like that. Besides, crimes of passion usually didn't involve poison—assuming somebody *had* poisoned Dirk. And when would he have had a chance to do it, anyway?

Tom was here that night, my mind whispered. *He could have snuck upstairs and done it.*

I squeezed a lemon, scolding myself for jumping to conclusions. The truth was, anybody in the inn could have snuck upstairs and doctored Dirk's personal stash of pills. Heck, I'd seen Elizabeth leaving his room the night before he died.

Elizabeth. I'd forgotten about her. Was her surreptitious visit to Dirk's room related to his death?

Why would she want him dead, though? Of all the people who would want Dirk out of the way, Elizabeth didn't seem anywhere near the top of the list. She was just a reporter—not his lover or his business partner.

I whisked the yogurt and lemon juice together, thinking more about Elizabeth. Maybe she hadn't poisoned the handsome trainer. But what *had* she been doing in his room?

———

By the time Gwen made it downstairs to the kitchen, dressed in a flowing skirt and a gorgeous velvet jacket, I was already cleaning up from breakfast. After the omelets, which had been remarkably tasty, Vanessa had led the guests on a jog to the cranberry bog, leaving the inn in peace for the first time since they'd arrived. I still hadn't seen John, but my eyes darted to his carriage house frequently as I rinsed the plates and tucked them into the dishwasher.

"Hey, Gwen. Thanks for your help last night—the kitchen looked great," I said.

"Did the walk help?" she asked.

"Sort of," I said.

"What does that mean?" she asked, pouring herself a cup of coffee from the carafe and grabbing a stack of gingersnaps from the jar by the door. I watched enviously as she bit into the first cookie: no veggie omelets for Gwen.

I sighed. "It looks like they think Dirk was poisoned," I said. "Gertrude Pickens wrote it up yesterday in the *Daily Mail*."

"Does John know anything about the lab results?" she asked.

"I don't know," I said, trying to sound neutral.

"Still haven't talked to him, have you?"

I shook my head.

"Aunt Nat ..."

"It's all right though," I said briskly, turning and grabbing the skillet from the sink. "I've got enough going on with the retreat anyway. I'm sure things will settle out soon." I busied myself scrubbing at a stubborn bit of cooked-on egg white and changed the subject. "Are you headed down to the studio this morning?"

"I could go either way," she said. "Do you need me here?"

"I think I've got it under control," I said.

"But it's not Marge's day."

"It's all right," I said. "You covered for me last night—besides, I need something to do to keep busy." What I didn't tell her was that I was interested in taking the opportunity to find out what kind of article Elizabeth was *really* working on. And to find out why she might have been poking around in Dirk's room.

"Well," Gwen said tentatively, "if you're sure..."

"Positive," I said quickly. "Go and take advantage of this gorgeous day." And it was a gorgeous day—the sun was sparkling on the water, and the breeze through the open windows ruffled the white curtains gently.

"Thanks, Aunt Nat," she said, taking a last swig of coffee and tucking the cookies into a pocket and coming over to give me a quick kiss. She smelled like soap and jasmine. "Call the studio if you change your mind, okay?"

"I will," I said.

She grabbed her portable easel and shut the door behind her a minute later, leaving me alone at the inn.

After one last glance at the carriage house, I shut the dishwasher and grabbed my cleaning supplies; then I headed to the front desk and tucked the skeleton key in my pocket.

Elizabeth might not want to tell me what she was doing in Dirk's room, but I hoped I was about to find out.

TWELVE

ELIZABETH'S ROOM WAS THE one nearest the stairs on the second floor, and even though I clean guests' rooms all the time, my heart beat a little bit faster as I let myself in this morning.

A pleasant lavender scent greeted me as the door opened, and if it weren't for that—and the lone book lying on the maple nightstand—I might have thought I'd let myself into the wrong room. The reporter from Portland appeared to be a neat freak; the bed was already made, the blue-and-white counterpane stretched without a wrinkle over the four-poster bed, and aside from the book, *A Pocket Full of Rye*, which I recognized as one of my favorite Agatha Christie mysteries, there was not a personal item in sight. Which made my cleaning job easier, of course—but made me a bit less comfortable about going through her things. If something is just lying out and you happen to see it, that's one thing—but despite the fact that I'd seen her sneaking into Dirk's room the night before he died, I still felt a little guilty as I locked the door behind me and hurried over to the desk by the window.

Elizabeth had filled the top drawer with empty notebooks and pens; the second drawer on the left, however, contained a stack of manila file folders, each one neatly labeled in her block print.

I sat down and lifted the stack to the top of the desk, listening intently for the sound of returning guests. Except for the cry of a gull and the soft sigh of the wind around the eaves, though, all was quiet.

The first folder was labeled "Lose-It-All"; inside was a stack of brochures on the program, a couple of company-issued press releases, and profiles of both Vanessa and Dirk.

I picked up Dirk's first. He had been photographed in a pair of running shorts and a short-sleeved shirt that showed his bulging pecs and biceps to good advantage. I suppressed a shiver at the sight of his blue eyes smiling out at me; they had looked very different yesterday, by the lighthouse.

"Dirk DeLeon brings twenty years of training experience to the Lose-It-All program," I read. "With a degree in kinesiology from Colorado State University and a masters in sports medicine from Virginia Polytechnic Institute, as well as years of experience training athletes at the high school, college, and professional level, Dirk has been helping people reach their fitness goals for more than two decades." There was nothing about his fancy supplement plan, I noticed. Elizabeth had circled Colorado State University for some reason; other than that, there were no notes on the page.

Vanessa's profile was equally vague. "The founder of Lose-It-All, Vanessa Tagliacozzi has long espoused the tenets of healthy eating for healthy living, and has helped thousands of people achieve their bodyweight goals." I glanced up at the picture; unlike Dirk, who was dressed to work out, Vanessa wore a revealing silky dress that barely covered her torso. Her gleaming black hair was slightly tousled, and her full lips were parted in a seductive smile. No wonder John was so happy to see her, I thought. Who could compete with that?

"With a degree from UCLA and years of hands-on experience, Vanessa has worked closely with the top names in the business to design a plan that has revolutionized the lives of thousands of Americans."

She certainly had revolutionized mine, I thought. And not for the better.

But I didn't have time to linger over Vanessa's sexy photo. The group would be back before long—and I still had a stack of files to get through.

I sifted through the rest of the file on Lose-It-All, but found nothing of interest. The second file in the stack was labeled "supplements." Inside were copies of several studies of weight-loss supplements, including a few of the ones Dirk had mentioned; I found a few referencing Creatine and catechins. At the bottom of the thick file was an invoice like the ones I had seen in Dirk's room, for a delivery of EPH, Creatine, and *Rhodiola rosea*. EPH was circled in ink. I flipped back through, looking for any studies that related to it, but there weren't any. Was the supplement too new to have been studied? Was that what Elizabeth was writing her article about—dangerous practices in the program?

I moved to the next file, which was labeled "press." Inside were two ten-year-old clippings about athletes who had died or become ill while taking illegal supplements. One of them involved an entire basketball team in Denver; when three of their members became ill, parents investigated, discovering that the team's coach, a guy named Frank Hobbes, had been giving them performance-enhancing supplements.

Another clipping was more heartbreaking—this one had occurred in a town just outside of Boulder. A young woman had died after taking supplements given her by her coach. A picture of the funeral showed a grief-stricken couple touching a white casket. The woman's face was streaked with tears; I could only imagine what hell she must have been going through. "Ashley Mickelson's parents mourn the death of their only child at Wednesday's funeral," said the caption. I stared at the grieving couple; they had caught the mother staring at the camera, and her eyes were haunted with pain and loss. I glanced over the article; apparently the coach, a young man named Dereck Crenshaw, had been imprisoned on manslaughter charges and was awaiting trial. I closed the file, relieved to be away from the woman's haunted eyes, and her face, which looked strangely familiar. How do you go on after losing a child to a senseless tragedy like that?

And what the heck did two ten-year-old articles have to do with the Lose-It-All weight-loss retreat?

The last file was labeled "legal," and contained copies of legal documents relating to the Lose-It-All company. Apparently it was registered under dual ownership, with Vanessa and Dirk owning equal shares. There was also a copy of another article, this one in New York, reporting that Dirk was being sued for using unauthorized weight-loss supplements at a gym in Concord, Massachusetts. The date on the article was only one month ago; apparently, one of Dirk's clients had experienced heart palpitations, and was suing both the gym and Dirk for giving him unsafe pills.

So I hadn't been wrong to be nervous about the pills Dirk was handing out like candy. Had his former client won the case against him, or lost? I wondered as I put the article back into the file and returned the stack to the bottom desk drawer, making sure they were in the same order that I found them. Maybe that was why he was looking so strained when he talked to Vanessa the other night. A lawsuit against Dirk would look bad for the company—and might even spark other complaints. Had Vanessa killed him to get him out of the way?

I grabbed the "legal" file once again, poring through the company information. Fifty percent of the company belonged to Dirk. But if something happened to Dirk, it all reverted to Vanessa.

I slid the file back into the stack and looked through the rest of the desk, but if Elizabeth had brought a laptop, she must have taken it with her. Likewise with the notebook I'd seen her carrying earlier. I did a cursory clean of the room, which it really didn't need, and ten minutes later I locked the door behind me, still thinking about the contents of those files.

Which led me directly to Vanessa's room. I was curious about those legal documents I'd seen; were they related to Dirk's lawsuit? Or were they connected to something else?

With the ownership of the company slated to go to Vanessa in the event of Dirk's death, she definitely had some motivation to slip a little extra something into the trainer's morning coffee. And the lawsuits couldn't have been good for the business, either—yet more incentive to get rid of a difficult business associate. Had the gorgeous Vanessa decided to get her deadweight partner out of the way?

Assuming, of course, Dirk was murdered, I reminded myself. But with the toxicology report pending, and the police questioning my guests, something told me it was only a matter of time before it moved from speculation to fact. And having the co-owner of a prestigious weight-loss retreat poisoned at my inn was not going to be good for business, regardless of the investigating officer's opinion of my food's safety.

Vanessa's perfume wafted out into the hallway as I opened the door to her room. I didn't bother with her dresser—no need to torment myself with the fact that she wore a size zero. Instead, after locking the door behind me, I made a beeline for the desk—and the stack of envelopes I'd shied away from earlier. Today, I opened them with no qualms.

The first two were letters from lawyers, complaining of clients who had experienced heart palpitations connected with the supplements Dirk was providing. Both threatened to sue for medical damages, which I could imagine would put a real damper on business profitability.

The third was a letter from Vanessa's lawyer, outlining the process for divesting Dirk of his ownership in the business. Which, according to the lawyer, would be a costly and difficult process.

I scanned the letter, my mind running through the events of the last few days. Vanessa and Dirk had had a heated conversation the night before he died. Had he discovered the letter? Was he threatening to retaliate? Had she decided to take the easy way out and kill him?

And what exactly *was* her relationship to her business partner? Her grief certainly had seemed real yesterday. But had it been an act?

I slid the letters back into the files and went through the rest of the paperwork, locating two more interesting things. The first was a copy of an e-mail from a national daytime television show inviting Vanessa to make an appearance; the second was a letter from a literary agent offering representation for a book titled *Dare to Lose-it-All*. I was about to slide it back into its file when I realized that Dirk hadn't been addressed in the letter; it had been to Vanessa alone. Did he know about the show and the book? I wondered. Or were they both Vanessa's private projects?

When I'd scoured all the files twice and failed to find anything else of interest, I did a quick wipe-down of the bathroom, still thinking of all I'd discovered this morning. Despite Dirk and Vanessa's cheery, can-do attitude, evidently there had been trouble in weight-loss paradise. Which might explain why one of them was now dead.

I closed and locked Vanessa's door, then eyed the next door down, which—until this morning—had been Dirk's. I was sorely tempted to pay it another visit, but Detective Rose had told me the room was off-limits. If—or when—they did determine Dirk had been murdered, the last thing I needed was to leave *more* of my fingerprints all over the place. In truth, there were probably too many already.

So I passed it by, instead doing the rounds of the other rooms. My heart sank a bit when I cleaned Greg's room; unless I was mistaken, one of Megan's long blond hairs was in the sink, and another lay on one of the pillows. It looked like their intimate conversations might have moved on to another level. *Even if they have, there's nothing you can do about it, Natalie. And it's not your business.* Still, it made my heart hurt for Carissa.

I half-expected to find my bags of chocolate chips—or at least the evidence of them—in Carissa and Megan's room, but while there was a mostly empty bag of mini Snickers bars tucked in the closet, my baking chocolate was nowhere to be found. I did think it was odd, though, that Carissa would raid the pantry when she still had chocolate in the room. Megan's bed was mussed, I was pleased to see. Even if she had taken the opportunity to visit Greg's room—which was pure speculation, based on a couple of hairs, I reminded myself—at least it looked like she'd spent some of the night here with her daughter.

The sorority girls' rooms revealed nothing of real interest, except that one of them—the pear-shaped one, Cat—seemed to have been stashing her pills rather than taking them, as there was a baggie of them poking out of the nightstand drawer. I found no indication of who my chocolate thief might be, though; whoever was raiding my pantry had done an excellent job concealing the evidence.

I had just finished the last room when the phone rang. I gathered my cleaning supplies and hurried downstairs, catching it just before it went to voice mail.

"Gray Whale Inn, can I help you?"

"May I speak with Natalie Barnes please?"

"Speaking."

"This is Carmen Bosworth from the *Bangor Daily News*. I understand there's been a suspicious death at your inn, and I wanted to ask you a few questions."

I sank down on the chair, hoping I was in a nightmare and somebody would wake me up soon.

———

I'd barely hung up the phone and was feeling like I'd been punched in the stomach—repeatedly—when it rang a second time.

I picked it up and croaked out my standard greeting, praying it wouldn't be Carmen Bosworth again.

Thankfully, it wasn't. "Hey, Natalie, it's Charlene."

"Thank God you're not the *Bangor Daily News* again."

"Oh, no," she breathed. "They called?"

"Yup. And they asked all kinds of interesting questions. Like if anyone had ever died or become sick after eating my food in the past, and whether the police were closing down my establishment pending investigation."

"You're kidding me."

"I wish I were. That Carmen Bosworth person makes Gertrude Pickens look like my best friend."

"I'm so sorry, Nat."

"Thanks," I said. "Now, what's up with you?"

"I was calling because I have a bit of news of my own—but I don't know if you'll want to hear it."

"Let me guess. *Good Morning America* is picking up the poisoning story," I joked.

"No," she said. "Not yet, anyway."

"That's comforting." I gazed out at the green field sloping down behind the inn, but the serene scene did nothing to calm my nerves.

"I was talking with Ernie, who has a friend on the force over on the mainland."

"And?"

"First, the toxicology report had a really high concentration of some chemical. So he either overdosed in a big, big way, or was poisoned."

"Wonderful. Maybe I should call Carmen back."

"But there's more," she said.

"How can there be?" I stared morosely at the calendar. I had several rooms booked for June and July—but if a story appeared in the Bangor paper, would the cancellations start rolling in?

"Here's the kicker," she said. "John's not allowed to have anything to do with the case."

My eyes jerked up from the calendar, and I gripped the phone tightly. "Why not?" I asked. As the island deputy, he wasn't overly involved in cases to begin with—but the mainland police had often included him as a source of inside information on local goings-on.

"Apparently, if it turns out to be murder—they're looking at him as a suspect," she said.

THIRTEEN

I CLOSED MY EYES, still clutching the phone like it was a lifeline. Even though the only news I'd gotten through it was bad. John was a potential *suspect*?

"Why?"

"The cops found out about his old connection with Vanessa, years ago. And somebody saw him arguing with Dirk."

"When?"

"I don't know. I'm just reporting what I heard."

"Hardly conclusive evidence," I said lightly, even though my stomach was churning.

"But enough to get him kicked off the case," she said.

"Trust me—there are a lot more compelling options out there than John," I said, trying to convince myself that it was true. Was it possible that my neighbor was a murderer?

Couldn't be, I told myself.

After Charlene promised not to pass any information on to her buddies at the store, I told her what I'd discovered upstairs in the rooms.

"I knew Dirk was too good to be true," Charlene said, sighing. "And Vanessa was trying to get rid of him—at least as far as the business was concerned. Do you think they were . . . well, together?"

"It's hard to tell," I said. "She did seem really upset when he died."

"Maybe her company ambitions overshadowed her romantic interests," Charlene suggested. "And it sounds like Dirk was getting into trouble with his diet pills. What do you think is in those supplements, anyway?"

"I saw the list—most of it is stuff that lots of folks use, but there's one thing I haven't heard of. Elizabeth's looking into it too, I think—I'm not sure what she's working on, but I don't think it's a travel article."

"Sounds more like an exposé on the weight-loss business, if you ask me."

"That's what I was thinking."

We fell silent for a moment, each lost in our thoughts. Then Charlene said, "Oh, I almost forgot to tell you."

"What?"

"Matilda was in here all excited a few minutes ago. You know that skeleton?"

"The one at the lighthouse?" I asked. As if skeletons were thick on the ground. Which, lately, they kind of had been, now that I thought of it.

"Well, you know how they think it's African-American, right?"

I gazed out the window at the lighthouse out on the rocky point. "Yeah."

"Matilda took that on as a challenge; she spent all day yesterday at the library, going through old documents and newspapers."

"Sounds thrilling," I said, my eyes still on the distant white building, the little keeper's house huddled up next to it. "Did she find anything?"

"That's the thing. There *was* one African-American here during that time. His name was Otis Ball. And you're never going to believe it, but he was a slave-catcher."

"A *what*?"

"Matilda told us that back in the time of slavery—about the time Old Harry disappeared, actually—escaped slaves would come north on their way to Canada, but their owners hired slave-catchers to follow and hunt them down. Otis Ball was one of them—and apparently he thought the Underground Railroad had a way station right here on Cranberry Island."

"You're kidding me," I said. "That's crazy. Why would anyone try to force their own people back into slavery?"

"That's what a lot of folks wondered, I'm guessing. And Matilda says it was pretty unusual—most of the slave-catchers were white. But the money was pretty good, so I guess he put his qualms aside."

"Did he ever find what he was looking for?" I asked.

"That's the thing; nobody knows. There was an article that said he was coming to town looking for some escaped slaves, but there's no other mention of him."

"Weird. He just vanished?"

"Who knows? Maybe he found the slaves and went home. Matilda's going over to the Somesville library to see if she can find anything else on him."

I shook my head. "The Underground Railroad—in Maine."

"Last stop on the way to Canada, I guess. And a coastal location was probably a pretty good thing, since you could travel by boat."

It made sense. "That hidden room in the lighthouse—do you think that might have been it? Do you think maybe Harry might have been hiding runaways there?"

"Could be," Charlene said. "If he was, and the skeleton *is* African-American, the question is, who was murdered? The slave-catcher? Or somebody he was looking for?"

"And we still don't know what happened to Harry," I said.

"It just gives you goosebumps thinking about it, doesn't it?"

Yes, it did. But as fascinating as it was, I had a much more recent mystery to worry about. "I've got to go, Charlene. But keep me posted, okay?"

"On the skeleton?"

"Well, that too, of course. But if you hear anything else about Dirk…"

"Will do," she said. As I hung up, I heard voices coming from outside. I peeked out the window; the retreat participants were coming down the hill. John had tagged along again this morning, walking very close to Vanessa, smiling. Two days ago the sight of John coming down the road would have made my heart feel light; now, seeing him so close to Vanessa, I wished he'd just disappear. Were the police justified in keeping him out of the case? I wondered, watching John's easy lope, and the way the sun gleamed on his sandy hair.

Had I been dating a murderer?

It's all speculation, Nat, I told myself, ripping my eyes from John—and Vanessa, who was inches away from him—and surveying the other guests.

133

A few yards back, Megan and Greg were practically holding hands while Carissa glowered a few feet behind them, her plump lips pushed into a pout. Cat, Boots, and Sarah were together, as always, and Bethany trailed the group. They all looked bright red with exertion—except Vanessa and John, I noticed. And Elizabeth, who was a few steps to the left of Vanessa, looking like the cat who'd caught the canary. Why? I wondered. Had she gotten another juicy tidbit to tuck into her article?

As I watched them approach the inn, my eyes riveted again on John and Vanessa, I suddenly realized that people who exercised are frequently hungry. I glanced at my watch; lunch was less than an hour away, and I'd been so wrapped up in my snooping—I mean, *cleaning*—I hadn't even thought about preparing food.

With one last look at the group coming down the road, I grabbed my supplies and hurried to the kitchen. I struggled to banish thoughts of John's potential suspecthood and the upcoming article in the Bangor paper from my mind—and breathed a sigh of relief that today's lunch was just a simple shrimp salad followed by the custards that were already made.

———

When I toted a tray of shrimp salads into the dining room less than an hour later—field greens, julienned veggies, and fresh shrimp drizzled with a yogurt-lime-chipotle dressing (I'd had to order the chipotles from Texas)—the mood of the guests was once again subdued. I wasn't sure if it was exhaustion from the morning excursion, though, or a reverberation from the trainer's death. John was nowhere in evidence; he had managed to pry himself away from Vanessa, at least for a few minutes, anyway. What exactly had

John and Tom been arguing about last night? Maybe once the retreat had moved onto the afternoon's "nutritional education" session, I'd steel myself to walk down to the carriage house and have a chat with my neighbor, who'd practically disappeared from my life the moment the retreat hit the island. Before I passed judgment, I should hear his side of the story, after all.

As I distributed the custards to my ravenous guests, including Vanessa, who had wolfed hers down almost before I'd handed out the rest of them, my eyes were drawn again to the lighthouse on the point. My thoughts turned to what Charlene had said about the Underground Railroad. Could it be that Cranberry Island had been a way station? If it was, how many refugees had taken up residence behind the white-painted façade?

I flashed back to the strange lights we'd seen the other night, and a shiver crept up my spine. The other question was, whose skeleton had the workers found hidden inside the lighthouse?

———

As Vanessa started droning on in the dining room about nutritional choices (not all carbs are bad, of course, but the less refined, the better), I tucked into my own shrimp salad at the kitchen table, eyeing the carriage house with trepidation. I knew I had to face John eventually. But it was going to be hard to control my emotions when I did it. Heck, I wasn't even sure what my emotions were. Anger, for sure. And hurt—even though, as Charlene said, there was no hard evidence to show that John and Vanessa were anything but friends. After all, my ex-fiancé had swept into town last fall, and even though he'd kissed me, it hadn't meant I was falling for him. If John had managed to overlook a kiss, I should be able to overlook him calling Vanessa *sweetheart*. And spending an hour behind closed doors in his carriage house with her. My blood pressure rose just thinking about it.

But there was another emotion I wasn't sure I wanted to deal with mixed in there. I wasn't sure, but I thought it might be fear.

As I finished my less-than-filling salad, my eyes strayed to the cookie jar. It was a good thing I'd taken those mint bars down to Charlene's, or I'd have plowed through the whole pan.

Instead, I turned my back on the jar's siren song and helped myself to the last remaining custard, which I'd tucked into the fridge next to a bag of lettuce. The smooth confection was missing some of the richness of the full-fat version, and the sweetener had a touch of aftertaste that wasn't my favorite, but I needed something sweet right now, and it filled the bill.

Finally, when I'd licked the last bit of custard out of the bowl (one of the benefits of dining alone, in my opinion), I realized I couldn't put it off any longer. With a tummy full of fat-free custard and fat-free shrimp, I checked my face for stray dressing, smiled into the mirror to make sure there was no salad stuck between my teeth, and headed out the door toward the carriage house.

I stepped out onto the porch off the kitchen, catching my breath at the gusts of wind off the water. Summer might be on the way, but the wind was still pretty darned chilly. And forceful enough to make my white-painted rockers rocket back and forth on the porch all by themselves. It was eerie, almost—as if they had invisible, highly agitated occupants. I glanced up at the lighthouse, white as bleached bones, in the distance. Then I wrapped my arms tightly around myself and forced myself to head down the path to John's carriage house.

———

"I hear you've been asked to leave the case," I blurted artlessly a few minutes later as I perched on the edge of John's couch. He winced slightly, and I cursed my poor choice of words. The room around me smelled faintly of fresh wood, like John himself, who was enamored of working with the natural material. Although he supplemented his income with his deputy position and the toy boats he made for Island Artists, his first love was working with the weathered wood that washed up on the rocks. He would spend months at a time transforming chunks of weathered wood from gnarled hunks of twisted branches into graceful sea creatures, several of which graced the bookshelves at the end of the room. John's first piece of driftwood art, a seal, still stood on the coffee table, its gray back smooth as silk. I reached out reflexively to touch it—it felt warm under my fingers.

I pulled my hand back and regarded the man on the other end of the couch, wondering at how quickly the intimacy of two days ago had dissipated. So far, our little meeting was not going as well as I had hoped. John had answered after the second knock; after a glancing kiss on the forehead, he'd invited me in, sitting down at the opposite end of the couch from me. Tension crackled in the air between us.

"Because I have a prior acquaintance with one of the people connected with the incident," John said in answer to my artless question, "they have asked me to disassociate myself from the case." He wore a flannel shirt and faded jeans, and the spray of yellow sawdust dusting his sleeve told me he'd spent some time in his workshop this afternoon.

"Do you mean Vanessa?" I asked, wondering if "prior association" was the only reason they'd asked him to step down.

He nodded, but I found myself unconvinced. Just because he knew her over a decade ago wasn't enough to get him removed from the case. Was there more than he was telling me?

"You never mentioned her to me," I said. "Why not?"

John sighed and leaned back into the cushions, his eyes fixed on the window behind me. "I don't ask about your past relationships, do I? Besides," he added, "it was just a summer thing. Puppy love, I guess you'd call it."

I tried not to flinch at the word *love*.

"Anyway, it was no big deal. We were both kids."

"You called her 'sweetheart' yesterday morning," I said, before I could help myself.

He flushed slightly. "I was trying to help her. She was obviously upset. She's going through a rough time right now." His green eyes slowly shifted to mine. "I'm sorry if you found it hurtful."

I sat quietly for a moment, trying to sort my emotions out. So far, I wasn't getting the warm and fuzzy feeling I'd been hoping for. Was John involved somehow in Dirk's death? Even if he wasn't—was there any way to fix this weirdness that had sprung up between us? Or had I already lost him to Vanessa?

"I saw you arguing with Tom last night," I said, failing to mention that I'd also seen him with Vanessa. Or that I'd sat on my bed with my eyes glued to his front door for more than an hour, feeling like I was about to puke. "Why?" I asked.

John's eyes grew suddenly guarded. "Tom has made some ... poor decisions lately."

"Like poisoning Dirk DeLeon?" I asked.

John drew back, startled. "No," he said shortly. "Nothing to do with Dirk—Tom didn't even know him."

He'd met him, though. And he knew he was Vanessa's maybe-boyfriend, I thought.

"I was trying to get him to think about what he was doing to his life," John said. "His ... actions have put his marriage in jeopardy. Not to mention his standing on the island. I was advising him to back off for a bit, really think about his decisions."

"Out of your feelings for his family? Or because you were interested in Vanessa yourself?" I asked, then wondered if I should go back home and tape my mouth shut. It was like I'd come down with an acute case of Tourette's syndrome on the short walk over here.

"So that's what this is about. You think I want to leave you for Vanessa?" he asked softly.

I shrugged, unable to meet his eyes. *Or that you were somehow mixed up with what happened to Dirk.* "The thought had crossed my mind," I admitted.

"There's nothing between us. Honest," he said. "I was comforting her, Natalie. She's been through a tough time, and she's got no one here. And she has to shoulder the retreat by herself."

Poor Vanessa, I thought. Rather uncharitably, I know, but I couldn't help myself. "So you're her rock, then. Just a good friend," I said, trying not to sound sarcastic.

"Exactly," he said, looking relieved. He moved closer to me, bridging the gap on the couch between us. Then he reached out to touch my chin, pulling my face up slightly to look at him. *Just like he did with Vanessa.*

"That was twenty years ago, Natalie," he said, staring into my eyes. Despite the long winter, his skin was still nut brown, and his sandy hair was still streaked in places, bleached by the sun. He was incredibly handsome—and despite my anger, something inside me tugged with yearning for this gorgeous, intense, incredibly sexy man. "This is now," he whispered, making goose bumps spring up on my arms.

Then he leaned forward and kissed me, slowly. His mouth was warm against mine, and his woodsy, masculine scent enveloped me.

My heart was pounding when he released me—partially from desire, but partially because I still wasn't entirely convinced that his feelings for Vanessa were platonic. And, if I was being completely honest with myself, partially because of the tendril of fear that had taken root in my heart. *I couldn't have been dating a murderer*, I told myself.

When I'd caught my breath, I asked, "There's nothing between you and Vanessa?" My eyes searched his for an answer.

"We're old friends," he said simply.

"What about Vanessa and Tom?" I asked. "Are they just 'old friends' too?"

John sucked in his breath, a pained look on his face. "Tom is still living a fantasy," he said. "He and Vanessa parted ways a long time ago, but I'm not sure he ever really gave up on her."

"I heard they'd been having an affair," I said.

He flinched a little. At least I thought he did—but maybe I was just looking for it. "He and Lorraine have a lot of things to work out," he said judiciously.

Based on the hungry look I'd seen in Tom's eyes when he looked at Vanessa, I had to agree with John.

The question was, was Tom the only one still carrying a torch for the island's summer seductress?

FOURTEEN

When I returned to the kitchen a few minutes later, my mind was whirling and my heart still pumping from that long kiss. But my doubts still lingered. Had the police really taken John off the case just because he and Vanessa were old friends? Or was it because they had had a more recent, intimate association? I never had asked him why Vanessa was at his carriage house the day she'd arrived. Or last night, for that matter.

Although I was sure I knew what his answer would be, anyway. "Catching up on old times," he'd say. Or "lending moral support." I tried to think positive thoughts, but found myself tearing open packages of ground turkey for tonight's low-fat white chili with a bit more aggression than usual.

Biscuit, who is always on hand when there's food to be had, sniffed out the prospect of a fresh bit of turkey immediately, sliding through the open kitchen door and meowing until I broke off a chunk and handed it to her. Then I dumped the rest into a pan sprayed with a tiny amount of olive oil and turned the burner on medium.

I was digging in the pantry for cumin and coriander when voices reached me over the sound of sizzling turkey.

"It's natural to miss her," said a low, female voice. "I don't think you ever get over that."

"I know," the other voice said. "I'm sorry. I don't know why I'm thinking about her so much. It's like losing an arm, or a leg or something—missing her is always there. Every minute of every day."

I sidled over to the door and peeked through it. It was Cat who was crying, slumped in one of the dining room chairs; beside her, concern in her eyes, was Boots.

"It's okay, sweetheart," Boots said, opening her arms to hug her friend.

"It's like a wound that never goes away," Cat snuffled into Boots's shoulder. "And I thought I knew how to fix it, but … it turns out it hasn't helped at all. I still feel hollow inside."

"Shhh," Boots said, stroking Cat's long brown hair. "It's okay, Cat. It's okay."

The sizzling from the stove grew ominously loud, and I tiptoed away from the door and stirred the turkey, wondering what it was Cat was talking about. Had Dirk's death brought back memories of her own loss? And who was the person she was talking about?

Turning down the burner, I crept back to the door, hoping to hear more. But the two women were leaving the dining room together, and out of earshot.

———

Cat seemed to have gotten herself back together by the time dinner was served; even though there was a melancholy look in her eyes, they were no longer red-rimmed, and her friends' efforts to cheer her up seemed to be working.

The turkey chili was a big hit, I was glad to see; I'd served the aromatic green stew over brown rice, accessorizing it with non-fat greek yogurt, reduced-fat cheese, and chopped green onions. I would have preferred full-fat cheese and a hefty helping of gua-camole—not to mention more jalapeno, which I'd cut back on in deference to northern taste buds—and a glob of sour cream. My guests thought it was deliciously spicy—Elizabeth, who had put up her notebook for a change, scraped every last bit out of her bowl and looked to be on the verge of asking for seconds. Back in the kitchen, though, I found myself dumping large quantities of hot pepper sauce on my own serving, along with the tiniest sliver of fresh avocado. And maybe just a little bit of real cheddar cheese. After all, I'd worked so hard cooking and cleaning all day, I figured I'd earned it. And if I fit in a little walk after dinner, it would erase *all* the extra calories. At least I hoped so.

When everyone had finished their chili and their melon plates and the kitchen was clean for the third time that day, I decided it was the moment to break free of the inn again. Gwen had come back from the studio and offered to do turndown for me, which I gladly accepted. The walk would help burn off my fat-laden indis-cretions; besides, I was curious about the lighthouse renovations.

I grabbed a flashlight and my windbreaker and headed out the kitchen door. After a moment's deliberation, I decided to ask John if he'd like to join me. Kind of an olive branch offer. And perhaps an op-portunity to find out more information, if I was being completely honest with myself. Walking down the path to the carriage house, I breathed in the salt air and admired the fresh green leaves on the beach roses, which I knew would soon be unfurling their gorgeous deep pink flowers. A couple of white strawberry blossoms peeked out from under tufts of grass next to the roses; my mouth watered just thinking of the little red berries that would replace them in June. Low calorie, too!

The carriage house was dark, but the lights were on in the workshop next door. I knocked on the door, and the smell of fresh paint wafted out as he opened it, paintbrush in hand. An endearing splotch of red paint decorated his nose; behind him, I could see a line of toy boats in various stages of completion.

"I was going to ask you if you wanted to go for a walk," I said, "but it looks like you're busy."

"The shop opens next week, and I'm trying to finish up an order," he said. "Maybe another night?"

"Sure," I said. We stood there for a moment. "There's leftover turkey chili in the kitchen," I said, "if you're hungry."

"Thanks," he said.

"Well." There was an awkward pause, and John glanced over his shoulder, obviously anxious to get back to his painting. "I guess I'll be going now," I said.

"Thanks for stopping by," John said. "I'd hug you, but ..." He opened his arms, showing me the splotches of wet paint on his shirt.

"No problem."

"Maybe next time," John said, reaching for the door. His green eyes looked troubled—or was I projecting?

As I turned up the hill alone, I found myself unsettled by the encounter. The feeling trailed me as I climbed the hill; not even the fresh piney scent of the towering trees and the tender green of the blueberry bushes flanking the road could erase it.

———

The lighthouse by night was far eerier than the lighthouse by day, and as I traipsed down the path to Cranberry Point, skirting the area where Dirk's body had lain—it was easy to see, as the bushes flanking the trail had been trampled—I found myself glancing up at the light uneasily, afraid it might start flashing at any moment.

A chill wind swept off the water as I grew closer to the old building, and the hulking construction equipment surrounding the lighthouse had an abandoned look that added to the brooding atmosphere.

A wire construction fence ringed the area, but it wasn't locked; I pulled back the gate and slipped through it, picking my way along the rocky area. Down by the water stood the remains of the keeper's boathouse—although the roof had caved in years ago, the walls were still bravely standing, if slightly tilted. To my immediate left was a roughly square patch of grass and weeds, now flattened by the tread of workers' boots, where Matilda had told me the keepers used to have a vegetable patch. Behind the grassy swatch stood the keeper's house, a little two-story building with peeling white paint, half of which had been stripped during the renovation process. The boards in the windows had been replaced with panes of glass that glowed in the last rays of the sunset, giving the appearance that a light burned somewhere inside. Down the hill a little way was the small stone building that the historian had told me was the oil house. For obvious reasons, the keepers stored the flammable substance away from the wooden structure of the house.

I tried the door to the keeper's house first. As I turned the knob and pushed the door, a gust of wind came off the water, yanking the knob from my hand and slamming the door open with a bang. I hurried inside, flashlight lit, and closed the door behind me. The difference in the air was instantaneous; the mildewed smell of old wooden building replaced the crisp sea air, along with a desolate feeling that gave me the creeps. I panned the flashlight around the room; several of the boards had been stripped from the inside, giving the place a skeletal appearance, and the floor had rotted away in large chunks. A jumble of furniture sat in the corner, covered with plastic sheeting; I could make out the shape of a table and a couple of spindle chairs, as well as the top of an old steamer trunk.

I walked around the two rooms of the downstairs—the one I entered must have been a living area, with a big stone fireplace at the end. That the other room was the kitchen was obvious from the rusted, antique wood cookstove and the blackened paint on the wall and ceiling above it. No sink, of course—the last keeper must have left before indoor plumbing became standard. I hadn't seen an outhouse outside, but there must have been one at one time. Unless they just squatted between a couple of rocks…

The stairs looked too rickety to risk, so I skipped the tour of the upstairs. I was guessing the hidden room wasn't to be found in the keeper's house anyway—unless the upstairs was significantly different from the downstairs, it would be almost impossible to find a place to put it. So I headed back toward the door, surveying the rooms a last time and shaking my head at the vision of the select-men. I could see the potential here—the antique wood floors were dirty and rotted in places, but what was left of them still gleamed with promise under the beam of light—and with a fresh coat of paint (and finished walls), the rooms could be bright and cheery. And a few well-planted window boxes outside would give new life to the house's Spartan exterior.

But I had nowhere near the energy—or resources—to even at-tempt such a huge undertaking.

The cold sea breeze was a welcome relief from the dank air of the keeper's house, but I knew the fresh air was short-lived; my next stop was the lighthouse itself.

As I traipsed down the short path from the keeper's house, I stared up at the cylindrical structure. For years it had been painted white with red accents, but the current coat of primer gave it a clean, stark feel.

Like the door to the keeper's house, the main door to the light-house was unlocked. Either the workers figured the gate would be deterrent enough to keep people out, or they'd picked up on the island's habit of not bothering with things like locks on doors.

The inside of the keeper's house had been bare, but the light-house itself was even emptier; all that the cylinder contained was a set of winding stairs leading to the light above. The same dank smell was here, too, and I had to fight the urge to flee. I wasn't leaving until I found that hidden room.

The wind whistled through a crack in one of the windows as I climbed the rusty metal stairs, pushing through the hatch at the top and stepping into the round watch room. Matilda had taken me on a tour once, telling me that this was where the keeper kept extra fuel and tended to the lanterns. It had been in this room that Harry had stood watch the stormy night he disappeared, I thought, a shiver passing through me that had nothing to do with the wind whipping by the windows. If he had, though, there were no signs of it; the room's brick walls were smooth and solid, and the wooden floor, while sound, was bare. The light was still there, though, right in the center, sprouting like a huge flower into the room above, held up by a cylinder in the center.

A small door led to a balcony encircling the light—for keeping the windows surrounding the lamp clean, I knew—but other than that and two small windows, the walls were solid brick. I took a deep breath; there was a hint of a kerosene smell on the air, along with the scent of fresh paint.

But there were no secret rooms to be found.

Another short staircase led to the lantern room above; I climbed it, poking my head through the half-rotted hatch, just in case maybe I'd missed something. The wind whistled through gaps in the windows ringing the room, which was empty except for the huge glass light that was still housed in the middle of the room.

I had seen a light flashing two nights ago. But the lantern was shattered, its metal frame twisted and rusted from the sea air, the floor around it littered with broken glass.

I stared at the broken light, feeling a chill pass over me.

If the lantern was in this condition, what had been the source of the light we'd seen two nights ago?

Fighting the crawling sensation that had started the moment I entered the lighthouse, I glanced around at the smudged, half-broken windows, searching for a hint of a hidden passageway. The jagged panes of glass gaped back at me. There was no room to hide another chamber here. I closed the hatch with a thud; bits of rotted wood rained down on me as I hurried down the short stairway. After another cursory search of the room, I headed back down the main staircase.

On the bottom floor, I trained the flashlight on the walls and floor one more time. And that's when I saw the hatch.

FIFTEEN

It was right under the bottom of the staircase, the crack in the boards outlining it almost invisible. It was obvious why it had escaped notice for so many years; now, though, a splintered area on one edge, farthest from the stairs, caught my attention. That must be where they had pried the door up. Holding the flashlight between my chin and my chest, I reached down and attempted to heave it up off the floor; on the third try, it came up with a creaking noise, exhaling a cold, earthy smell that made me think of basements.

Which made sense, because in a way, that's what the tiny chamber was.

I trained the beam of the flashlight into the yawning gap, illuminating a small, irregular chamber that had evidently been hewn from the rock below the lighthouse. Even though I knew the skeleton had been removed, I was terrified of seeing something—a finger bone, or a pool of dried blood—to remind me of what had lain here for so long.

But the room's rocky floor was empty, its occupant relocated to an antiseptic laboratory somewhere on the mainland.

Propping the door of the hatch up against the back of the stairs, I descended the wooden steps and stood on the dirty floor. The crude room was small, but deep, about six feet in diameter and eight feet high. I flashed the light around the rocky walls, looking for some indication of who might have hidden here, but nothing but bumpy dark granite stared back at me.

Had Harry been harboring a slave in this tiny room? I wondered. If he had, how long had the poor person been forced to stay here, in this little dark cell hewn into the rock? It must have been bitterly cold in winter; there was no place for a fire, and the granite would have been as frigid as the ice and snow outside.

A couple of shelves had been hewn from the rock, at around shoulder-level. If they had held anything, though, it had either disappeared long ago or been taken during the restoration. I ran my fingers over the rough shelves, which were more like alcoves, wondering what secrets they had held. Had the man who owned the skeleton been murdered in this little room? Or just hidden here, later? Had his death had something to do with Harry's disappearance?

I stood in the room for a long moment, trying to imagine it as it had been when the work crew discovered the body. My fingers trailed over one of the rocky shelves; when I pulled them back, they were coated with grime. Wiping my hand on my jeans, I turned and climbed the stairs, turning halfway up to get one last look at the room. I flashed the beam around—and stopped.

Unless I was mistaken, something wooden was jammed into a crevice near the ceiling. I concentrated the light on it for a moment longer, thinking it must just be a chunk of wood wedged in to keep the floor supported.

But most wedges of wood don't have keyholes.

My heart pounding, I hurried down the stairs and trained the beam on the corner of the ceiling where I'd seen the wood. From this vantage point, it was invisible. And, unfortunately, unreachable.

Should I tell Matilda it was here, and let her get it?

I could—in fact, I probably should. But I was far too curious. I jumped up a few times, trying to reach it, but it was too high, so I came up with another plan.

A stack of chairs had been in the keeper's house, I remembered, covered with plastic. Would they be strong enough to hold my weight?

There was only one way to find out.

I hurried back up the steps and crossed the short distance to the keeper's house, pulling my windbreaker tight around me to shut out the cold. The sky had darkened to black while I was in the lighthouse, and the white stars shone cold overhead, obscured occasionally by a tattered wisp of cloud. I pushed through the door to the pile of old furniture, feeling only slight qualms as I pushed aside the steamer trunk—which was interestingly heavy, making me wonder what was inside it—and grabbed what looked to be the sturdiest of the chairs. Which wasn't saying much, unfortunately.

The wind buffeted me as I carried the rickety chair back to the lighthouse; once inside, I hauled it down the short flight of stairs, the flashlight clenched between my chin and my shoulder. Then I placed it as evenly as I could on the lumpy floor and climbed onto it gingerly, wincing at the loud creaks the old wood made from the weight. I transferred the flashlight to my left hand, and while the wind moaned overhead, reached out for the box with my free hand.

If the box hadn't been quite so wedged into the rock, everything would have been fine. But my gentle efforts to dislodge it didn't work, and a moment later, the chair protesting loudly below me, I was forced to set the flashlight on the shelf and grab the box with both hands, tugging hard.

The first two times, nothing happened.

The third time, however, the box came rocketing out of the wall. At exactly the same moment, the ancient chair gave way beneath me. The chair's wooden leg splintered, sending me plummeting to the room's rocky floor. An instant later, something exploded next to my head, glancing my temple.

I had had more head injuries since coming to this island than most professional football players experience in a career, I thought as I lay in the darkness, staring up at the beam of the flashlight, which lay out of reach on the high shelf.

I remained prostrate for a few minutes, trying to get rid of the dizzy feeling in my head before attempting to sit up. The room spun a bit as I finally levered myself upward, looking for the box.

The fall had broken the brittle wood, and the top of the box had popped free, releasing a sheaf of papers that had scattered on the floor. I bent to pick them up; they were handwritten, and both the ink and the paper appeared brownish. Then again, it could just have been the dim light. I gathered them together gently, trying not to damage the documents, and laid them into what was left of the base of the box, which was about eighteen inches long, a foot wide, and a couple of inches high. Without the flashlight in hand, it was too dark to read the archaic script, but I could make out dates; it appeared to be a log of some sort. I had gathered half of the papers, laying them carefully in the box and hoping I hadn't gotten them terribly out of order, when I found the cover—a piece of rotted leather that had evidently housed all the pages. I groaned, realizing I'd inadvertently destroyed a historic book, and felt around on the floor to see if I'd missed anything else. Or inadvertently decimated anything else.

I was about to give up when my left hand encountered something rough and cold in one of the corners behind the stairs. I closed my fingers around it and then jerked them away, realizing what it was I had touched.

It was a manacle.

I reached out to touch it again, and realized it was still shackled to its twin. *Wait until Matilda hears about this!* I thought, lifting the heavy metal rings off of the rocky floor. Then it occurred to me that my method of recovering the information—breaking an antique chair, shattering an antique box, and then scattering the contents of a historic handwritten book all over a dirty floor— would be enough to have the local historian bar me from her circle of acquaintances for life. She'd done a good bit of archeological field work before taking up residence on the island, and had made it clear more than once that she was a wee bit compulsive when it came to handling artifacts.

Which I apparently was not. Even if it wasn't my fault that the chair had broken and the box had gone winging across the little room.

I looked up at my now-unreachable flashlight. Should I leave the broken box and its contents here for the workers to find and report to Matilda—along with the flashlight and the remains of the chair? Or should I take everything back to the inn with me—and then hand it over to her the next day?

It was a tough call. If I left it here, Matilda couldn't be mad at me for tampering with artifacts, but there was always the chance that someone might not bother to pass it on. If I took it with me, maybe I could tell her that I had just found it all lying around, and that I had no idea how the box got destroyed. Maybe in the construction, somehow…

A few minutes later, I was traipsing back to the keeper's house in the dark, trying not to get spooked as I fumbled the second-sturdiest chair from the pile and hauled it back to the lighthouse. It held me long enough to get the flashlight and feel around to see if I'd left anything behind. There was a scrap of fabric tucked into the back of the shelf, balled up at one side and tied with a piece of rough twine. I stuffed it into my pocket and climbed down again. It took a few trips to return the chair to its home in the keeper's house, along with what was left of its companion. Then I laid the manacles and the bit of fabric in the box, gathered the pieces together, and with the heavy box in one hand and the flashlight in the other, hoofed it to the chain-link fence. I was relieved to pull it closed behind me and step back into the twenty-first century.

———

My right arm felt like it was about to fall off by the time I made it back to the inn about a half hour later. Who needed to lift weights when you could cart artifacts across the island? I thought as I let myself into the kitchen and laid the broken wooden box on the table.

My nighttime visit to the lighthouse seemed far less spooky in the warm light and faintly spicy aroma of my familiar yellow kitchen, but as I opened the box, the musty odor of the underground room wafted out of it, sending chills up my spine once again.

The manacles were on the top of the box, made of iron, and rusted all over. I lifted them from the box carefully; they clanked open as I laid them on the table, trying to imagine whose wrists had once been imprisoned in them. Or ankles, I realized, examining the short chain between the bigger rings.

Next was the scrap of fabric I'd found tucked into the corner of the shelf. On closer inspection, it appeared to be a homemade doll, its head stuffed with some soft material, like cotton. The fabric was calico, its tiny rosebud pattern smudged with dirt and yellowed from handling or age—it was hard to tell which. A crude smiling mouth had been inked on the head, along with two black eyes. A child's doll. A slave child's only possession? Had the slave-catcher come to Cranberry Island to return a child to shackles?

I shivered, laying the little doll next to the manacles, where it smiled up at the lights, eyes staring blindly among the faded roses. Then I turned to the papers in the box.

As I had suspected, they did seem to be a log.

There was no name on the pages, but there were dates on each entry. I shuffled through the old papers, trying to find the earliest entries, which turned out to be in November of 1836. Each day was recorded, with a quick bit about the weather. I read through, feeling my excitement dim, because the references to weather went on for entry after entry. "High winds" were common, as was "rain" and "snow," but after about sixty pages of meteorological observations,

I started to wonder if there would be anything of interest. Then, in January of 1839, there was a different kind of entry.

"The M___ delivered two parcels from South Carolina today, to be held until the S___ returns for pick-up, Wednesday next. One sustained some damage during the voyage; I have endeavored to mend what I could. Have stored both in the cellar to await transport."

Excitement coursing through me, I flipped the page and ran my finger down the page to Wednesday.

"The S___ picked up the parcels from South Carolina today, amid northeasterly winds and a storm. Shipped out for Halifax at 03:00."

Three o'clock in the morning?

I flipped through several more pages. Every six weeks to two months, there was another reference to a shipment, always delivered by the M___, and always picked up at the dead of night by the S___. And all headed toward Nova Scotia. No mention of money passing hands; just references to parcels. A few of them seemed to be moved from the lighthouse—assuming that was the "cellar" referred to in the entry—to Hatley's Cove to await transport. Could that be a reference to Smuggler's Cove, which was hidden near the Gray Whale Inn and had been known as a prime spot for the transport of illegal goods? I'd been in there once before—it had a room-like cave deep inside it, including two ancient iron rings for boats to tie up at, so the story made sense. I'd always assumed the smuggled goods were rum, or sugar, or tobacco, or something. But could it have been people the smugglers were moving? I looked up the source of the "parcels." They were mainly from South Carolina, but some came from Alabama, and there was one set of six from Mississippi.

Why would he—or she, or whoever had kept this record—have written all of this down? There was no reference to money, or payment, or the type of goods transported. But every parcel arrived and left in the wee hours of the morning, and every one came from a southern state. The "parcels" were recorded in batches ranging from one to as many as seven. Was it possible that seven people had huddled together in that cold dark basement under the lighthouse, waiting for a ship to come and take them to freedom?

I leafed through all of the documents, up to the last pages, which were dated February, 1841. "Three parcels arrived from South Carolina," read the top entry on the second to last page. "Some indication that route has been compromised. Departure scheduled for February 10 may be delayed until the situation is resolved."

The next entries were simply records of the weather, which was evidently less than favorable, with lots of squalls and north winds. There was no further mention of the "situation." The entries led up to the day before the scheduled departure, in which I saw a hint of emotion for the first time. The neat, methodical hand was hurried in the last entry—almost a scrawl. "Observing much caution—visitor has particular interest in these parcels. Am fearful that the code has been compromised, and the station is no longer safe. Will attempt departure tonight, despite foul weather from the north; further delay may be catastrophic."

I flipped through the rest of the pages, searching for a hint of what might have happened next.

But the rest of the book was blank.

SIXTEEN

Next morning's breakfast of cracked wheat with Greek yogurt, a smattering of honey, and frozen Maine blueberries from last summer started off well enough, with lots of lively conversation in the dining room. My thoughts kept returning to the two mysteries on the island—both Dirk's death and the skeleton in the lighthouse—but my guests seemed more focused on calories than corpses. Now that the initial shock of the trainer's death had passed, everyone seemed to be relaxing a little bit—and even though Vanessa still wasn't back to her previous level of perkiness, which in my opinion had been inhuman anyway, at least she didn't seem quite so strained.

That was before Detective Rose appeared at the door, carrying a search warrant and trailing a team of forensics experts. Half of them peeled off and headed toward my kitchen.

"Where are they going?" I asked.

She ignored the question. "You haven't tampered with the victim's room?" she asked me as the rest of the forensics team traipsed up the stairs, presumably toward the late trainer's room.

"I've kept the room locked since you were last here, like you asked. But why are they in my kitchen? And what do you mean, 'victim'?" I asked. "Did the autopsy results come back then?"

She nodded brusquely. "They did a rush job, since the guests are only here temporarily; we got the results in late last night. We're treating the case as a potential homicide."

Despite the chill coming through the still-open front door, my palms began to sweat. "May I ask what the cause of death was?" I asked, thinking, *please, please, please don't let it be poison*.

"The victim ingested large quantities of a toxic substance," she said.

"You're kidding me," I said, waiting for the other shoe to drop. Namely, that the fact that the forensics team was investigating the food prep area meant they were closing down my kitchen.

Detective Rose eyed me coolly. "I'm afraid you'll have to make alternate arrangements for food preparation," she said, "while we inspect your kitchen."

"For how long?"

"Until we have determined that the source of the poison was not your kitchen," she said, "you're going to have to shut down your food service operation."

I felt like the earth was falling out from under me. "But how are the guests supposed to eat?" I asked.

"I'm afraid you and the retreat leader will have to make other arrangements," she said. "I saw a restaurant down by the pier. Perhaps they will be able to handle the food service."

"But they're closed until June!" I said. This retreat, which had seemed like the answer to my prayers, was turning into a nightmare.

"I'm sorry for the inconvenience, Miss Barnes," she said. "But we are dealing with a murder investigation, and must take all the proper precautions. Now, if you have a few minutes, there are some more questions I'd like to ask you."

"Sure," I said weakly. "Can we at least do it in the kitchen, so I can clean up?"

"Not until the forensics team has been able to examine it," she said. "Do you have an open guest room?"

I sighed and opened the cabinet, plucking the key out and handing it to her. "Here's the key to the Blueberry Room—it's the last one on the left, on the first floor. I'll be there in a minute, if that's okay. I'd like to check on my guests and call the restaurant to make arrangements; lunch is in a couple of hours, and I don't think they even have any food on hand. We may have to settle for sandwiches from Charlene's store." Which were anything but dietetic, unfortunately, consisting as they did of white bread, globs of mayonnaise, and American cheese.

"I'll wait for you in the room," she said.

The guests stared at me as I walked through the dining room— they had seen the forensics team trooping into the kitchen, and it appeared to have put them off their food. Elizabeth looked keenly interested in the happenings, but everyone else seemed slightly dazed, even fearful; I heard a spoon clatter to the table as we marched past the sorority sisters and into the kitchen.

After refilling coffee mugs and reassuring everyone that the investigation was "routine" (hardly), I scurried down to the front desk and called Evie Spurrell. When she didn't answer, I called Charlene down at the store.

"I've got a problem," I said in a low voice. "Dirk was poisoned, and they've shut down my kitchen indefinitely."

"No," she breathed.

"I can't get in touch with Evie. Can you see if you can find her? I need to have someone else prepare lunch and dinner."

"I can do sandwiches if you need me to," she said.

"Thanks," I said. "I may have to take you up on it. I suppose I could bring something in from the mainland for dinner, if I needed to…"

"If I can't get in touch with Evie, we'll work something out here. But I'm sure she'll be happy to help out. And there's still time to order supplies from the mainland."

"Thanks a million," I said. "Keep it quiet, if you can."

"I'd like to," she said, "but I'm afraid once I ask Evie to cover for you, it will be the equivalent of announcing it with a bullhorn."

"I know," I said. "Thanks, Charlene. You're a lifesaver." I glanced at the door to the guest room, where I knew the detective was waiting for me. "I have to go answer more questions now. I'll call you later," I said.

"This will all get worked out," she said. "Don't worry. It's just a glitch."

"I hope you're right," I said, hanging up the phone and preparing myself to face Detective Rose.

———

Her questions, fortunately, had less to do with my food than I had feared. Instead, they focused primarily on who had had access to

Dirk's room, which was comforting; it meant they suspected that was the source of the poison. I told her I'd seen Elizabeth coming out of Dirk's room the night before he died, and that the skeleton keys—along with several spare room keys—were generally kept at the front desk, where anyone would have access to them.

"You leave the keys out in the open?" she asked, blinking at me with watery eyes. The morning light through the window behind her made her kinky silver hair glow like a halo around her sharp face.

"Not exactly," I said. "They're in a cabinet."

"But the cabinet isn't locked?" she asked.

"No," I admitted sheepishly.

She let out a long sigh. "So any of your guests could have had access to Mr. DeLeon's room." She made a few notes on her notebook as I shifted uncomfortably in my wooden chair. "What about \Tom Lockhart? Was he at the inn at any time that you know of?"

"Yes," I said, feeling a coldness inside me. At her request, I told her about his visit with the gift of lobsters. Which were still waiting in a pot down by the dock, I realized. With my kitchen closed, maybe I should just let the poor things go.

"And John Quinton?" the detective asked, and the coldness in my gut turned to a block of ice.

I nodded, and she made a notation on her pad.

"When was he present?"

"He was in and out a few times," I said lightly. "He lives just next door, and we're … good friends," I added lamely. Since at the moment, I wasn't sure exactly what the status of our relationship was. Even if he *had* kissed me last night.

"Was he here at all the day before Mr. DeLeon died?"

I thought back. "He was here in the afternoon," I said. "He helped transport the guests, and hung around the inn for a while afterward. I don't think he was here in the evening, though."

"Does Mr. Quinton have a key to the inn?" she asked.

"Yes," I said, feeling my stomach sink. "He does."

"So he could have come in at any time. And is he aware of the location of the skeleton key?"

I nodded, and she took down more notes.

"Was there any strife between Mr. Quinton and Mr. DeLeon?" she asked, pen poised over her notebook.

"Not that I know of," I said. "They really didn't know each other."

"I understand Miss Tagliacozzi and Mr. Quinton had a prior relationship," Detective Rose said, her keen eyes glued to me. "How much time did they spend together after her arrival?"

I shrugged. "Not much, I don't think." Then I remembered Gwen telling me Vanessa had been down at the carriage house the day she arrived. "I think Vanessa went down to visit him after they got here—once they figured out they knew each other."

"She was unaware of Mr. Quinton's presence before her arrival?"

"Yes," I said, suddenly wondering if that was true. Was finding John here really such a surprise? If Vanessa had been corresponding with Tom Lockhart, surely she knew John was still here. Was it because of him—or Tom—that she had decided to host the retreat here?

"You don't seem quite certain about that," the detective said. Either I was an awful actress or she had very good instincts.

I arranged my face into a pleasant expression and said, "I'd heard she was still in touch with some of the islanders, so she may have known. But both of them seemed surprised."

"Did you notice any intimacy between the two?"

"Between Vanessa and John?"

"Yes."

"They spent some time together the last few days," I said. "I don't know what they talked about."

"Did John mention anything about Dirk in your presence?"

"Not that I recall," I said. "Then again, I've been very busy with the inn; we haven't talked as much the last few days." Then I blurted out, "I know there was some strife between Vanessa and Dirk—you should definitely ask her how things were going with the business. I think she was trying to cut him out of it—she didn't like the supplements—and he was giving her a hard time about it."

She made a note on her pad as I rambled. The cool breeze from the open window behind her brought her Ivory soap scent to my nose.

"And Bethany, the guest who had a crush on Dirk?" I continued, looking at her pink, scrubbed face.

"What about her?" the detective asked.

"She has a whole shrine to Dirk. She's obsessed with him—she followed him here, is convinced that he loved her, even though he was with Vanessa," I said, the words tumbling out.

The detective gave me a sharp glance. "How do you know all of this?"

"I clean the rooms," I said. "So I see a lot of things. And there was another thing I've been meaning to ask: do you know when he died?"

"I'm afraid I'm not at liberty to say," she said.

"But he was poisoned. By what?" I asked.

"Again, I cannot share that information."

Which was completely unhelpful. I made yet another gambit. "If he'd been poisoned by the food he'd had at the inn, wouldn't he have died the night before?" I asked.

She shook her head. "Some poisons take several hours to take effect."

I sighed. "Still. If it was my kitchen that caused the death, don't you think some of the other guests would have been sick?"

The detective looked at me with pity in her eyes. "Miss Barnes, I appreciate your situation—and the difficulty this case is causing for your business—but we must take precautions. We will do everything we can to get you back up and running, but you'll have to be patient."

I closed my eyes for a moment. "The *Bangor Daily News* is calling. I'm afraid when this gets out, it will ruin my business."

"We're doing everything we can," she repeated. She reviewed her notes once more. "I know you have guests to attend to, so I don't want to keep you. I think we're done for now … if I have more questions, I know where to find you."

"Thanks," I said gloomily, then forced myself to look on the bright side. Even though it wasn't a very big bright side. Detective Rose might have closed down my kitchen, but at least she was much easier to deal with than her predecessor, Grimes. For starters, she didn't look at me like she was sizing me for orange coveralls.

"I will need to talk to your neighbor, though," she said as I turned to go, and something in her voice sent a shiver down my back.

"He works from home," I said, "so he should be in."

"Thank you," she said with a chilly smile, shuffling her papers together as I walked out of the room. Perhaps she wasn't sizing *me* for a jumpsuit. But I wasn't sure the same could be said for my neighbor.

I hurried into the tense dining room, where I retrieved three more empty bowls and stacked them on the buffet by the kitchen door.

"What's going on?" asked Sarah, who was comforting Cat. "Why are the police in the kitchen?"

"Apparently Dirk died from ingesting a toxic substance," I said. "They're doing a routine check to make sure everything is in order." No need to go into the whole "kitchen closed" thing right now. I glanced at Cat, whose large eyes were swollen. Sarah had stretched a protective arm around her shoulders. "Is everything all right?" I asked.

Boots took me by the arm and led me aside. "Cat lost a daughter once, years ago, and today's the anniversary of her death."

I looked at Cat's haunted face. "Oh, my gosh. I'm so sorry..."

"It's okay. It's just that this is a tough time of year for her," Boots said. "And with another death..." She shook her head, and her bobbed hair swung back and forth. Even though she must have been in her fifties, she still had some of the look of a college student, I thought. A certain vitality to her ... "The timing couldn't be worse," Boots continued. "The whole reason she wanted to come to the retreat this week wasn't really the reunion; it was to take her mind off of her daughter."

"When did she lose her daughter?" I asked quietly, the forensics unit in the kitchen forgotten for the moment. My heart went out to the poor woman, who was clearly still bereft. As I would be too.

"It's been several years now," she said.

No wonder Cat had been so upset last night, I thought. She'd come to the retreat to forget about her personal tragedy, only to be faced with another. I glanced at the poor woman who had lost her daughter; the empty, lost look on her face was somehow familiar. Probably because I'd had to spend so much time staring across a table at Charlene's haunted eyes, just a few months ago, after Richard McLaughlin had died. Grief, unfortunately, was universal.

"If there's anything I can do to help," I said, "let me know."

"Thanks," she said. "Do you know if the detective is going to want to question us again?"

"I'll ask her if she can skip Caterina," I said. "She's been through enough already."

"Thank you," Boots said, giving me a grateful smile. Then she returned to the table to comfort her friend while I headed back to the guest room where the detective had installed herself.

She opened the door a second after I knocked.

"Are you going to question the guests again?" I asked as she stood in the doorway, still holding her notepad, and hitched up her belt.

"I'm afraid I'll have to," she said.

"I wanted to let you know—one of my guests lost a daughter on this day several years ago," I said. "Her name is Caterina. She's having a rough morning—all of this seems to be bringing the old memories back."

The detective blinked at me. "What bearing does that have on the case?"

"It doesn't," I said. "It's just … could you be particularly gentle with her?" I asked.

"I'll do the best I can," she said. "I assume all of your guests are at breakfast?"

"Yes," I said. "Most of them, anyway. Hey—can I at least put the dirty dishes in the kitchen?"

She hesitated.

"I just don't want them cluttering up the dining room," I added.

"I suppose that will be all right," she said.

"Thanks." It wasn't much, but it was a small triumph.

As she plucked the first guest from the dining room—Bethany, whose moon-shaped face was still pale and blank with grief—I gathered up a stack of dishes and headed into the kitchen. Two people, a man and a woman, looked up as I entered.

"Sorry to interrupt," I said, "but the detective said I could at least put the dirty dishes in the kitchen. Can I put them on the counter by the sink?"

The woman nodded brusquely and returned to the work of bagging a marshmallow from a bag she'd pulled from the pantry, setting it on a growing stack on my kitchen table. If I had to wait for them to do a chemical analysis of every foodstuff in my kitchen, I realized, I'd be closed for months.

Fighting the wave of despair that threatened to engulf me, I deposited the first load of dishes on the counter.

On my way back out the door, I paused at the cookie jar. God, I needed a sugar hit. I didn't bother asking. As the woman bagged a raisin and her helper dug through my refrigerator, I plunged my hand into the jar to grab a handful of cookies—but found only the jar's ceramic bottom.

Somebody had eaten all of the cookies.

I tilted the jar, just to be sure there wasn't one hiding in the corner, but even the crumbs were gone. I jammed the lid back on and headed into the pantry. What else had the midnight thief taken?

And would any of his or her haul turn out to be the source of the poison?

SEVENTEEN

MARGE SHOWED UP SHORTLY after Detective Rose arrived, coming in through the main door when the forensics people rebuffed her from the kitchen. Gwen hadn't made it out of bed yet—which was amazing, considering the noise coming from the kitchen—but since it was her morning off, I couldn't blame her. I'd have slept in too, if I could.

"What's all the commotion then?" Marge asked as she hung her pea-green jacket on a hook behind the front desk.

"Apparently the guy who died the other day may have been poisoned," I said. "They're going over the kitchen with a fine-toothed comb and questioning all the guests again." I lowered my voice. "My kitchen is closed—I can't cook anything for anyone until they've looked at everything. But please don't say anything. I don't want the *Daily Mail* to get wind of it."

She tsked. "Bad business, then. Can I still do up the rooms?"

"I hope so," I said. "They let me in to clear the dishes at least; maybe they won't give us a hard time about getting cleaning supplies from the laundry room.

"Good. I've got another job this afternoon at two, if I can get everything done in time. Opening up a house for one of them summer families."

"Seems a little early for summer visitors," I said, since the temperature had been in the high forties when I'd stepped out earlier that morning.

"It may not be warm like in Texas, maybe, but it's coming along," she said. "We'll be seein' lupines soon enough."

"I hope so," I said.

"By the way, Miss Natalie. You told me if I saw anything peculiar, I should let you know."

My heart rate picked up a bit. "Did you see something?"

"Heard something, more like. One of the ladies, that dark-haired one, was talking on her cell phone. Asking somebody to look into some legal stuff. And there was a name she'd asked about, too."

I felt adrenaline pulse through me. "Do you remember what it was?"

"It was a man's name," she said. "Something Kershaw. Eric, maybe—I couldn't quite catch it."

Eric Kershaw. "What was she asking about?"

"Wanted to see what someone could find on it. She said something about the town he lives in, but my hearing's not as good as it was, I'm afraid."

"Did she say anything about the state?"

Marge shook her head. "Not that I could hear." I smiled, but couldn't keep the disappointment off my face. "But I'll keep listening and looking," Marge said eagerly. Ever since our harrowing near-death experience last fall, she had seemed anxious to help me in any way possible. "Don't worry. If I hear anything, you'll be the first to know."

"Thanks, Marge. And thanks for all of your help around here—you've been a godsend."

"You think?" she said, her dour face brightening into a small smile. "I know your niece don't think much of me, but I do try."

"Don't worry about Gwen," I said. "We're both delighted you're here," I said, stretching the truth just a bit.

Marge smiled. "I'd better get to it then," she said. And unless I was imagining things, there was a new spring in her step as she headed for the kitchen.

When she was gone, I sat down behind the front desk, feeling restless—and helpless. John was a suspect in a murder investigation. And as much as I wanted to believe he was absolutely innocent, his behavior had been so strange these last few days, I wasn't quite sure. I racked my brain, trying to think of who might have wished Dirk harm—other than Vanessa, perhaps, or even Bethany. If Bethany had killed him in a fit of passion, though, I wouldn't have guessed she'd use poison. Passion generally involves instant gratification—something like a knife, or a gun, rather than a time-release capsule.

I sighed, trying to come up with other possibilities. But aside from Dirk's former disgruntled clients, I couldn't think of any.

Dirk's former disgruntled clients, I thought suddenly, and sat up straight in my chair. Was it possible that one of them had come to the inn? Or was that entirely too far-fetched? I thought back to the letters I'd seen. People had gotten sick, to be sure—even suffered heart attacks, at least in one case—but no one had died. Would someone commit murder in revenge for a non-fatal heart attack?

Could it be that there were cases I didn't know about?

I glanced up at the clock; lunch was at twelve, and I still needed to get in touch with Charlene to come up with something that would work, but with Marge doing the rooms, I had a couple of free hours before it was time to serve dinner. And since I wasn't going to be doing the cooking, I might have enough time to head over the mainland and find out what I could about Dirk DeLeon.

My thoughts turned to the Somesville Library—and to Audrey Fedders, the fabulous librarian who had helped me do research in the past. Maybe if I called her, she could see what she could find; there were so many things to track down, I wasn't sure I'd have time. It was worth a shot, anyway—and I could always pay her with a batch of her favorite cranberry walnut muffins.

I picked up the phone and dialed the library, asking for the reference desk.

"Somesville Library," said a bright voice. I could picture Audrey with her sparkly reading glasses and ready smile; we'd become friends over the winter, when I'd spent a lot of time searching the stacks for good books.

"I've got a big favor to ask," I said.

"Does it have anything to do with that handsome man who died near the inn?"

"How did you guess?" I asked.

"Everyone's talking about it. Since I don't have much on today, I'll do whatever I can," she said.

"Are you sure?"

"It's more interesting than tracking down knitting patterns," she said, and a moment later, she agreed to see what she could find on the names I gave her.

"I'll bring over a batch of cranberry muffins sometime soon—I'd do it today, but I'm short on time." And a kitchen, of course. "I probably won't get over there until about two. Will that give you enough time?"

"I'll see what I can do," she said.

I hung up the phone, thinking wonderful thoughts about librarians in general and Audrey in particular, and knocked on the door to the blueberry room to see if Detective Rose needed anything else from me. When I told her I was heading out for a while, she nodded. "Just don't stray far," she said, and returned her attention to Cat, who was huddled in the chair across from her, as I closed the door behind me.

I was about to call Charlene when the phone rang. Cringing, I picked it up, praying it wasn't the Bangor paper.

Thankfully, it wasn't. "Nat," Charlene said. "Evie Spurrell has agreed to open the restaurant for dinner, and I'm going to send over sandwiches on whole wheat bread with some fruit for lunch."

"You're a godsend," I told her.

"Anything else you need?"

"Can she do lunch and dinner for the next few days? Just in case?"

"She says she'll do whatever you need," Charlene replied.

Thank goodness. "I'm going to call and thank her right now," I said. "She's a lifesaver."

"Any more news at the inn?"

"Nothing yet," I said. "I'll let you know as soon as I hear anything, though."

After hanging up with Charlene, I called Evie to thank her for helping out. "Can I come down and cook?" I asked. After all, Detective Rose hadn't told me not to cook; just that I couldn't do it in my own kitchen.

"I'll take care of the cooking," she said. "I need to get warmed up for the summer season. But if you'll serve, that would be great!"

"I'll put an order in for the food and get the recipes to you," I said, hoping her insistence on cooking had more to do with feeling territorial about her kitchen than concerns that I might poison yet another guest. "We may have to do this for a few days, if that's all right with you."

"Whatever you need, Natalie. I'm happy to help out with lunches, too, if you need."

"Thanks a million," I said, wondering what I was going to do about tomorrow's breakfast. Maybe I could work something out with Charlene. "I'll drop by in a little bit with the menu, and I'll order the food now." Which was frustrating, since I had several pounds of expensive food already purchased and stowed in the freezer, just steps away. Oh, well. "Dinner is scheduled for 6:30; I think it's grilled scallops tonight, which is easy."

"Perfect. See you in a bit, then." I headed back to the kitchen and retrieved my menus, trying to ignore the chaos that had descended on my favorite room—and the fact that my freezer door was just standing open, allowing everything in it to thaw. Including five pounds of scallops. I had just called to place the food order— it would be over on the 2:00 mail boat, they assured me—and had my hand on the doorknob, wondering if I could get the police to reimburse me for lost food, when I realized there was another stop to make while I was out.

I hurried up the stairs to retrieve the broken box I'd gotten from the lighthouse.

While I was out, I might as well make the trek to the Cranberry Island Museum.

———

After dropping off the menus with Evie, who had greeted me with a hug and smile that warmed my heart, I headed down toward the pier—and the museum—feeling a little bit more hopeful. Maybe it was Evie's willingness to come to my aid, or the buds on the gnarled apple trees along the roadside, or the warmth I could finally detect in the breeze off the water, but I felt as optimistic as it was possible to feel when you're an innkeeper and the police have shut down your kitchen because one of your guests was poisoned.

Matilda answered the door in a turtleneck and jeans, a pair of wire-rimmed glasses perched on the end of her long nose. "Natalie!" she said, her thin face breaking into a smile. "Come on in. Sounds like you've had lots of excitement up there at the inn this week."

"A bit too much, if you ask me," I said.

She laughed. "I'm sure everything will work out all right—even though it's a shame about that poor man dying. Anyway, what can I do for you?"

"I wanted to show you something," I said.

"Oh?" she said, her eyes sparking with interest. "Did you find that diary you lost last fall?"

"Uh, no," I said.

She sighed heavily. "I was afraid not," she said as I followed her through the door of her little yellow house and into the dining room, where stacks of old papers were carefully laid out on the cherrywood table. The walls were adorned with old photographs of the island as it had been; I recognized several of the houses, which were still standing today.

"I took a walk down to the lighthouse yesterday," I said.

"It's really coming along, isn't it?" she asked. "I can't wait to get to work on recreating the interior. They're going to let us use it as an extension of the museum."

"Yes, that will be lovely," I said. "Anyway, while I was there, I decided to take a look at that little hidden room ..."

"You found it?" Her eyes were bright. "The skeleton was such an amazing discovery. Most of the clothing was rotted away, but there were still scraps."

All I could think was, *blech.*

"If only there had been more information available," she continued, "to help us figure out what happened."

"Have you found anything in your research?" I asked, gesturing toward the stacks on the table.

She walked over to the table and pointed to a copy of an old newspaper article. "Nothing other than this reference to a black slave-catcher named Otis Ball. I'm surprised to find a black bounty hunter—they were almost invariably white, for obvious reasons. But evidently he was here in 1841—caused quite a stir."

"Who was he looking for?" I asked.

"Two adults and a child," she said. "Their names were James, Emma, and Sadie. No last names, of course—slaves didn't have them—but they belonged to a family called Dixon, in the Carolinas." She pushed her glasses up and shook her head. "Slavery was such an awful institution. To think your own child could be sold ... I'd try to escape, too, if my daughter's life was at stake. Even with the risks."

I stared at the article. *Slave-catcher pursues runaways to Cranberry Island*, read the headline. The slaves—ages twenty-three, twenty-five and seven—were suspected to be hiding somewhere on the island.

"Apparently he thought there was a way station hidden here on the island," Matilda said. "But I've never heard or seen any mention of it, which makes me wonder. Usually, something as unusual as that would have at least a few rumors associated with it. And African-Americans weren't exactly common in this part of the world—you'd think something like that would be noticed."

"Did the Underground Railroad come this far north, then?" I asked, clutching the handle of the canvas bag I carried.

"There are a couple of hundred recorded in Maine. This was one of the last stops before Canada, which is where many of the runaways were headed—slavery was illegal on that side of the border." She glanced over the article again. "I don't think he found what he was looking for, though. I couldn't find any other articles about him, and I'm sure if he'd tracked them down, it would have been big news." She finally noticed the bag in my hands. "But I'm nattering on, and you said you had something to show me. What's in the bag?" she asked.

"It's what I came down to talk to you about," I said, setting the canvas bag down on the table, amidst all the papers. "I found it on a shelf in that little underground room."

She gave me a confused look. "But the shelves were all empty," she said. "I checked them."

"There was one right at the top—you could only see it from the ladder," I said, pulling the box from the bag and setting it on the table. "This was wedged into it."

She glanced down at the box with barely contained excitement, but shot me a sharp look as she noticed the broken lid. "And you didn't leave it there?"

I shrugged. "I probably should have, in retrospect, but didn't know what it was."

She touched the splintered wood. "Was it like this when you found it?"

"It happened while I was taking it out," I said.

"What did you do, take a sledgehammer to it?" Her voice had more than a little edge to it.

"Look and see what's inside," I said, ignoring the barb. Even though I probably deserved it, at least a little bit.

Matilda adjusted her glasses and lifted off the broken lid, drawing in a sharp breath when she saw the manacles. "Heavens," she whispered. She touched them gingerly, as if they might bite, and laid them carefully on the table. Then she picked up the little bit of calico with the crude face. "A child's doll," she said. She touched it gently; then she turned to the pages on the table. I didn't say anything as she leafed through the log. I was curious to see if she came to the same conclusion I had.

"What a strange document," she said, turning the pages carefully. "From the dates, assuming it was penned by the keeper, it would have been Harry Atherton. I'll have to check the handwriting, to see if it matches."

"But what *is* it exactly?" I asked.

"I don't know. It resembles a lighthouse log—I have two of them down in the museum—but the entries are all wrong. The weather is there, which is fine—but all this stuff about parcels is very strange. Always the same ships," she said, "and always at night. It almost looks like he was smuggling."

"Read the last entries, and see what you think," I suggested.

She flipped through to the last part; I could hear the excitement in her voice. "Natalie, if this is his handwriting—goodness me, he must have written this just before his disappearance!" She looked back down at the page, biting her lip. "The question is, though, where did he go? Did he vanish because someone found out what he was doing, and threatened to turn him in?"

"The log's date is pretty close to when the slave-catcher was in town," I pointed out. "And there were the other things in the box, too."

She looked at the doll and the manacles, and her eyes widened. "The way station on the Underground Railroad..."

I nodded. "That's what I was thinking, too."

"That would explain the body, too. Why it was an African-American." She bit her lip. "But who was it?"

"I was hoping you could help me figure that out," I admitted.

She shook her head. "The problem is, we don't know exactly when the body was placed there; we only have a general time period. There's no way to know when he died."

"But he was in the same room with the log," I said. "And the log ends with the storm. Don't you think the two must be related?"

She shook her head. "It's impossible to know. It could have been two separate incidents. Still, though..." Her lined face was alive with excitement. "It almost looks like Harry was using the lighthouse as a way station on the Underground Railroad! This is so exciting, and historically important." She ran her finger down the page again, reading the entry a second time.

"Have you ever heard of Hatley Cove?" I asked as she turned the page. "He mentions it a lot as a pick-up and drop-off point."

"No, but that doesn't mean there isn't a reference to it somewhere. One of the islanders may know about it. Maybe it's on one of the nearby islands, even; he could easily have used a boat to go to and from it." She pursed her lips. "I do wonder about that body, though. If he was harboring runaways, could it have belonged to one of the slaves?"

"Or maybe even the slave-catcher," I said.

Matilda sighed, cradling the scrap of calico with the crudely drawn face in her hands. "We may never know, unfortunately. So many mysteries. Whose doll was this?" she wondered aloud. "And why did she leave it behind?"

I glanced at the manacles. They were still menacing, even now. "Let's check the handwriting on the lighthouse log—see if it matches."

"Good idea. It's down at the museum," she said, gently placing the items I had brought back into their broken box, cradling it in her arms as I followed her out the front door and down the short hill to the Cranberry Island Museum.

It was a small brick building, most of which had been financed by the Selfridges, a prominent family on the island. One of the Selfridges had built the Gray Whale Inn, in fact—it had started life as a captain's house, placed far from the pier so that the missus wouldn't have to suffer the stink of fish.

The smell of dust and age wafted over us as Matilda turned the key and opened the door. Old fishing implements—rusty hooks, rotted nets—adorned the walls, along with photos of the island as it had been more than a hundred years ago. The clothes had changed, as had the style of lobster traps—the metal ones had supplanted the traditional wooden pots—but everything else was eerily similar, down to the ridges of the mountains on the mainland, framed in the distance.

"It's over here," she said, picking up a large, leather-bound book that was almost identical to the one I'd found in the hidden room. She picked up the top sheet from the box and compared the handwriting. "The dates and the handwriting match; this was written by Harry."

"Is there an article about Harry's disappearance?" I asked. "So we can confirm the date of the last entry?"

"Well, the last entries match," she said, flipping to the end of the lighthouse log. "Both of them ended in February of 1841. She began rummaging around in the stacks on her crowded desk. "I had a copy of the article on Harry Atherton's disappearance here somewhere. I also want to check the dates and see if I can find out if there's any record of a boat starting with 'S' landing in Halifax, coming from the Maine area, around these dates."

"You can do that?"

"I have a colleague up in Yarmouth who specializes in maritime history," she said. "I'll give her a call and see what she can come up with. It's a long shot, but you never know." She looked at the doll and the manacles. "I'll have to see if I can find out anything about these, too. You're sure they were in the box?"

"The manacles were—I'm pretty sure, anyway. The doll was stuffed in behind it, on the shelf."

Matilda touched it gently, reverently. I wished its crudely drawn lips could talk. "Do you think the doll belonged to the little girl?" I asked.

"Perhaps," she said. "We may never know. And if so—why would she leave it behind? It seemed to be well-loved—the fabric has seen a lot of wear."

"Maybe whoever owned it had to leave in a hurry," I said, thinking of the body that had lain in the lighthouse for so long, and the log hidden on the shelf.

"Or maybe it was a mother's memento, of a lost child," Matilda theorized, tracing the hand-drawn features. "If only she could talk," she said, echoing the thought I'd had just a moment earlier.

My eyes shifted from the doll to the manacles, and a shiver passed through me as I thought of the body in the lighthouse.

Even if the doll could talk, I wasn't quite sure I wanted to hear what she had to say.

———

By the time I left the museum, it was almost eleven-thirty—time to head over and see if Charlene needed help with the sandwiches. I couldn't cook in my own kitchen, but at least I could do something.

I was still thinking about my lighthouse find when I stepped into the Cranberry Island Store about ten minutes later. Several pairs of eyes swiveled to the door as I entered, but there were more smiles than speculative looks, I was happy to see. Charlene was in the kitchen area, making sandwiches.

"Where have you been?" Charlene asked, slapping a few slices of turkey on a piece of brown bread. "I called the inn, but Marge said she couldn't find you. Gwen's worried, too."

"I went down to the museum," I said, washing my hands at the sink and stationing myself next to her. As I turkeyed a sandwich, I said, "I found something down at the lighthouse yesterday, and I wanted to talk to Matilda about it. Why? What's wrong?"

"Natalie, it's not good news." She bit her lipsticked lip; something about her expression sent a needle of ice through my heart.

"What is it?" I asked, afraid to hear the answer. Had someone else died?

She cast a glance over her shoulder at the group assembled on the couches, all of whom were eyeing us with curiosity. Then she leaned over and whispered, "They've taken John and Tom to the station on the mainland. They're interrogating them right now."

EIGHTEEN

My MOUTH FELT SUDDENLY dry, and the hand holding the turkey started to shake a little bit. "Why did they take them to the mainland?" I asked in a low voice. "Why not question them here?"

"I don't know," she murmured. "They must really think they're involved, somehow. I heard the police also got search warrants for both places—they're probably at John's carriage house now!"

I closed my eyes, trying to steady myself. In the last three days, my life had turned upside-down. My kitchen was temporarily condemned, the poisoning at the inn was big news in the paper, and now John was a serious suspect in a murder case. What did the police know about him that I didn't? "I don't understand," I said. "What did they find out?"

"I don't know," she said, "but I thought you should hear it from me, rather than through the grapevine." She added lettuce to a sandwich and turned to me, concern in her blue eyes. "Are you okay?"

"I'm fine," I said, although in truth I felt completely disoriented—as if the ground was disappearing from under my feet.

"What did you find at the lighthouse?" Charlene asked.

"I found a log of sorts," I said, although I was no longer very concerned with events that had happened so long ago. Not when people I cared about were threatened in the here and now.

"Is it connected with the skeleton?"

"Maybe," I said. "There was also a doll, and some manacles. I found them hidden in the room where the skeleton was."

"Creepy," Charlene said, shivering.

"No kidding."

Before we could say more, selectwoman Ingrid Sorenson came over to grill me over what was happening at the inn. I dodged as many questions as I could as we wrapped up the sandwiches and stowed them, along with some fresh fruit and several bottles of water, into a crate.

"Take the truck," Charlene said, tossing me the keys. "And take your time—I don't need it today."

"Thanks," I said, grateful to be leaving the store—and the hungry eyes of the islanders.

———

The dining room was empty when I got back to the inn, but once word spread that food was on the premises, the vacant chairs filled quickly. Gwen and Marge had been waiting for me by the front door, and I had to face a scolding from my niece before I could ask if there were any messages. "Why didn't you tell Marge where you were going?" Gwen asked, her dark eyes stormy. "I was worried sick about you!"

"I'm sorry, Gwen. I didn't think."

"You've got some messages, I'm afraid," Marge said. "Phone's been ringing off the hook."

"Reservations?" I asked hopefully.

She shook her head. "Reporters." I cringed as she ran down the list. Apparently in the brief time I was gone, the Bangor paper had called twice, and the *Daily Mail* three times.

"Please tell me you didn't tell them anything," I said.

"I just told them they'd have to talk to you," she said.

"Hopefully I can come up with a good spin before the next phone call." I turned to Marge. "Can you let everyone know that food is here?"

"Sure, Miss Nat," she said, and headed for the stairs.

"Are you sure you're okay?" Gwen asked as Marge lumbered to the second floor.

"They're interrogating John," I said in a low voice.

Gwen's hand leapt to her mouth. "No. Do you think... do you think he did it?"

"No," I said. "Maybe."

Her eyes widened. "Maybe?"

"He's been acting so strange lately. I just don't know what to believe anymore. But I just can't imagine that John would..." The sentence trailed off, leaving us in an awkward silence.

"Is that lunch?" Gwen asked finally, pointing to the crate of food.

I nodded. "We can't use the kitchen, so dinner will be down at Spurrell's, too."

"This retreat is turning out to be a total disaster, isn't it?"

I sighed. "All we can do is manage it the best we can." With that, I hauled the crate into the dining room to face my guests, trying to forget that they had paid top dollar for this retreat—and were being served processed turkey on store-bought bread.

"Sandwiches?" Carissa asked as I laid out the simple meal on the buffet.

"We had something more elaborate planned," I said, "but we had to improvise. Dinner should be marvelous though—we're going to eat down at the pier."

"It will be good to get out of here," Megan said, glancing around. "It's like living in a death trap."

I gave her a brittle smile and handed her a sandwich.

A moment later, Detective Rose appeared at the doorway, accompanied by Greg, who hurried over to join Megan while Carissa glared at him.

"Would you like a sandwich?" I asked, turning my attention to the detective. Charlene and I had made extras for the officers, in the interest of public relations.

"Thanks," she said, taking one and heading back toward the guest room.

Before she could disappear, I said, "I hear John Quinton has been taken to the mainland for questioning—and that you've got someone searching his house."

"That is correct," she said in a flat tone of voice that told me I wasn't going to get much from her.

"Why is he a suspect?" I asked.

"Miss Barnes," she said, "As you know, I am not at liberty to share the details of the case with you. But since I know you have some involvement with Mr. Quinton…" She paused, and I think

I saw a flash of pity in her gray eyes. "You might want to start distancing yourself a bit."

"What do you mean?" I asked, feeling like she had punched me in the stomach.

"I believe there may be more to their relationship than you are aware," she said, reaching up to push a clump of iron-gray hair behind one ear. Then she started for the door again. "Thanks for the sandwich."

"My pleasure," I said, feeling sick as she flashed me another look of sympathy before leaving the dining room.

———

An hour later, the lunch cleanup—which consisted of throwing wrappers into the trash—was finished, and I was at loose ends again. *At least you're getting a break from dishes*, I told myself. But it was cold comfort.

Everyone who could had deserted the inn—the guests had gotten permission to join Vanessa on another walk around the island, Gwen had headed to visit her boyfriend, and Marge had left for her other job—leaving me alone with the police.

After checking to make sure I was free to leave the inn, I headed down to my skiff. I couldn't do anything here; but maybe the librarian had turned something up that would help exonerate John.

The motor revved on the first try, and I wrapped my jacket tight around me as I steered it away from the inn. My eyes were drawn to the little carriage house hunkered down next to the inn, remembering all the good times John and I had had there together. Lobster dinners in his cozy dining room, late nights watching old

Audrey Hepburn movies and eating popcorn together while a storm raged outside, my head nestled into his warm shoulder...

He couldn't have murdered Dirk.

Could he?

I forced my eyes from the carriage house, and they moved instinctively to the lighthouse. Yet another unsolved mystery. Why couldn't anything be simple? I wondered. After a last survey of the island, its houses huddled around the pier, the gray wall of cliffs near the inn, I turned to face the mainland.

The little boat slapped down on the whitecaps as I steered it around a trio of gulls bobbing on the water. As much as I loved the island, it was good to be away from it for a little while—even though the thoughts racing around in my head made it hard to enjoy the scenery.

As the fresh air buffeted my face, I tried processing what Detective Rose had told me. What had she meant when she told me I should distance myself from John? Had she discovered something about him that I didn't know? Did he, like the lighthouse, have a secret past?

I thought about raven-haired Vanessa, her supermodel figure and her dark exotic eyes. Everything had started with her arrival at the island; she had stirred up all kinds of problems. Had she come back to chase a lost summer romance with John? But in truth, he didn't seem her type—as handsome as he was, he wasn't the sort of highly driven man I would expect Vanessa to be drawn to. But I could be wrong about that; after all, as they say, opposites do attract.

But if the two of them had a relationship, why bother to hide it? After all, it's not like either of them were married. If they wanted to be together, there was nothing stopping them—other than an awkward break-up conversation between John and me, and maybe Vanessa and Dirk. Certainly no legal proceedings.

By the time I docked at Somesville a half hour later, I had done nothing but tie myself up in mental pretzels, and was even more worked up than I had been when I left Cranberry Island. Once the skiff was tied up, I hopped off onto the dock, admiring the little town with its white-painted wood houses and picturesque bridge as I headed for the library. A couple of people smiled as I passed, but without the avid interest I'd experienced earlier at Charlene's store. As much as I loved Cranberry Island, it was refreshing to not be in a place where almost every person I met stared at me with curiosity—and maybe a hint of suspicion. I pushed the wooden door to the library open a few minutes later; the building still had the serene feel of the church it had been in a previous life. I fervently hoped Audrey had found some answers to my questions.

And if not answers, at least a clue that would point me in the right direction.

The research librarian greeted me as soon as I came through the door, eyes shining behind her rhinestone-studded glasses. "Natalie! So glad you could make it."

"Me too," I said, following her to her desk, where she picked up a sheaf of papers. "I haven't had a chance to make muffins yet," I said, omitting the fact that the reason I hadn't had a chance was that the police were inspecting every inch of my kitchen, "but I'll get them to you soon."

"No worries," she said. "And you don't need to bring me anything—I had fun!"

"Looks like you were pretty successful," I said, eyeing the pile in her hands.

"I found all kinds of things for you," she said, handing me the stack. "I don't know if any of it will be useful, but you never know!"

I studied the top page, which was a news article on Bethany Thomas. "Interesting," I said.

"What?"

"Bethany Thomas. She's got a history of obsessions, it seems."

"And at least two restraining orders to go with them," Audrey said, raising an eyebrow.

"Delightful," I said, shivering as I thought of the shrine she'd set up on her dresser. "No wonder Dirk wanted to steer clear of her."

I flipped through more of the pages, and found several articles by Elizabeth. Evidently the reporter at the inn used to work for one of the daily newspapers.

"You found the articles by your reporter," Audrey said. "She covered the traffic beat."

"Not very glamorous work, is it?" I leaned over the counter and looked through the rest of the pages. Not much on Boots or Sarah—just a couple of newspaper commendations for volunteering. Cat had evidently been very active in the Junior League in a town called Evergreen, but that was about all there was on her. Megan and Carissa were also minimally represented; Megan's wedding announcement had appeared in an Oregon paper in the late '80s, as was Carissa's birth a few years later, but that was all.

Greg, on the other hand, turned up some surprises.

"Greg is a private investigator?" I asked.

"If it's the same person, he's out of Boston," she said. "Which is interesting. Several of the lawsuits I found against Mr. DeLeon originated in Boston."

"So do you think one of his former clients may have sent him to check up on Dirk?"

Audrey shrugged. "No way to know, unfortunately. He does a lot of infidelity work, according to his web site—I printed his photo."

I glanced down at the color print of a good-looking man in a coat and tie. It did look like Greg—only a few years younger and several pounds thinner than he currently was. Maybe his reason for going to the retreat really was to take off some excess poundage. But the fact that he was a private investigator made me suspicious.

"Did you find anything on Eric Kershaw?" I asked.

"Maybe," she said. "But I'm not sure it's relevant. There's an English musician by that name."

"Really? Where does he live now?"

"Nowhere. He passed away in 1983, I'm afraid."

"Oh. Maybe I got the name wrong." I stifled my disappointment. I had had high hopes that we would uncover something interesting about Eric Kershaw that would somehow pertain to Dirk's death. On the other hand, Audre had found a lot of good information on Bethany and Greg, so it hadn't been a total loss. "What about Dirk and Vanessa?" I asked, paging through to the end of the stack of papers. Of all the names I'd given her, these two seemed to have produced the most information.

"There's plenty on both of them. Dirk had a couple of lawsuits written up in the press—no judgments against him, at least not that I could find, but there are a few still pending. He seems to have been in Boston for the last six years—before that, I can't find anything."

"His bio says he's been a personal trainer for many years," I said. "Maybe he was working for a small gym somewhere."

"Vanessa, on the other hand, has had quite a history. She was engaged to marry a big shot in New Jersey about two years ago, but called it off." Audrey took the papers from my hand and flipped through to an engagement announcement featuring a picture of Vanessa, her hair longer than it was now, glowing next to a handsome blond man with a very toothy smile.

"Did you find anything more on it?"

She shook her head. "Nope. But unless the wedding is still on hold, it never happened. I checked the date."

"I heard her say she was engaged to a real estate mogul," I said. "I wonder what put the brakes on?"

"Hard to tell," she said. "But she seems to have done quite well for herself since then. She's been interviewed in all kinds of articles, and her business seems to be getting a lot of good press."

She certainly did; the program—and Vanessa—had been featured in *Cosmopolitan*, *Self*, and even *O! Magazine*. No wonder the literary agent was interested in her proposal; if she could wangle a spot on Oprah, Vanessa's book would be golden.

I leafed through the pages again, thankful that Audrey had taken a couple of hours of her day—and her superior research skills—to come to my aid. "This has been a huge help," I told her. "I can't thank you enough."

"If you need anything else, let me know," she said. "I've been getting a lot of requests from Cranberry Island these days."

"Really? Who else have you been talking to?"

"Matilda Jenkins," she said.

"Of course. The lighthouse."

Audrey nodded. "Exactly. Matilda is obsessed with that building—always has been. And now that they've found that body there..." She shivered. "Have they found anything else out?"

"The first lab results show that the bones are African," I said, "but they're getting a second opinion. Matilda found a reference to a black slave-catcher who was here around then, and she thinks there may have been an Underground Railroad way station on Cranberry Island—maybe at the lighthouse. Have you ever run across any mention of one?"

She shook her head. "No, but then I haven't looked. Tell her I'll poke around a little and see what I can find."

"She'll be delighted to hear that, I'm sure. She won't be happy until this mystery is put to rest!"

Audrey peered at me over her sparkly glasses. "And I hope for the sake of the inn that you put your mystery to rest, too. I've been telling people all day that Gertrude doesn't know what she's talking about, but you know how folks are. I wouldn't be surprised if it turned up in the *Bangor Daily News* soon."

"Let's hope not," I said, conveniently ignoring the fact that they were already calling. Repeatedly.

"I hear two of the islanders have been taken to the station for questioning," she said as I shuffled the papers together.

I glanced up. "I heard that too."

"Somebody said one of them is the head of the lobster co-op over there on Cranberry Island," she said. "He was having an affair with that Vanessa woman, I heard—and he wasn't the only one.

Apparently the other fellow they hauled in was seeing a bit of her, too."

"Really?" I asked, feeling my throat close up. "Where did you hear that?"

"Oh, I don't know. Lots of folks are talking about it—not much else going on right now, so it's big news. It may just be a rumor, but I'd be willing to bet there's some truth to it."

"You think?"

"Almost always is, it seems." She shook her head. "I guess it's not too surprising that one of her fellows turned up dead. I just hope it's not one of ours that did the deed."

NINETEEN

When I made it back to the inn about an hour later—I'd stopped at one of the stores in Somesville to pick up some snacks to keep up in my room, just in case they banished me from the kitchen overnight—I was hoping to find the place still deserted, so I could revisit Greg's room and see if I could turn up a connection to Dirk.

Unfortunately, I was out of luck. Detective Rose was gone, but the guests were in the living room, lifting weights under Vanessa's direction. Despite the recent tragedy, she was dressed for spring in a fuchsia spandex exercise top and skin-tight shorts that showed off the kind of honed physique I could never hope to have. I had to give the woman credit—she was still doing her very best to give the retreat participants what they'd come for, even though her hearty "One, two, three, fours!" seemed strained.

Several pairs of eyes flicked nervously to me as I entered— maybe because Dirk had been poisoned and I was the cook. I told them in cheery tones that we'd be dining at Spurrell's that night.

Then, after checking the messages (three more from Bangor, two from Gertrude) and saying a brisk 'hello' to the two officers who were destroying my kitchen, I high-tailed it to my room.

Ripping the wrapper off a Snicker's bar—by now, all thoughts of dieting were long gone—I peered through the curtains at John's carriage house. Was he back yet? I finished the bar and then crept down the stairs and out the door, my heart hammering in my chest as I tapped at the door. But the only thing that greeted me was the wind, moaning eerily around the corner. I tried again, and then went to the workshop next door. But no one answered there, either. Something tightened inside me as I knocked a fourth time before conceding defeat.

Was he still being questioned at the station? I wondered. And if so, why?

The only thing you can do to help him is to prove he didn't do it, I told myself as I headed back up the green slope to the inn. I was still smarting over Audrey's comment about John's supposed affair with Vanessa. Even if things between us were beyond repair, though, that didn't mean I was going to let him be arrested for a crime he didn't commit.

Assuming I was right—and John was innocent.

———

A little while later, as I walked through the living room, checking on the guests, I examined the portly, reddish-haired Greg—who was snuggled up with Megan on the couch—with new interest. Was he really just here to lose weight and chat up attractive fellow dieters?

Or had he come to find out more about Dirk for a client?

But Dirk was dead, and Greg was still here. Which didn't make sense if he was here just on business. Unless he had stayed because he had fallen for Megan. I watched the two of them talking in low tones on the couch; even with Boots, Cat, and Sarah eyeing them, there was an air of intimacy that made it uncomfortable to be near them. Megan's blond head was inches from his, and the two of them were deep in intense discussion. Carissa was nowhere to be seen, but that wasn't surprising—she tended to avoid Greg, and I imagined she was seeking solace in a Snickers bag in her room somewhere. Vanessa was absent, too.

"Where's your fearless leader?" I asked Boots, who was relaxing on the couch under the window with her sorority sisters.

"She went upstairs to take a shower," Boots said.

"And to escape that reporter," Sarah added, adjusting her over-sized pink sweater. It was bulky, but the color brought life to her pale face and light hair. "That woman has been hounding poor Vanessa all day. I don't think she's writing a travel article."

"Do you think?" Cat asked from a wingback chair. She still looked a bit haggard, but she didn't appear to have been crying recently.

"I'm positive," Sarah said. "She's been asking some *very* personal questions."

"Like what?" I asked.

Boots leaned forward. "Like whether or not she and Dirk were dating. And whether there were any disagreements between them over how to run the business."

"What did Vanessa say?"

"Not a whole lot. A polite version of 'no comment.' I think Elizabeth's getting frustrated, to be honest," Sarah said.

Boots stood up then, straightening her fine-gauge turtleneck, which was cut perfectly for her curvy figure, and patting her stomach. "When did you say dinner was?"

"In a couple of hours," I said. "Down at Spurrell's Lobster Pound."

"Oooh, does that mean we're having lobster?"

"Not yet," I said, hoping that the cops would open my kitchen in time for me to prepare the lobsters Tom had brought. "Scallops instead."

"With brownies for dessert?" Sarah asked hopefully.

"Not till you get home, I'm afraid. Or unless you can manage to sneak over to the store," I joked.

"I just might get hungry enough to do that," she said. "How late are they open?"

Boots tsked at her. "No cheating, Sarah. We're here to lose weight, not gain it. Remember that reunion!"

———

Vanessa trotted everybody out for one last exercise session before dinner—the whole group trooped out of the inn carrying objects that looked like rubber hoses with handles, and I wondered exactly what they were planning on doing with them. She informed me that a bunch of bicycles would be coming over the next day, and I knew what to do with those, but how exactly did you exercise using hoses with handles?

As they all puffed up the hill together, toting their lengths of rubber, I was glad not to be joining them. And thrilled that I would finally have an opportunity to check Greg's room.

Grabbing the skeleton keys from the cabinet by the front desk, I headed up the stairs, trying to look nonchalant. I didn't have particularly high hopes for this visit; after all, I'd been through his room many times before and seen nothing untoward—with the exception of a couple of stray blond hairs, that is. On the other hand, I hadn't really been looking.

Today, though, was a different story. Locking the door behind me, I headed first for the desk, hoping to find some explanation for why Greg was here—other than the need to drop thirty pounds, that was.

Unfortunately for me, all of the desk drawers were empty. Nor was there a briefcase in the room—or anything else to indicate he was at the retreat on anything business-related.

Maybe my instincts were wrong, I thought, crossing my arms and surveying the room to see if I'd missed anything. Maybe he really *was* here just to drop some excess weight.

As a last-ditch effort, I peeked into the shallow drawer of the nightstand next to the bed. I don't know what I expected to find—I was hoping for Carissa's sake it wouldn't be condoms—but what I did find was a moleskin notebook, like the ones they sell in bookstores.

Perching on the edge of Greg's bed (which had no more blond hairs on the pillow, I was happy to see) I picked up the book and leafed through it. The first few pages had been torn out, but there were several remaining, all with dates and times on listed them. And short entries such as "Tuesday afternoon, April 20. Went to movie at mall alone at 12:05—shopped at Lane Bryant, returned home at two."

Lane Bryant? That was a plus-sized women's clothing store. Why would Dirk be shopping there?

202

I flipped through the rest of the pages, which read like a surveillance report. But why would anyone want a report on someone whose most interesting outing consisted of a trip to an Outlet Mall?

The entire document was about as exciting as the lighthouse log had been—only with trips to various shopping centers and restaurants recorded instead of weather reports. And there were absolutely no references to possible smuggling activities—or anything else illicit, for that matter.

On the sixth or seventh page, the word RETREAT was listed in block letters. The date was listed as two days ago. "Established contact with subject today," read the first entry. "Made initial overture; response was promising."

I flipped the page to see what was written down for the next day, but that was the end of it. Greg hadn't written anything after the initial opening. Which was strange, because up until then, he had recorded his subject's every move in mind-numbing detail.

Was the sudden halt because Dirk—the subject—had died?

I leafed through the strange notebook one more time, then returned it to its drawer in the nightstand before slipping out the door and closing it gently behind me. I glanced down the hall toward Dirk's door. The forensics people weren't in there anymore, and for a moment I considered doing another investigation of my own. But in truth, I doubted I'd find anything that I hadn't already discovered—and if there was anything, I was sure the police had probably taken it.

Instead of slipping back through my former guest's door, I headed down the stairs and into Bethany's room; other than Vanessa and possibly Elizabeth, she was my best option for the position of murderer.

The room looked just the same as it had the other day—pictures of Dirk smiling out from a dozen frames on the dresser—but with one difference. The smell of something burning filled the air. I sniffed a few times, scanning the room for smoke, but the air was clear, so I headed for the nightstand, anxious to get a look at Bethany's journal. If she had killed Dirk, would she have recorded it? It certainly would make solving the case easy if she had, I thought.

The journal was no longer on the nightstand, so I opened the drawer, expecting to find it hidden there. But the drawer was empty. I searched the entire room—under the mattress, under the bed, in her suitcases—but it was nowhere to be found. Then I noticed a pile of ashes in the fireplace, and a scorched fragment of paper, and realized why I hadn't been able to find the journal.

Bethany had burned it.

I poked around in the ashes to see if any of it had survived, but other than a few blackened bits of leather and a couple of curls of scorched paper, the book was gone.

But why?

Had there been something Bethany hadn't wanted the police to find?

I left Bethany's room in deep thought, wishing I could tell Detective Rose about the diary, but afraid that if I did, it would look bad—like I'd been rooting around in my guests' things. Which, to be honest, I had.

I thought again about the restraining orders Bethany had had in the past. Why had the objects of her attraction resorted to court orders? Had she threatened them?

And there was one more thing I needed to ask about, too, I realized as I locked Bethany's door behind me. I'd given Audrey the names of all of my guests to research, but I hadn't asked her to find out what she could about the mystery ingredient in Dirk's weight loss supplements: EPH.

———

By the time the guests had returned, looking winded, their rubber hoses draped over their shoulders like strands of limp spaghetti, the forensics folks had packed up and given me permission to put my kitchen back together, even though I wasn't allowed to cook in it. Not for guests, anyway. The police were gone, but the kitchen was still a jumble, and after calling the library to ask Audrey to look up one more thing, I spent the next hour trying to bring some order to the chaos.

I was trying to organize my spices when the kitchen door nudged open and Vanessa slid into the kitchen, slim and lithe as a snake.

"Oh!" she said with a start. "I didn't know anyone was in here!"

"Can I help you with something?" I asked.

Her dark eyes darted to me. "Oh, no," she said, looking … shifty, somehow, I realized. She surveyed the counters, which were still covered with packages of food from the pantry. "I was just going to see if I could get a glass of water."

"Glasses are above the sink," I said. "Help yourself."

"Thanks," she said.

This was the first time I'd had an opportunity to question Vanessa alone, I realized. As she retrieved a glass and filled it, I tucked a bottle of nutmeg onto a shelf, trying to decide which of the many questions to ask first. As much as I wanted to dive in and ask the big ones—like, *Did you kill Dirk?* and *Are you and John seeing each other on the side?*—I decided to ease into things.

"How are you holding up?" I asked solicitously as she turned off the water.

"All right, I guess."

"You're doing a great job keeping things going, with everything going on. It must be hard losing your business partner—*and* your boyfriend, all at the same time."

"Dirk and I weren't really ... *together*," she said. "But we *were* close."

"You and John seem to be pretty close, too," I said, trying to keep my voice light.

"We've had a good time catching up. And he's really been a rock for me this last day or two."

"I understand you two were an item for a while, way back when," I said.

"I guess we dated one summer, but nothing ever came of it," she said offhandedly. As if she hadn't spent almost every moment of her free time down at John's carriage house since she'd arrived.

"How about with Tom Lockhart?" I asked. "I heard you two were out catching up on old times the other night."

"What?" she said, jerking her head up sharply.

"You know," I said. "The night you went out for a walk—your first day here."

"I was alone," she said, the friendly tone vanishing from her voice. "I told you—I just went out for a stroll. Now, if you'll excuse me, I have a retreat to run." She finished her water in one gulp and high-tailed it toward the door.

"I notice you haven't been giving out Dirk's supplements since he died," I said before she could leave. "I'm kind of surprised; I thought that was a big part of the program."

She turned to face me, her smoky eyes flashing with suppressed anger. "I appreciate your concern for the retreat," she said, "but I think you might want to leave the weight-loss business to the professionals." She raked a critical glance up and down my less-than-streamlined form, then swept out the kitchen door.

Once I'd recovered from her quick exit—my cheeks still burned when I thought about her scornful glance—I thought about the sudden change that had come over her once I started talking about Tom.

And the weight-loss supplements she'd stopped handing out.

——

By the time the retreat trooped into Spurrell's Lobster Pound a few hours later, Vanessa had recovered her sangfroid, and other than a chilly glance my way, had reverted to her normal perky, encouraging, disgustingly skinny self. I seated everyone at little wooden tables and brought them seltzer water; Evie had taken over the food preparation, so I was limited to serving and cleaning up. I hoped it wasn't because she believed everything she read in the *Daily Mail*.

I was worried that the change of venue would be a problem, but the guests seemed charmed by the little restaurant—the white-clothed wooden tables and the gingham curtains at the windows gave the dining area a cozy, welcoming feeling, and the delicious aromas wafting from the kitchen had everyone's mouth watering. There would be none of Evie's delicious lobster bisque—or her melt-in-your-mouth parkerhouse rolls and butter, unfortunately—but since my guests didn't know what they were missing, they wouldn't mind. And for a low-fat menu, tonight's dinner smelled pretty darned fabulous.

As strange as it was not to be cooking, I was thankful to have my menu in the hands of such an accomplished cook. The salads she had plated were gorgeous, bursting with color from the yellow and red cherry tomatoes, purple onions, and the gleam of a raspberry vinaigrette.

"Looks great!" I told Evie, whose round face was red from the heat of the kitchen.

"I just followed your recipe," she said, smiling.

"You're a lifesaver," I said. "I owe you—big time."

"Don't worry about it," she said, turning back to the stove, where a batch of scallops were browning in a pan.

As I served the salads, I scanned the room. Greg and Megan were attached virtually at the hip, oblivious to Carissa, who was glowering at them across the table. If nothing else, I told myself, at least the presence of Greg had diminished the amount of criticism Megan directed at her overweight daughter. Still, Carissa looked miserable. What was she going to tell her father when they got home? Even if nothing had happened between Greg and Megan, there was obviously some kind of mutual fascination going on.

I looked at the private investigator, thinking of the journal I'd found in his room. I still hadn't figured out his connection with

Dirk. Even if the trainer *was* the "subject" mentioned in the notebook—why make contact? What was the goal?

There were so many things that didn't make sense, I thought as I returned to the kitchen for more plates. Including the question of John and Vanessa. And why John was currently being questioned on the mainland.

I pushed thoughts of my neighbor from my mind, grabbed a few more plates, and headed back out to the dining room.

The three sorority sisters were reminiscing as I served them their salads.

"Whatever happened with you and Roy, anyway?" Sarah asked Cat, after complimenting me on the salad and grabbing a fork. What was it someone said? That hunger makes the best seasoning?

Cat pushed at a cherry tomato with a fork, looking uncomfortable with the direction the conversation had taken. "We kind of fell apart after ... well, you know."

"After you lost Ashley," Sarah said sympathetically.

"Yes," Cat said.

"Does his family still own that lumber business?" Boots asked. "Mickelson's Lumber, I think it was called?"

"As far as I know," Cat said. "We really don't keep in touch."

Boots shook her head. "All ancient history, I know. So much has changed over the years, hasn't it?"

"It has," Sarah said. "But let's talk about the future. As in, who do you want to see at the reunion?"

Cat shot her a grateful glance as I laid the last plate in front of Boots and returned to the kitchen. Something they had said rang a bell, I realized as I headed back to the kitchen again. One of those names; I'd heard or seen it somewhere before.

The question was, where?

TWENTY

By the time I left the restaurant, after thanking Evie about a million times and making sure the schedule was set for tomorrow, it was well after dark.

"I feel awful about intruding on you this way," I said. "Please let me reimburse you for your time—and for using the restaurant."

She smiled at me and untied her apron from her ample middle. "You're an islander now, Natalie. This is what we do for each other—always have."

"But …"

"When someone else is in need, you'll do the same. You've already done it with Marge," she pointed out.

"They may close my kitchen for the rest of the week, though."

She shrugged. "It'll get me back into the swing of things," she said.

"Are you sure?"

"Positive," she said. "Maybe you can help me with some of the desserts this summer—but you don't have to."

"As soon as my kitchen is open," I said, "you're welcome to anything I can make."

"How about some of those famous Blackout Brownies?" she asked.

"Consider it done," I said. As I zipped up my jacket and headed out into the darkness alone, I couldn't help smiling. Things might be going south at the inn, but the islanders were rallying around me. I would never be a native, but they were starting to view me as one of their own.

———

The retreat members had headed home with Vanessa while I stayed to clean up, and by the time I crested the last hill before the inn, the moon was up and the inn's many windows were glowing. I hoped Gwen had remembered to do turndown service.

I glanced down the hill as I unlocked the kitchen door, and my heart seized in my chest. It wasn't just the inn's lights that were burning; the windows of John's carriage house were lit as well.

Gwen jumped and whirled around as I pushed open the door. "Aunt Nat!" she said, sagging against the cluttered countertop. Several canisters and bags of dried fruit were still scattered haphazardly around my normally immaculate kitchen. "You scared me!"

"Sorry about that," I said. My eyes scanned the counters, but my mind was still on the carriage house—and John.

"Do you know where the sugar-free mints are?" she asked.

"I'm guessing the police hid them somewhere," I said. "You'll just have to skip it tonight."

"How did dinner go?" she asked.

"Fine," I said, anxious to go and find out what had happened with John. "It looks like John's back—I'd like to go talk to him."

"I saw him in the living room a few minutes ago," she said.

"With Vanessa?"

She nodded, pity in her brown eyes. "I think he went back to the carriage house, though."

"Alone?" I asked.

"Yes," she said.

I took a deep breath. "Do you have things under control here?" I asked.

"I'm fine, Aunt Nat," she said, her eyes following mine to John's windows. "Go talk to him."

"Thanks," I said, walking back through the kitchen door and down the hill, feeling numb. I dreaded talking to him—but I needed to know what was going on.

John answered almost immediately, looking haggard and weary.

I stood there, tongue-tied, hugging myself against the cold wind off the water.

"Hi," he said.

"Hi," I said. "You're back."

"Yes," he said. After a pause, he said, "Would you like to come in?"

"Sure," I said.

As I walked into his jumbled living room, he removed a pile of cushions from one of the couches, gesturing for me to sit, then pulled up a chair across from me. The smell of fresh wood did nothing to soothe me today, and the seal sculpture that usually sat on the coffee table had been relocated somewhere. The picture of

John as a child, standing beside a sailboat with his grandfather, still had pride of place among the bookshelves, but everything else was still in disarray. "You'd think they'd put things back when they were done," I said, glancing around the mess they'd made of his usually neat living quarters and trying to ease the tension that had sprung up between us. "I may never get my kitchen back into shape."

"They went through your kitchen?" he asked.

"They closed it," I said. "That's why we ate down at the restaurant."

"Vanessa told me about that." His green eyes flickered slightly.

I nodded abruptly, and we lapsed into silence again. I broke it a moment later. "Why did they question you on the mainland?" I asked. "And go through your house?"

He didn't answer for a moment. Then, his eyes focused on a spot on the wall behind me, he said, "They think either Tom or I killed Dirk."

I swallowed hard. "Is there something you need to tell me?"

His face went very still. "Do you think I murdered Dirk De-Leon?"

"I don't know what to think," I said. "Ever since Vanessa turned up on the island, you've been—not yourself. Distant."

He didn't say anything.

I stared at the sisal rug. "I heard you might be having an affair with Vanessa," I said.

"I'm not," he said quietly.

I looked up at him, wanting with all my heart to believe him. But his ready smile was nowhere to be seen—in fact, his tanned face was closed to me. "It is true that Vanessa and I had a relationship one summer," he said, "about twenty years ago. I think you know that."

"And since then?"

"We've talked a couple of times, but lost touch over the last five years or so."

"So she didn't know you were here when she scheduled the retreat," I said, staring at the rough texture of the sisal rug again. I couldn't bear to look him in the eye—perhaps because I was afraid of what I might see.

"Tom may have told her I was here."

I looked up. "So there *is* something going on with Tom."

"Yes," he said. "They've been ... in contact ... for some time."

"Just via e-mail?"

"Not entirely," he said.

"But you haven't talked to her in years," I said, feeling anger and hurt roiling inside me. "And that's why the police had you over on the mainland for questioning all day."

"I know it looks like things might have been ... rekindling between us," he said awkwardly. "But really, I was just trying to be a friend."

"Why were you arguing with Tom the other night?"

He bit his lip and ran a hand through his short hair. "Tom is still hung up on Vanessa—hung up enough to risk everything, even though she doesn't want to continue the relationship. His family, his livelihood—he's throwing it all away."

"Why does she want to end the relationship?" I asked. *Is it because of you?* I thought but didn't add.

"I don't know," he said.

"Do you think Tom killed Dirk?" I asked.

John looked up at me. "No," he said. "He's obsessed, but he's not violent."

"Poison isn't violent," I pointed out. "What exactly was going on between Dirk and Vanessa? Did she tell you?"

"She was engaged to be married to some guy in New Jersey, apparently, but then she met Dirk and they fell for each other, so she called off the wedding."

"So they *were* involved," I said.

"For a while. Then they started the business together, and things started going south. He was going nuts with all this supplement stuff, and it was starting to cause problems—apparently he'd run into trouble with it before, and Vanessa wanted him to lay off."

"What kind of trouble?" I asked, thinking of the articles on lawsuits I'd seen in Elizabeth's room. And wondering how John knew all of this if he and Vanessa had just reconnected a couple of days ago.

"There were health risks, apparently." He leaned back in his chair. "Vanessa thought it was too dangerous to use them, particularly as the business started taking off—but Dirk saw it as a big money-making opportunity, and didn't want to let go of it."

"No wonder Vanessa stopped dishing out pills after Dirk died," I said. And before that had contacted her lawyer about kicking him out of the business. "But how did Tom and Vanessa manage to have an affair?" I asked. "I mean, I think everyone would notice if she was making clandestine trips to Cranberry Island."

John studied the wall behind me. "They ran into each other down in Boston, and Vanessa told me they kind of picked up where they had left off. Tom had been married for a long time, and things had started deteriorating with Dirk, so Vanessa was vulnerable."

Vulnerable? Yeah, right. "So they started seeing each other?" I asked.

"She'd come up to Mount Desert Island on weekends, and he'd head over and visit her. Told Lorraine he was out fishing."

I thought of John's occasional trips to art studios on the mainland. Had he been meeting clandestinely with Vanessa, too? But I took a deep breath and said, "Is that why she decided to hold the retreat here on the island? Because Tom was here?"

He nodded. "Initially, yes. But he started talking about leaving his family, and Vanessa started pulling back. She wanted the excitement of an affair, I guess, not a lobsterman husband with two kids from a prior marriage."

Infidelity was a terrible thing, but I still felt bad for Tom, who evidently was going through a bit of a midlife crisis. Not to mention poor Lorraine. If they did manage to cobble their marriage back together, it would never be the same.

On the other hand, if he spent the next fifty years in prison, that would make reconciliation really, really hard.

And if John spent the next fifty years in prison, our relationship would have a hard time moving forward, too.

"Did Tom think Dirk was his competition?" I asked.

John nodded. "That's why he's still at the station."

"What do you mean?"

John looked pained. "They found some of the supplement pills at his house. He says he got them for Lorraine—she was always trying to lose a few pounds—but the police think he may have doctored some of them and exchanged them for Dirk's pills."

"So is that what killed him?" I asked.

"They found massive quantities of ephedrine in Dirk's system," John said.

"Ephedrine?" My mind clicked back to the list of supplements I'd seen in Dirk's room. "Do they sometimes call that EPH?"

He nodded.

"He had it in the supplements he was giving to the guests!" I said, my spirits lifting a little for the first time since I'd knocked on John's door. "Maybe nobody poisoned him—he just probably took too much."

John shook his head. "He'd been working with the stuff for years—but the amount they found in his body was off the charts. Enough to cause a cardiac arrest, which is what he died of."

"But how come the guests didn't die?"

"He kept his pills separately," John said. I thought back to what I'd seen of Dirk's room and realized John was right. He *had* kept a stash of pills for himself, away from the supplements for the retreat. "When the police searched his room, they found several pills filled with huge doses of the stuff among his personal items— enough to kill someone bigger than Dirk. The pills looked identical, but few of them had huge doses of ephedrine."

"So it looks like someone slipped in some bad pills and poisoned him," I said. "Does this mean they'll let me reopen my kitchen?"

"I wouldn't count on it," he said. "They tend to be cautious with things like that."

"But why do they think it was Tom?" I asked.

John sighed. "Because Tom was here the night before Dirk died. And they found a big supply of ephedrine at his house, at the same strength as the stuff in the pills. He says he used it sometimes on the boat, when he hadn't had a lot of sleep, but..."

"The police aren't buying it," I said, suddenly feeling sick. The police had let John off the hook, but Tom...

"No, they're not," John said quietly. "Which is why they've arrested him," he continued, "for first-degree murder."

I closed my eyes, wishing it wasn't true. But when I opened them, John was still looking stricken.

"What are we going to do?" I whispered.

John shrugged, looking defeated. "I don't know, Natalie. I just don't know."

———

My head was still reeling as I headed back to the inn a few minutes later. They had arrested Tom Lockhart for murder. If he was convicted, he would be separated from his family for life—and the island would never be the same. My heart broke when I thought of Lorraine, with Tommy Jr. and his younger brother Logan, growing up knowing their father was in jail for murder. And Lorraine herself, who would go through life as a single parent, believing the father of her children was a murderer.

Tom might have been going through a midlife crisis; and he might have done some irrational things. But I knew he wasn't a murderer.

Unfortunately, unless I could prove it, I didn't think anyone else would believe me. At least not the people who mattered.

What about John? my mind whispered. *There's still something he's not telling you; is it that he's the one who murdered Dirk?*

"Everything okay, Aunt Nat?" Gwen asked when I closed the kitchen door behind me, barely feeling the cold breeze.

"They've arrested Tom Lockhart," I said tonelessly.

The color drained out of her face, and the pot she was washing slipped out of her hands, clattering onto the counter. "No," she breathed.

"Yes," I said mechanically. "I'm going to head upstairs for a bit—let me know if you need me." I climbed the stairs to my bedroom as if in a trance, then sat down on the bed, staring out the window at the cold dark water below.

I stared out the window for about fifteen minutes. Tom couldn't have murdered Dirk over Vanessa. He might have been obsessed— but obsessed enough to risk losing his kids? I just couldn't believe it. Again, I found myself wondering about John . . . and banished the thought.

I grabbed a notepad and a pen and tried to put my thoughts in order. I had to help Tom. Just had to.

And the best way to do that was to find out who had *really* murdered Dirk. Something told me I already had the key to the murder; I just had to sort through and find it.

I chewed on the cap to the pen for a moment, then started to write. First on the list was perky, beautiful Vanessa, who of all the people on the island had the clearest motive for getting rid of the trainer. Not only was her personal relationship with him troubled, but she evidently viewed him as a business liability, too, if the letters from her attorney were anything to go on. There was also the potential book deal, from which Dirk's name was notably absent. Did he find out about it—or the letters from the attorney—and threaten to do something to her? Did she respond by getting rid of him before he could cause more problems?

I thought about the way Dirk had died—not by a knife or gun, which is what you would expect of a jealous person—but by poison. Which had always seemed to me the method of a calculating person—not the weapon of choice for a crime of passion. And as far as access was concerned, I was guessing that wasn't a problem for Vanessa.

The wind sighed around a corner of the inn as I tried to piece things together. There was no way to know for sure whether Vanessa had had access to Dirk's supplements, but since they were working closely together, it was a good bet. Was the cost of buying him out of the business too high for her? And Vanessa had told John that she wanted to end things with Tom, but her cheeks had been glowing after her late-night sortie. Had Dirk been interfering with her romantic plans as well?

If she had murdered Dirk in order to clear the way for her relationship with Tom, though, she'd have to be awfully mercenary to let him take the rap for the crime. Was she cold-hearted enough to let her lover take the fall for her? I didn't know, but I decided it might be time to search Vanessa's room again. Just in case.

I forced my thoughts away from the dark-haired retreat leader. As tempting as it was to limit my suspicions to her, she wasn't the only one with a motive for killing Dirk. There was also Bethany, whose obsession with Dirk—not to mention the burned journal I'd found in her room—made her a prime candidate. Particularly with her colorful history of past one-sided relationships, along with the restraining orders to go with them. Had she been jealous enough of Dirk's attention toward Vanessa to get rid of him? Had he told her to leave him alone—that he wasn't interested in her? If Bethany couldn't have the object of her desire, perhaps she had decided that no one would. Normally I'd expect her to have gotten rid of the competition—in this case, Vanessa—but if Dirk had spurned her, perhaps her anger had been enough to obliterate him entirely. She certainly had obliterated her journal. The crime didn't have the hallmark of a crime of passion, and I couldn't think of a way to prove that she had done it—I had no idea how she'd get access to ephedrine, or if she knew where the inn's keys were located. Still, she was definitely a candidate.

I looked out the window, my eyes tracing the line of craggy mountains on the mainland, turning the problem over in my mind. Bethany might not have known where the keys to Dirk's room were, but someone else at the inn definitely did—in fact, I'd seen her leaving Dirk's room the night before he died. *Elizabeth*, I wrote, underlining the name twice.

Although she was theoretically a reporter, I had never confirmed that she was with *Maine Monthly Magazine*. And she *had* shown an inordinate amount of interest in the Lose-It-All business—and Vanessa.

But why would Elizabeth kill Dirk? Reporting on a weight-loss retreat didn't seem in any way to lead to a motive for murdering one of its leaders. Unless she wasn't what she purported to be. Was she masquerading as a reporter in order to gain access to Dirk, to exact her revenge? Had someone in her family, or someone she loved, been damaged by Dirk's supplements in the past? I made a note to call and confirm that she was in fact employed at *Maine Monthly*. And maybe find a chance to chat her up and ask some questions ...

My mind sorted through the other guests at the inn, trying to think of who else might want Dirk dead. Megan and Carissa seemed too embroiled in their own affairs to care much about Dirk, and the three sorority sisters were focused on their upcoming reunion—and supporting one of their number through a tough time. Greg was a possibility. But would a private investigator take it upon himself to murder on his client's behalf? It didn't make sense.

I sucked on the end of my pen for a moment, struggling to come up with another possible suspect.

What about John? My mind skittered away from the thought, instead turning to the police's number one suspect: Tom. And his wife, whom I'd never seriously considered—although perhaps I should. The ephedrine had been found in their house, after all. But how would she have gotten the pills here? And why kill Dirk, and not Vanessa—or Tom? Unless the pills had somehow ended up in the wrong person's possession ...

No, I thought. Lorraine was almost certainly innocent. She was still worth talking too, though. If nothing else, I could show her my support through what must be one of the most trying—and mortifying—times of her life.

I resolved to visit Tom's wife tomorrow with a batch of cookies—provided I could actually use my kitchen—then spent another ten minutes trying to come up with another suspect. I eventually gave up, tucking the notebook back into my drawer and heading downstairs to check with Gwen.

"Are you okay?" she asked as she stowed two of the canisters in the pantry.

"I guess so," I said. "I'm just trying to figure out a way to get Tom off the hook."

"Do you really think they're going to convict him?"

I told her what I had learned of Tom and Vanessa's relationship, then relayed what John had told me about Dirk's death—including the stash of ephedrine the police had found at the Lockharts' house. "I've been trying to come up with a list of other suspects."

She sucked in her breath. "Poor Lorraine."

"I know," I said. "If they'll let me use my kitchen, I'm going to thaw some chocolate chip cookie dough and make a batch to take over tomorrow." I'd hidden the frozen dough behind a big bag of corn in hopes that my midnight marauder would miss it. So far, the ruse had worked. "I've been meaning to ask: have you seen any of the guests in the kitchen?" I asked Gwen.

"Today it was just the police," she said.

"I mean before that?" I said.

"Not that I can think of," she said. "Why?"

"I'm missing some of my baking supplies. I think we may have a compulsive eater at the inn."

"What's gone missing?"

"Chocolate chips, some sugar, crackers, molasses, my ginger-snaps ... whoever it is even took all of my unsweetened baking chocolate."

Gwen made a face. "Honestly?"

"No kidding," I said. "I'm a pretty serious chocoholic, but even *I* wouldn't be that desperate." I opened the freezer and started digging for the bag of frozen dough. I was worried I might have lost half my inventory, with the police keeping the door open for what seemed like hours at a time, but it didn't look like things had had a chance to thaw out.

"Do you need me to help with breakfast tomorrow morning?" Gwen asked.

"No. Evie is bringing up oatmeal and blueberry compote."

"What about coffee?" she asked.

I grimaced. "I guess I'll just have to bend the rules a bit."

"Let's just hope nobody else ends up dead," Gwen said with a rueful smile.

—

After a long, much-needed bath and a couple of hours with one of J. B. Stanley's Supper Club mysteries—her characters were all struggling to lose a few pounds themselves, and I needed something to salvage my flagging motivation—I eventually fell into a fitful sleep with Biscuit curled up at my side.

I was dreaming about a lighthouse filled to the lantern with skeletons and bits of cloth when a crash pulled me out of my dark, eerie dream world and back to the inn. I glanced at the clock—it was 2:30 a.m. Biscuit, too, was awake, green eyes glowing in the gleam of the alarm clock's digital face.

In seconds, I was grabbing a robe and heading down the stairs, heart thumping in my chest.

TWENTY-ONE

THE KITCHEN WAS DARK as I raced downstairs, the treads squeaking noisily under my feet. I hit the light as soon as I reached the base of the staircase, hoping to catch my kitchen kleptomaniac, but the only sign of the intruder was the still-swinging kitchen door.

I ran over and pushed through it, hoping to find the culprit in the dining room, but my intruder was long gone. A moment later, I heard the sound of a door closing somewhere in the inn.

I let go of the swinging door in defeat, turning to survey the kitchen.

It wasn't nearly as bad as it could have been—the raccoon that had plagued my pantry last fall had done much more damage. The only thing out of place was the sugar bowl, which had been knocked off the end of the counter. It must have been the bowl shattering on the wooden floor that had awakened me. After sweeping it up, I opened the refrigerator door; as I suspected, the bag of cookie dough was gone.

Who was raiding my kitchen? I wondered. Was it Carissa, upset over her mother's interest in Greg? Or was another guest secretly hiding a sugar obsession?

As curious as I was to find out who was stealing my food, it really was the least of the mysteries facing me. So after a quick inventory of the fridge—the cookie dough appeared to be the only casualty, fortunately—I replaced the sugar bowl with a spare one and headed back upstairs, thankful I'd had the foresight to hide the chocolate I'd bought on the mainland in my room.

I'd need it when I was making a second batch of dough tomorrow.

———

Vanessa had given everybody a chance to sleep in—the first event of the day wasn't scheduled to start until ten thirty—so breakfast was more of a staggered affair than usual. Evie had brought a crockpot of oatmeal over at eight thirty, along with a saucepan of blueberries she had heated and spiced. I had taken the liberty of brewing up a big pot of coffee; police orders or no police orders, there was no way I was going to serve breakfast without caffeine.

The guests were cheery, even with the simple breakfast—probably because the blueberries were a perfect foil to the slightly cinnamon-spiced oatmeal. I had to hand it to Evie. She was one heck of a cook.

To my surprise, Dirk's murder wasn't at all a topic of discussion in the dining room that morning. Only when I was refilling coffee cups the third time did I realize why: none of the guests knew there had been an arrest. And I didn't want to ruin the morning by reminding them of what had happened just a few short days ago.

Besides, it made me sick just thinking about Tom locked up in a cell somewhere, for a crime I was sure he hadn't committed.

At nine o'clock, the phone rang. It was Matilda. "I just got off the phone with the lab," she said.

"What did they say?"

"The bones are definitely African-American or African. But the most exciting thing is that they've confirmed his age."

"How old do they think he was?"

"From what they can see in the cranial sutures and the ribs, they're guessing mid-thirties."

I thought about the newspaper article on the slave-catcher. "The male slave—James—was only in his twenties, though. At least that's what the paper said. Do you know how old the slave-catcher was?"

"That's the mystery," she said. "I can't find anything that mentions it. But since it looks like the age rules out the male slave he was looking for ..."

"Then either it was the slave-catcher or somebody else," I finished for her.

"Exactly. And I can't find another reference to an African or African-American in the area at the time, so it's looking like it may be Otis Ball."

"The question is, if it is—who killed him? And why?"

"We may never know," she said. "Maybe he found what he was looking for—and the escapees killed him rather than go back into slavery."

"But what happened to Harry Atherton, the keeper?" I asked. "Was he the murderer? Is that why he left? Or did he die in the storm, like the legend says?"

"We may never know," she said. "But I'm hoping there will be a clue in that article—I've decided to go over to the mainland and get it myself today. I've also got a call into my friend in Yarmouth; she's going to check the shipping records for that time period, and see what she can find."

"Keep me posted," I said, glad for a momentary distraction from more recent events.

"Don't worry," she said. "I will."

"Did you hear about Tom, by the way?"

"I did," she said, all the excitement draining from her voice. "I just can't believe it."

"Me neither," I said. And it was true: I didn't believe it. Not for a moment.

I hung up the phone and started another pot of coffee, gazing out the window at the lighthouse in the distance. We might not be making any progress figuring out who had murdered Dirk, but it looked like Matilda was shedding some light on what had happened 170 years ago. Still, odds were good that we would probably never know what really happened to the body in the lighthouse.

I just hoped the same wouldn't be said for the island's more recent tragedy.

———

By the time nine thirty rolled around, everyone had made it downstairs except Boots and Bethany. I needed to close up the kitchen at ten, so I decided to wait until nine forty-five before sending someone up to wake them.

Bethany wandered into the dining room ten minutes later, looking like she hadn't slept a wink. After serving herself a third big bowl of oatmeal—"after all, with Dirk gone, why bother losing weight?"—she retreated to a corner table and resumed eating mechanically.

When Boots hadn't rolled downstairs by the appointed hour, I stopped by the table where Cat and Sarah were finishing up their oatmeal. I refilled their coffee cups, then asked if they would mind checking on their friend. "I don't want her to miss breakfast," I explained.

"Sure," Sarah said. "I'll run up and check on her."

"Thanks," I said, refilling Cat's coffee.

"I wonder where she is?" she said, sipping it. "She's usually an early bird. This isn't like her."

A twinge of misgiving passed through me, but I dismissed it. If Boots was my late-night marauder, maybe she was sleeping off a chocolate hangover. "I'm sure she just forgot to set her alarm clock. And when people are on vacation, sometimes they relax their schedules a bit."

I had barely finished my sentence when there was a scream from upstairs.

Cat's face blanched. "Boots," she whispered, and then we were both in motion, running for the stairs.

At first glance, it looked like she'd died in her sleep. She was stretched across the bed, one limp hand dangling over the edge of the side, her friend doubled over her, calling her name again and again. Sarah's moaning voice sounded eerily like a chant.

But Boots wasn't ever going to answer again. Nor, I realized with a sick feeling in my stomach, was she going to make her college reunion.

I reached out to draw Sarah away from her friend's body, but she wouldn't let go of the woman's cold hand.

"There's nothing you can do," I said soothingly. "She's gone."

"But ... but she can't be dead!" Sarah wailed. "She just can't be! We were going to go to the reunion together!" Cat came forward, tears in her huge eyes, and drew her friend away from the inert form on the bed.

The oatmeal I had eaten a half hour earlier seemed to congeal in my stomach as I took in the scene. Boots was dressed in a blue nightshirt, as if she had been asleep when she died. But other than the pillow that had been pulled from the top of the bed and placed beneath her head, the bed was still neatly made—and her pale face was mottled with purplish spots I hadn't seen before. Alarm bells went off in my head at the wrongness of the scene: the body askew on the bed, the covers still in place, the purplish splotches ... A disturbing thought stole into my mind.

Had she fallen victim to the same person who had murdered Dirk?

And if so—why?

———

Within ten minutes, John had secured the room and was on the phone with the mainland police, who were sending the coroner—and the forensics team—over to Cranberry Island once again. The guests were in the dining room, talking in hushed murmurs about the discovery upstairs; when I'd picked up the last of the breakfast dishes, Sarah and Cat had been huddled together by the window, their faces streaked with tears. I eyed Vanessa closely, looking for signs of something—guilt, maybe?—but nothing looked out of

231

the ordinary. She looked solemn and in control as she went from table to table, checking up on her clients.

The 10:30 jog was delayed, obviously, in light of the morning's discovery. The retreat was turning out to be a total disaster. Should I throw in the towel and make a batch of cookies to comfort everyone? I wondered. Then I remembered that the bag of cookie dough was gone, so I would have to make them from scratch. Besides, my kitchen was still officially closed. Stacking the last of the dirty bowls, I retreated to the kitchen, seeking solace in the routine of washing the dishes—and praying Boots hadn't been poisoned.

John pushed through the swinging door as I loaded the last dish into the rack. Although his presence, as always, sent a little charge through me—today he wore a pine-colored wool sweater that intensified the green of his eyes and a pair of faded jeans that fit him perfectly—there was still a huge wrongness between us. And this morning, his expression chilled me. There were deep furrows in his brow, and below those green eyes, his lips were a tight line.

"Do you want some coffee?" I asked, rinsing my hands at the sink and trying to sound normal.

"Sure," he said, pulling a chair out at the table and sinking into it with a weary sigh.

I grabbed two mugs from the cabinet and filled them, then sat gingerly beside him at the table. The smell of sawdust, along with John's clean, masculine scent, was faint, but enough to subtly charge the air in the kitchen—at least for me. Had he stopped to comfort Vanessa before coming to visit me in the kitchen? I wondered.

"What do you think happened?" I asked as he closed his hands around one of my white porcelain mugs.

"It looks like we're dealing with another murder," he said, confirming what I already suspected.

"Why do you think that?" I asked.

"The position of the body—and the purple spots on her skin."

"I noticed them, too," I said, shivering as I recalled the little livid splotches marring her pale skin. What had caused them? "What are they from?" I asked.

John shook his head grimly. "It's often a sign of asphyxiation."

I thought of the pillow that had been tucked neatly under Boots' head. "Do you mean ... she was suffocated?"

"I can't be sure," he said. "We'll have to wait for the coroner's report. But that's what it looks like to me."

"At least it wasn't poison," I said. "So Gertrude can't blame the food. And I guess that exonerates Tom." As the words left my mouth, I realized the implications of what I'd just said. Tom hadn't been on the island last night—but John had. And as of yesterday, John had been what the police call "a person of interest." Which meant he might be rocketing to the position of number one suspect all over again.

Was John involved in Boots' death? I thought of the crash in my kitchen last night, and the sound of a door closing. Last night, I had assumed it was my midnight marauder. I realized with a chill that it could have been John, leaving through the front door.

But what possible motive would John have had for killing Boots?

"That's assuming both murders are linked," John said. "And that Boots *was* murdered. We don't know that for sure yet."

"But it's looking that way," I said.

"Yes," he said. "It is."

As we sat in silence, brooding over the poor woman upstairs, I thought about what John had said about the two murders not necessarily being linked. Was Boots' death related to Dirk's? Or was the reason for her death unrelated? As far as I knew, there was no real connection between the former sorority sister and the hunky trainer.

Unless she had seen something that the murderer considered a threat, I realized. Had Boots seen the murderer leaving Dirk's room?

I thought about Elizabeth's surreptitious exit from the trainer's room.

Had *I* seen the murderer leaving Dirk's room?

I took another sip of coffee, thinking of the list of potential suspects I'd made last night. Obviously, with the new information in hand—the death of yet another guest—it could stand some updating. But I still hadn't called *Maine Monthly Magazine* to check up on Elizabeth. Since business hours were well underway, I decided there was no time like the present. And I was dying to confirm that someone other than my neighbor had a strong motive for murder.

"I'll be back in a moment," I told John, running upstairs to grab my most recent issue of *Maine Monthly*. I glanced over the masthead; no sign of an Elizabeth Green. The business number was listed at the bottom, and I carried the magazine downstairs and picked up the kitchen phone.

"What are you doing?" John asked.

"Checking on something," I said, dialing the number and taking another sip of coffee as it rang.

"Good morning, *Maine Monthly Magazine*."

"Hello," I said. "I'm trying to get in touch with one of your reporters—Elizabeth Green."

"Elizabeth Green?" the woman repeated.

"That's right," I said. "She's doing an article on Cranberry Island right now—about a weight-loss retreat."

"I don't recognize the name—but maybe she's new. Hold on a moment," she said, and Wings came on, singing "Band on the Run" as I waited. Finally, after what seemed an interminable time—we'd moved on to the Bee Gees—she came back on the line. "I'm sorry," she said. "You must be mistaken. There's no Elizabeth Green working here."

TWENTY-TWO

So Elizabeth Green wasn't a reporter for *Maine Monthly Magazine* after all. "Thank you," I said. "I must have been mistaken." Then I hung up and turned to John.

"What is it?" he asked.

"The reporter—Elizabeth Green?"

"What about her?"

"She claims she's a reporter for *Maine Monthly Magazine*," I said. "Lose-It-All comped the trip so she could do an article. But I just called the magazine's office, and they've never heard of her."

"Interesting," John said, sitting up a little straighter in his chair. "Why is she here then?"

"I don't know," I said. "Maybe she wanted a free ride, so she passed herself off as a reporter. Or maybe she's got another reason." I sat back down at the table across from him. "I saw her coming out of Dirk's room the night before he died."

His green eyes were still. "Do you think she's the one who killed him?"

"I don't know," I said. "But I think we need to let Detective Rose know she's not who she says she is."

———

By eleven o'clock, the inn was swarming with officers and the guests were being questioned one by one. Nobody had officially confirmed John's murder diagnosis, but from the grim looks on their faces, I was guessing he hadn't been far off.

I'd tried to catch Detective Rose's attention, in part to share what I'd learned about Elizabeth and in part to see if Tom Lockhart had been released, but I hadn't been able to get her to spare a moment—which gave me some comfort, since I presumed that meant I wasn't at the top of her list of suspects. And John, I was happy to see, hadn't been carted off the island in handcuffs, either.

Gwen had appeared downstairs not long after the police arrived, wondering what all the commotion was about.

"Another murder," I said. "It's not official, but ..."

"Who was it?" she asked, brown eyes wide.

"Boots," I said. "One of the sorority sisters."

She sucked in her breath. "Is it related to the trainer's death?"

"We don't know yet," I said.

She poured herself a cup of coffee and reached for a ginger-snap, but of course they were all gone. "There are muffins in the freezer still," I said. "At least I think there are—somebody swiped a bag of cookie dough last night."

"Mysteries all over the place here," she said.

"I'm a bit more concerned about the guests dying, though."

"Any idea who did it?"

I shook my head. "John thinks she was asphyxiated," I said with a shudder.

"So it wasn't poison," she said. "And unless she choked on something, it couldn't have been your cooking."

"That's something, at least. But I have a feeling they're not about to let me open up shop quite yet."

Unfortunately, I was right.

———

While the police questioned the guests, I sat in the kitchen, nursing a cup of coffee and dreading a phone call from the *Daily Mail*—or worse, the *Bangor Daily News*.

I was on my fourth cup when Marge knocked at the kitchen door, dressed for a day of work in a faded, overlarge T-shirt and cotton pants that appeared to have had several run-ins with a Clorox bottle.

"What's all the hubbub?" she asked.

"Another guest died."

"Here? At the inn?"

I nodded.

"Murder?" she asked, jowls wobbling.

"Looks that way," I said.

She drew in her breath and tsked. "Bad news comes in threes," she said ominously. "Let's hope there's not a third body to come."

"Can we count the one in the lighthouse?" I said hopefully. The last thing I needed was another dead body on the premises. Or close to the premises. I shivered again, thinking of Boots' inert form.

"Gertrude called you yet?" she asked.

"No," I said gloomily, "but I'm sure she will."

"She's no help at all, that woman. All this reporting ain't good for business," she said, adjusting her faded cotton shirt around her solid body as she entered the kitchen.

"It's good for the paper's business, unfortunately, which is why I'm guessing she'll be on the horn as soon as she figures it out." I sighed and changed the subject to something I actually had some control over. "Thanks for coming today, Marge—but I'm afraid you'll have to talk to the cops to see if you'll be able to get into the rooms to clean them."

"I'll manage somehow," she said. "The police won't be here forever. I'll stay late if I need to."

"Maybe you could do the living room floor if you can't get into the rooms. With all the traffic, that floor could probably use it."

"I'll get right on it," she said. She hesitated for a moment, then asked, "Kitchen still closed?"

"Indefinitely," I said. "If it weren't for Evie Spurrell, I'd be sunk."

Marge's broad face was sympathetic. "Things will turn around, Miss Nat. Just give it time."

"Let's hope so," I said.

Marge had just trundled out of the kitchen when the phone rang. I cringed, but forced myself to answer it. If it was Gertrude Pickens, I could always say "no comment."

Fortunately, it was Charlene. "What's going on over there?" she asked before I could even spit out my normal "Good morning, Gray Whale Inn" greeting.

"Another murder, it looks like," I said.

"Who?"

"One of the sorority sisters. Boots."

"Poisoned?"

"Suffocated, John thinks."

"How awful," she said. "Did it happen at the inn?"

"Unfortunately, yes. Her friend Sarah found her on her bed."

"Poor thing. Wait till Gertrude gets hold of this one," she said, echoing Marge's earlier comment.

"At least it wasn't poison," I pointed out.

"I guess there's a silver lining," she said. "And I guess that lets Tom Lockhart off the hook."

"Presuming the murders are related."

"Why wouldn't they be?"

"I don't know," I said. "I don't know anything, it seems like. None of this makes sense."

"Who do you think did it?" she asked.

"I wish I knew," I said. "But I did find out a few interesting things." I told Charlene what I'd learned about Greg's profession— and the burned diary in Bethany's room. Then I relayed what I'd learned that morning about Elizabeth's false credentials.

"Why do you think she's here, then? Just a free ride?"

"If that were the case, why would she be asking so many questions?"

"Keeping up the façade?"

"I have a feeling there's another reason," I said. "I just can't think what it might be."

"I can understand that a few people might have wanted Dirk dead," she said. "But why kill Boots?"

"I don't know. The only thing I can figure is that she knew something the murderer didn't want her to."

"But with Tom Lockhart already in custody, why bother?"

"Good question," I said. "Maybe the two murders aren't related." I leaned against the wall, then froze. "Wait a minute," I said. "This morning, when I served breakfast, no one knew Tom had been arrested."

"So maybe the murders *are* related," she said. "If the murderer didn't know that the police had already arrested someone…"

"But who do you think did it?"

"Well, Vanessa's the obvious choice," she said. "She had the most to gain for getting rid of Dirk."

"What about Bethany?"

"The burned journal is weird, I'll admit. And the restraining orders don't help, either. But if she thought Dirk was hung up on Vanessa, why not kill her instead, and then try to be the shoulder for him to cry on?"

"Unless he really spurned her," I said.

"But wouldn't she just haul off and whack him with something? Poison takes planning—I think Bethany would have been more… impulsive, somehow. Honestly, I think Elizabeth is a more likely suspect than Bethany. After all, you *did* see her coming out of Dirk's room."

"And she's obviously here under false pretenses," I said.

"Maybe she's working undercover for another publication."

"Or maybe she's linked to one of those old cases," I said. "You know—the ones where people were hurt after taking supplements?"

"Maybe." I heard a voice in the background, and Charlene responding. "Who's that?" I asked.

"It's Ernie—apparently the mail boat is here, and it's so overloaded with lumber for the lighthouse there was no room for all the groceries." She sighed. "I'll be so happy when that renovation is done."

Lumber. Something in the mention of lumber sparked something in my mind, but I couldn't place it.

"Nat, I hate to run," Charlene said, "but I've got to go talk with Tania. Can I call you later?"

"Sure," I said.

"I'll call later to find out if there's any news!"

I hung up the phone a moment later, still thinking about what Charlene had said. I *had* seen Elizabeth coming out of Dirk's room the night before he died.

Was she the one who had spiked his pills with ephedrine? And then smothered Boots to cover the crime?

What I really needed to do was to slip back up to Elizabeth's room and do another search. I didn't know what I might find, if anything—I'd been pretty thorough last time—but I wasn't sure what else to do.

I was about to grab a skeleton key and head upstairs when something caught my eye. It was two police officers, and they were escorting someone down the path to their launch.

John.

I raced to the back door and hurtled down the stone steps, huffing as I caught up with them. "Where are you taking him?" I asked.

"To the station, ma'am," the taller of the two told me, looking like he was assessing me for risk potential.

"Why?" I asked.

"Natalie, it's fine," John said. But something in his face told me otherwise.

"They're *arresting* you?" I breathed, feeling my lungs close up.

"It's a big mistake," he said. "One of the guests claimed she saw me in the inn last night, coming out of Boots' room."

"But you weren't," I said. Then I remembered the door I'd heard closing the night before, after the crash in the kitchen. Had that been John, leaving through the front door of the inn?

"I wasn't," he confirmed, as if sensing my doubt.

"Let's go," said the shorter of the two officers gruffly. As I stared in disbelief, they led my neighbor down the path, escorted him onto the launch, and untied the ropes. I stood staring as they revved the engine and headed toward the mainland, taking John farther and farther away from me.

TWENTY-THREE

My heart pounded as I walked back into the inn, struggling to breathe. *They'd just arrested John.* What was I supposed to do now? Did he have an attorney?

And why had they arrested him?

Marge wasn't in the living room—I assumed that meant she had gained access to the guest rooms—but most of the guests were there, attended by a stolid-looking officer in a too-tight polyester uniform. Conversation, as you might imagine, wasn't particularly bright; in fact, the silence was oppressive.

"Can I get anybody some coffee?" I asked, trying to act as if everything was normal, when in truth things were about as far from normal as possible. "There's tea over here, too," I said, feeling like a robot.

The dieters shook their heads—almost everyone was in the room, reading or staring out the window, including Elizabeth, who, uncharacteristically, was nose-deep in a rather dry-looking paperback, which must have been why she didn't notice them arresting my neighbor.

Sarah and Cat were sitting beside each other wordlessly, still looking stunned, while Bethany wore the same depressed look she'd had for days. Only Megan and Greg looked content in their seats by the corner, holding hands.

What was I going to do about John? *Elizabeth's busy*, I thought. *Why don't you go see what you can find in her room?*

"Let me know if I can get you anything," I sang out, then raced to the front desk and grabbed the second skeleton key.

I was halfway up the stairs before I realized that it might be a good idea to have something with me when I went into Elizabeth's room—like cleaning supplies. Since the police were gathered right down the hall and all.

I retraced my steps, tossing a couple of spray bottles and a sponge into a bucket, and headed back upstairs, almost running into Marge as I turned the corner at the top.

"What's that for?" she asked.

"Oh," I said, glancing at the officer outside Boots' door, "I thought I'd take care of some of the rooms, to help out."

"I've already done them two," she said, pointing to Elizabeth's and Vanessa's.

"Great," I lied.

"And you got the wrong stuff," she said, jabbing at the two bottles of window cleaner in my bucket.

"You're right," I said woodenly. "Silly me."

The officer down the hall was watching us, I realized, so I turned and greeted him. "Can I get you officers anything?" I called down to him, trying to sound relaxed, even though I felt so tense I might shatter at any moment. "Maybe a drink of water, or some tea?"

"I wouldn't object to a pot of tea, if you're offering," the red-haired man said with a smile.

"Let me just take care of a few things and I'll bring a pot right up," I said. "How many cups?"

"Three would be good," he said. "Thanks for offering." Marge gave me a dubious look as I turned back to her. She knew I was up to something. "I'll just go over the mirrors and windows up here, okay?" I said, feeling sweat spring up on my brow.

Marge gave me a slightly affronted look and harrumphed as she let herself into Sarah's room. I, on the other hand, walked as casually as I could to the end of the hall and unlocked the door to Elizabeth's room.

Once the door was locked behind me again, I made a beeline for the desk.

The stack of files had moved from the bottom drawer to the desktop, which made things very convenient for me. I tore through them all again, to see if there was anything new. Unfortunately, there wasn't—until I got to the last page of the press file.

The articles hadn't changed, but as I scanned the last one—the manslaughter case in Boulder, Colorado, I noticed several places where the name of the coach accused of the crime had been underlined. *Dereck Crenshaw*. I suddenly remembered the name Marge had told me Elizabeth was asking about on the phone the other day: *Eric Kershaw*.

Could Marge have misheard the name?

My eyes scanned the article again. Something else stuck out at me: *Mickelson*. I knew I'd heard someone mention that name before. But who?

I stared at the clipping one last time, and then, in a split second, everything clicked.

When I let myself out of Elizabeth's room a moment later, the policeman was no longer stationed outside Dirk's room, and Marge was nowhere to be seen. Should I go find the officer and share my suspicions?

No, I decided. First I'd confirm it.

I walked a short way down the hall and knocked at another door. When nobody answered, I put down my bucket of supplies and unlocked it, slipping into the room and locking it behind me.

The desk was my first stop, and my hands shook with excitement—and fear—as I pulled the drawers open one by one. But they were all empty.

Frustration mounting, I yanked open the nightstand drawers, again coming up empty. It wasn't until I got to the makeup kit in the bathroom that I found what I was looking for.

It was in the bottom of a makeup kit, and if I hadn't been looking for it, I never would have found it.

It was just a scrap of paper adhered to plastic—the remnants of a blister pack that had evidently been thrown away. But the letters 'edrine' were printed on it.

I set down the makeup bag and headed for the door, ready to tell the police what I knew. But just as I left the bathroom, the doorknob jiggled—and Cat walked into her room.

She narrowed her eyes at me.

"What are you doing here?" she asked, closing the door softly behind her.

"Just cleaning up a little," I said.

"You left your cleaning supplies outside," she said.

"I just realized that," I lied. "I was heading out to get them. Sorry to disturb you."

Her eyes flicked from me to the picture on her bureau, and mine followed involuntarily. It was of a teenaged girl, her eyes the same color as her mother's.

I dragged my eyes away a second too late.

"What are you doing in my room?" Cat asked again, her voice deadly quiet. Her face was eerily blank; it sent a chill down my spine.

"I told you. I was just cleaning."

"What were you looking for?"

I swallowed. "Nothing." She took a step toward me. "The police are right down the hall," I said, trying to forestall her from trying anything.

"No they're not," she said with a smile. "I just saw them heading downstairs."

"I'd better go get them tea, then," I said, walking toward the door and trying to pretend I didn't know she was a murderer.

"You're going to tell them, aren't you?" she asked in a dreamy voice.

"Tell them what?" I said, heart pounding in my chest. The air in the room had changed, and there was no doubt that I was dealing with a severely unhinged woman.

"He deserved it, you know. He killed my daughter, and never paid the price. If I didn't stop him, he would have killed again."

"I don't know what you're talking about," I lied.

"Yes, you do. You know. And then when Boots made the connection, I had to make her go away, too. She would have spoiled it all. Fortunately, the police believed me when I told them I saw your boyfriend leaving her room last night. And I sprinkled a tiny bit of sawdust in her room, just to be sure."

She was the reason they'd arrested him, I realized. Rage bubbled up alongside the fear inside me. "What connection did she make?" I asked, surreptitiously scanning the room for something I could use as a weapon. Now that she'd confessed, she'd never let me out of here alive—not if she could help it, anyway.

"My daughter's death," she said. "He poisoned my little girl, you know. Poisoned her, and walked away scot-free."

"How awful," I said consolingly, eyeing the door behind her. Could I get past her and raise the alarm?

"And the supplements," Cat went on. "She started making the connection after Dirk died. Something I said tipped her off—she came to ask me about it, last night. I had to drag her all the way back to her room, you know. I don't look strong," she said, her large eyes unfocused, "but a mother will do anything for her child. *Anything*," she whispered, stepping toward me.

"You changed your name," I said.

"That's right," she said. "After the divorce, I went back to my maiden name. Never liked Mickelson anyway. And it made it so much easier when I signed up for the retreat. The jerk didn't even recognize me—and he'd killed my child!" She was revving up again—her eyes burned in her pale face.

"How did you get Dirk to take the ephedrine?" I asked, stalling for time. *The lamp on the nightstand.* I took a step backwards,

249

edging toward it. She didn't have a weapon that I could see—but she'd managed to kill Boots without one. If I grabbed it and hit her over the head ...

"It was a problem, I'll admit," she said. "I needed to get him to take a lot of them. But he took all those supplements, you see, so I just ground up all those pills and stuffed his little capsules with them." She smiled at me—an awful, empty smile. "You made it so easy, leaving those keys down there where anyone could get to them. I did it while you were downstairs talking with your neighbor friend, and Vanessa." She paused. "She really should thank me, you know. If I didn't stop him, he would have killed again—and she would have been an accessory."

She'd poisoned him that first night, I realized.

"What did he do to your daughter?" I asked, hoping to jolt her out of her daze.

"She was so beautiful," Cat said. "She was the light of our lives. We were so proud of her when she joined the varsity team. And Dirk was her coach ... only he had a different name then. Dereck. Dereck Crenshaw."

The *Eric Kershaw* Marge had heard Elizabeth asking about on the phone the other day. Elizabeth had been onto him, too.

"So he gave your daughter too much of something?"

Cat nodded, the same haunted look on her face I'd seen the other day—and subconsciously recognized from the article I'd found in Elizabeth's room. "The same thing he died from. It was to help her win a race. Only she never crossed the finish line. She had a heart attack fifty yards in." Her face was stricken. "Her last race."

"So you were afraid he'd strike again," I said. "Why wait so long, though?"

"He changed his name," she said. "I didn't know where to find him—he disappeared after they dropped the charges."

"They dropped the charges?"

"No evidence," she said, her voice hard. "But I knew. I knew."

"How did you find him again?" I asked.

"I saw his picture in a magazine, and I recognized him immediately. He was back to his old tricks, killing again—and he never paid for what he did to my darling." Her eyes drifted to the photo of the bright-eyed girl on her dresser. "I signed up for this retreat and planned what I was going to do. And it would have worked, too." She seemed to remember suddenly that I was still in the room with her. "Still will."

She stepped toward me.

"Don't be stupid, Caterina. The police are right downstairs. They'll hear you—and besides, we're in your room."

"They'll never know," she said dreamily. "They won't hear, and I'll be sure to relocate your body when it's over. No one heard Boots with the pillow over her face. I hated to do it, but I had no choice." She advanced toward me, grabbing a pillow from the bed. I backed up, stumbling over a hitch in the rug. She darted forward, her hand closing on my arm just as I grasped the solid brass lamp.

I swung it at her, but she ducked. The shade glanced off her shoulder and tumbled to the floor. I swung again wildly, but missed. Then, with a strength that amazed me, Caterina shoved me onto the bed. I got one look at her wild eyes; there was nothing human left in her. Then she smashed the pillow into my face, throwing her body on top of it.

I struggled, thrashing against her, scratching at her arms, pulling at her shirt, trying to get her off me. But the pillow just came down harder.

My lungs burned, and I sucked in a deep breath—but there was no air. Nothing. A wave of dizziness overtook me—and the sudden, savage urge to live. I flailed at my assailant, but she was made of iron—unflinching, unmoving. Finally, I gathered all I had and pulled my right arm back, balled my hand into a fist, and swung with all my strength.

There was a cracking sound, and an explosion of pain in my hand.

But the pressure lightened.

I pushed against the pillow as hard as I could; it moved a bit, enough for me to get a lungful of air, before it came down hard, again.

I swung again, but hit only air. And again. I was about to succumb to darkness when my fist made contact one more time—and this time I heard the crack of the bones in my fingers. But the pressure faltered—this time, enough for me to shove the pillow off my face.

With the pillow off my nose and mouth, I gasped for breath and rolled off the bed, struggling to get to my feet. Caterina was up, blood running from her broken nose, eyes just as wild as before. She reached for the lamp on the floor—before I could stop her, she had it in her hand and was swinging it at me.

"Help!" I yelled, my voice hoarse. I ducked just in time and stumbled toward the door. "Help!" My voice sounded like it was coming from the bottom of a well.

"Shut up!" she hissed, advancing on me as I scrabbled at the door. I was trying to turn the knob when there was a crack, and pain exploded in my head.

"No," I said, my knees buckling beneath me. Then I was on the hard, cold floor, looking up at Cat's mad eyes as she dropped to her knees beside me, reaching for the pillow on the floor behind her. She smashed it into my face again, but I scooted backward and kicked out with everything I had, feeling the soft, sickening thud as my foot made contact.

There was a short gasp. Then the pillow fell away and Caterina crumpled to the floor beside me.

I was struggling to my feet when the doorknob jiggled. "Open up!" came a voice from the other side.

I reached for the knob, and realized hazily that the door was locked. It took three tries before I managed to slide the deadbolt back; then the red-haired cop exploded into the room.

"What happened?" he asked, taking in my wild appearance, the woman sprawled on the hardwood floor, blood leaking from her smashed nose.

"She killed Dirk," I whispered. "Ephedrine—in her makeup bag, in the bathroom. Killed Boots, too," I said. "John—he's innocent. She framed him."

"Calm down, ma'am," he said. "I need to get a paramedic out here—both of you look like you're in pretty bad shape."

"She's a murderer," I said, my voice hoarse. I pointed at the pillow on the floor beside Cat. "She tried to kill me with that. Just like she killed Boots."

"Let's get you settled down," he said, "and you can tell me everything. From the beginning."

TWENTY-FOUR

ONCE THEY'D MADE SURE I wasn't suffering from any potentially fatal injuries—I had a mild concussion from the lamp, and some bumps and bruises—I'd told the police everything I'd discovered. They'd searched Caterina's room, and after finding the scrap of ephedrine packaging in the bathroom—and getting something of a confession from Cat herself—they'd escorted her from the inn in handcuffs.

I knew because I'd heard her yelling all the way down to the path. "He deserved it!" she screamed. "He killed my daughter! My only child!" Then, a moment later, she started moaning. "Ashley. Ashley. I miss you so much…"

Goosebumps rose on my skin at the plaintive call. Her cries were heartrending—but not enough for me to regret that she was being escorted off the premises. The woman had, after all, just tried to kill me.

They took me to the mainland hospital for a checkup, then spent an hour or two quizzing me on the details of what had happened upstairs with Cat, but I was back on the island—and in my re-opened kitchen—in time to cook dinner. Gwen had insisted I lie down, but I couldn't bring myself to do it; concussion or no concussion, I still wanted to make things right at the inn. And I was still upset because I hadn't heard from John. I needed something to distract me.

Tonight, I'd decided, I was boiling up the lobsters Tom had caught earlier in the week. Of course we wouldn't be using melted butter, but I was looking forward to a dinner of the sweet, tender meat with fresh corn on the cob on the side.

Since three of our guests wouldn't be joining us, there were more than enough lobsters to go around, so I asked Gwen and Charlene to join us; Marge had already left for the day, and I hadn't been able to get in touch with her. I'd wanted to ask John, too, but he hadn't turned up. And there was no way I was going down to talk with him—even though Gwen told me he was back on the island. Why hadn't he come to see me? I wondered, feeling acid burn in my stomach.

Gwen had run upstairs to grab a sweater when I heard a male voice on the other side of the kitchen door.

I walked to the door, my heart in my throat, hoping it was John, and pushed it open.

Greg stood there, his broad back to me, talking on a cell phone.

"I'm telling you, I can't continue to represent your interests. Her behavior has been above reproach," he said, pacing back and forth across the peach and blue rug. "Even in very trying circumstances. But yours, sir—you ought to be ashamed of yourself."

There was silence yet again, and then he said, "You've been a serial adulterer! She told me about the phone bills, about the credit card charges for hotels, the trip to Hawaii with your 'business associate'. She knows you were planning to divorce her and abandon her, along with your only child. You were trying to entrap her when she was at her most vulnerable." His voice rose so that he was almost bellowing, and I eased the door partially closed.

There was another pause; then he said formally, "I must inform you that I am resigning from the case, effective immediately. I will return your deposit when I get back to my office." After another moment, he said, "And a very good day to you, sir!" and jabbed at a button on the phone with an index finger, breathing heavily.

I slid away from the doorway and busied myself shucking corn. So *that's* who Greg had been investigating! It hadn't been Dirk at all; it had been Megan!

Well, I thought as Gwen hurried down the stairs behind me, that was one mystery solved.

But there was still another that remained unresolved. And I wasn't thinking of the body in the lighthouse, either.

My eyes drifted to the window—and John's carriage house down the hill. I knew John had been released, but I still hadn't heard from him. And despite my relief at the discovery that he wasn't involved in Dirk's death—or Boots'—my heart ached that he hadn't come to see me.

Maybe, I thought, my heart feeling swollen and painful, it really was over between us.

"I almost forgot to tell you," Gwen said as she filled a huge pot with water. "Gertrude called again—so did someone from the Bangor paper. I told them both there had been an arrest, and that

256

you—and the inn—had nothing to do with it. You might want to talk to them, though."

"I'll call them tomorrow," I said, my eyes still glued to John's front door.

"I still can't believe her own friend killed her," Gwen said, shaking her head as she walked up beside me. "Dirk I can understand—but poor Boots. She didn't deserve what Cat did to her." Gwen paused, peering at me as I stood staring at a half-husked corncob. "Are you okay?"

"Fine," I said, swiping at my eyes and tearing off another wad of husk. "Just fine."

"Are you sure you don't want to go upstairs and lie down?"

"Positive," I said, pasting on a smile. "Let me just finish husking this corn and we'll put together a salad, okay?"

My niece assented, shooting me worried glances as she filled the second pot and pulled a bag of lettuce out of the fridge.

———

Just as I was about to put the first lobsters into boiling water—feeling guilty, as I always did, at being the agent of death—there was a knock at the kitchen door.

It was John.

I put the lobster back into the sink and walked over to answer it, feeling both numb and apprehensive at the same time.

He was wearing a red T-shirt and a pair of jeans, and the wind filled the steamy kitchen with his clean male scent as I opened the door.

"Hi," he said, his eyes darting to the lump above my right eye. He reached out to touch it, but I shied away.

257

"Come in," I said tonelessly, and as he closed the door behind him and slid into one of my kitchen chairs, I grabbed the lobster again.

"Are you doing okay?" he asked. "I heard she gave you a concussion."

"I'm fine," I said, closing my eyes as I put the first lobster into the pot.

"Good," he said.

The kitchen was silent except for the bubble of the water as I put the rest of the lobsters into the big pot and then dropped the corn into the smaller pot next to it. When everything was in, I set the timer and turned to look at him. "Why did they arrest you?" I asked.

"They found sawdust in Boots' room," he said. "Caterina put it there. She knew I was a suspect—she was trying to frame me."

I nodded, then took a deep breath. "I need to know, John," I said, focusing on his deep green eyes, his familiar, weathered face. "If you want to be with Vanessa, that's fine. But tell me the truth."

"I want to be with you, Natalie," he said, and I could hear the urgency in his voice. It pulled at something deep inside me.

"I want to believe you," I said. "But I can't."

"Why not?"

"Because I've seen you together. You hugged her, in the doorway of your house that night—when you argued with Tom." I looked away from him, at the grain of the wood on the floor. "And you called her 'sweetheart,'" I whispered.

He let out a long, deep breath. "Many years ago, we had a summer together. It was fun, but … we're not right for each other. We both know that."

I said nothing.

"After Dirk was found dead, Vanessa came to me with a problem—she asked me not to say anything about it."

"What problem?"

"Nat," he said. "If I tell you, you must promise not to breathe a word."

I swallowed. What could it be? Everyone knew she was having an affair with Tom. "Promise," I said.

"Vanessa is a bulimic," he said. "Her entire business is built on her ability to stay thin—and she's suffered from an eating disorder for years."

I blinked. "She eats and throws up?"

He nodded. "After every meal. Sometimes she takes laxatives, too—but she left them home on this trip. She's taking in almost no calories, and she's destroying her throat—that's why her voice is so rough sometimes. From the acid."

"You're kidding me," I said, trying to grasp the fact that beautiful, totally together Vanessa was actually spiraling out of control.

"She was going to try and get over it on this retreat, but she's been stealing food since she got here. She's so distraught she's almost suicidal."

I thought of the disappearing chocolate, the missing cookie dough—and the shifty look on Vanessa's face when she'd come into the kitchen the other day. "I never would have known," I said, leaning against the counter.

"She was struggling when she got here. She was getting so much attention for her program—book deals, attention from Oprah—and the whole thing was based on a lie. It was getting harder and harder for her to keep things together. Then, when Dirk died, she kind of went over the edge."

"So you've been counseling her," I said. "All those times she went to visit you, you were counseling her."

He shrugged. "She didn't have anyone else to talk to. And then there was this business with Tom, and that reporter following her around and asking all kinds of questions, on top of everything else. I wanted to tell you, but I'd promised not to."

"Why tell me now, then?" I asked.

He stood up and closed the distance between us. "Because I was afraid if I didn't, I'd lose you," he whispered.

As the corn bobbed in the pot next to me, he leaned down and kissed me gently. Warmth spread through me at his touch, and for the first time in days, I felt myself truly relax.

When we came up for air, I said, just to be sure, "There's really nothing between you and Vanessa?"

"No," he said. Then he reached for the pocket of his shirt. "I was planning on waiting awhile to do this, but I think this may be the time." As I watched, he pulled a little box out of his shirt; then he dropped to one knee in front of me and lifted the lid.

A small diamond glinted up at me from a bed of dark blue velvet.

"Natalie Barnes," he said, his voice husky with emotion, "will you marry me?"

At that moment, Gwen pushed through the kitchen door. She took in the scene and gasped—then, blushing, hurried back the way she had come.

I looked down at the man kneeling before me, his dark blond hair, the smile lines on the corners of his deep green eyes, the hopeful look in his face. I believed what he had told me about Vanessa; there had been no lie in his eyes.

And he had just asked me to marry him.

"I know it's kind of sudden," he said, the hope in his eyes starting to dim a little. "If you want to think about it..."

I thought of Vanessa, and the way he'd distanced himself from me after her arrival. I shook my head slightly, just thinking of it.

He seemed to deflate. "No?"

"No... it's not that. It's just..."

"You want to think about it?" he asked, looking hopeful again.

"Yes," I said, staring down at the ring he held in his hand. A small stone winked up at me from an antique silver setting.

"It was my grandmother's," he said.

I closed his hand around it and kissed him on the forehead. As much as I was yearning to say "yes," I couldn't. Not yet.

"Thank you for asking," I said. "Give me a little bit of time, okay?"

"As long as you need," he said. He rose to his feet, touching my chin gently, then tilted my head toward him and kissed me. I don't know how long the timer had been going off when he finally let go. And to be honest?

I really didn't care.

TWENTY-FIVE

Four months later...

As I poured a creamy tarragon dressing—full fat, thank good-ness—into a bowl filled with chopped onion, walnuts, and chunks of cooked chicken breast, I glanced out at the maple tree near the kitchen window and realized that the leaves had started to turn dusky red at the edges. It seemed that summer had begun just a few weeks ago. Now, too soon, it was almost over.

I had just finished scraping out the measuring cup when John came up and wrapped his arms around me, smelling of fresh wood from the boats he'd been carving down in his workshop. My heart, as always, skipped a few beats at his touch. "What are we cooking for dinner?" he asked, kissing the top of my head.

"I picked up some crab on the mainland yesterday," I said. "How do you feel about making crab cakes?"

"Sounds good to me," he said. "With a little remoulade sauce ... de-licious. How many guests?"

"Ten for lunch," I said. "If I'd known how good that lighthouse renovation would be for business, I would have pushed for it last year." The full meal service had helped too, I knew. Not long after our engagement—and after everything on the island had settled down—John and I had decided to turn the inn into a full-service establishment. I handled breakfast and lunches, and John, who was an excellent cook, took care of most of the dinners. And despite my fears that the murders at the inn would quash bookings, the opening of the lighthouse—and the still-unsolved mystery of the disappearing keeper and the skeleton in the hidden room beneath it—had caused a spike in tourism on Cranberry Island.

"Megan and Greg will be here this weekend, right?" he asked.

"On their honeymoon," I said. Evidently the two had continued to hit it off after leaving the island in the spring, and had recently celebrated their nuptials. Carissa was still warming up to the idea, but she was starting to come out of her shell—and even drop a few pounds—now that her biological father was out of the mix. Apparently Megan's ex-husband hadn't just been having affairs, but had been emotionally abusing both Megan and Carissa for years. "I hope Carissa warms up to the idea of a stepfather."

"She'll be here the second half of the week," John said, "so I guess we'll see how it's going."

"I still can't believe all that happened just a few months ago," I said.

"Things have changed a lot since then."

He was right. Not only had John and I gotten engaged—and taken the inn to a whole new level—but Vanessa had come clean about her bulimia and checked herself into a treatment facility.

It wasn't good news for Elizabeth, who had been planning to break the news—and a bunch of other dirt on the program—in a big article for the *Boston Globe*. Fortunately for Elizabeth, though, she instead got to do an exclusive on the murders at the inn, along with Dirk's shady past, and now she was a regular contributor.

To Vanessa's surprise, the announcement of her eating disorder had been more of a boost than a detriment—her story had landed her a six-figure book deal and guaranteed her a spot on several of the major morning talk shows. I'd seen an article about her in a magazine a few weeks ago, at the Somesville library. She was a bit plumper than the Vanessa I remembered, but just as beautiful—if not more.

I, on the other hand, had somehow managed to lose a few pounds over the hectic summer. Not enough to appease my doctor, of course, but since my numbers were in better shape, he couldn't complain too much. I hadn't been very successful cutting back my food intake, but the long walks John and I had been taking every evening after dinner had helped.

"It's different without Gwen here, isn't it?" he asked.

"Yeah," I said. Gwen had gone back to UCLA to finish her degree just two weeks ago, and although she'd be back to the inn—and to spend time with Adam—next summer, I already missed her. As did Adam, who was evidently running up a huge phone bill calling her twice a day.

"I ran into Adam yesterday, down by the pier. He was still mooning over Gwen—but when I managed to get him off the subject of your lovely niece, he told me Tom seems to be coming around."

"I'm glad to hear it," I said. Now that Vanessa was off the scene, Tom and Lorraine were working hard to put their marriage back

264

together, and they seemed to be making progress. I'd seen the entire family down at the store the other day; Tom had regained his customary twinkle, and even Lorraine had had a bit of a smile. They weren't out of the woods yet, but they were headed in the right direction.

I sighed, leaning back into John's arms. "All's well, that ends well. But duty still calls; I need to finish getting lunch ready," I said, although I was reluctant to separate from my handsome fiancé. The term was still an exciting one, even though I'd been using it for three months. We hadn't set an official date yet, but were thinking about tying the knot next spring.

"You can't spare just a few minutes?" he asked, nuzzling my neck in a way that made me forget all about the ten guests who would be heading to the dining room expecting lunch in just a few minutes.

I was about to surrender when someone hammered at the kitchen door. We both jumped; John released me, and I turned to see who was knocking. It was the town historian, her eyes bright with excitement.

"Hi, Matilda," I said, opening the door. She burst in, clutching a letter in her hand.

"Remember my friend up in Yarmouth?" she asked breathlessly.

I stared at her blankly.

"You know," she said. "The one who was going to look into the shipping records for me?"

"Oh, yeah." I focused on the letter. "Did you hear from her?"

"She just sent me the documentation," she said, showing me the pages, which were photocopies of what appeared to be a log of sorts, with archaic, faded handwriting. I squinted at the page, but it was hard to make out. "What is it?" I asked.

"It's hard to read, I know. But apparently there was a boat that ported in Halifax several times, up from Maine, during the 1830s and 1840s. It was called the *Stalwart*."

"And?" I asked.

"Well," she said. "The last time it docked was 1841, a few weeks after Harry disappeared. And do you know who was on it?" she asked, eyes sparkling.

"Who?"

"Three young African-Americans and a man named Harold Atherton."

"Harry," I said.

She nodded. "She's spent the last few months trying to track him down—found out that he bought a house in a small town called Lubeck."

"So he didn't die that night. He just escaped."

"And he married," she said, flipping through to another copy of an official document, dated 1842. "Here's the certificate. A woman named Emma Jones. And the church records show that they baptized a girl named Sadie Atherton, age eight, six months later."

"You're kidding me," I said.

"There's no way to be sure, but she probably took the surname 'Jones' to fit in. And here's the best part. The family stayed in Lubeck—one of the only families with African-American blood in the area. My friend went and talked with them, to ask them if they had heard any stories about their heritage. And you're never going to believe it ... but they did!" she said, cheeks flushed pink.

"How did you find all this out?"

"My friend was so intrigued by the story that she tracked down Harry's great-great-granddaughter ... she's in her late eighties now, but she remembers a story that her mother used to tell her, about how one of her ancestors escaped a black slave-catcher—that he'd almost caught them, but that they'd gotten away just in time."

"Did they say where it happened?"

"She didn't say it was in Maine, but there was a story about a lighthouse—how they escaped in the middle of the night, in a storm, in a boat that almost went aground … and barely made it to freedom."

"What about the other slave? James?"

"Apparently, he headed west to find work after they landed in Nova Scotia. The family doesn't know what his name was, and I haven't managed to track him down yet, but I'm working on it. I thought he might have been Sadie's biological father, but the way the family story goes, they weren't able to get her father out; he was sold to another plantation before they could make their escape."

"How sad," I said, feeling my heart tug for the little family. "Still, at least Emma and Sadie made a life for themselves." I thought about the drama that had happened so many years ago—and the still unsolved mystery on Cranberry Island. "Nothing about the body in the lighthouse, though?"

"No," she conceded. "But if you'd murdered someone—even if it was a slave-catcher—would you pass that information on to your children?" she asked.

"True," I said.

"The shipping records show them landing in Halifax a few weeks after Harry disappeared—and his name was on the register, along with three unnamed African-Americans. I think we can put the rest together."

"So?"

"The slave-catcher was chasing three slaves. After showing up on Cranberry Island looking for them, he was never seen again."

"You mean?"

"One of them must have killed him and hidden him in the room below the lighthouse, and then they all fled north. They must have been in a hurry if they left the doll and the log."

"And the manacles," I said, shuddering.

"Why would Harry leave?" John asked.

"Well, there was a murdered man on the premises, of course," Matilda said. "He could easily have left because of that. Or maybe it was because he fell in love with Emma," she said. "After all, records indicate they married. Also, if Otis Ball had found the way station, there was a risk that Harry's secret was out. He could be punished for harboring runaways, you know—in addition to murder, if they found the body."

My eyes strayed to the window—and the lighthouse in the distance. I thought of the mystery that had lain hidden under the floorboards for more than a century. "We never will know exactly what happened, will we?"

"Not for sure," she said. "But I think we know as much as we can."

"What are you going to do with the doll?" I asked, thinking of the well-loved little calico figure with the crudely drawn face.

"We're going to set up a little exhibit at the lighthouse," she said. "As one of the northernmost way stations on the Underground Railroad. We'll tell what we know of the story of Harry and Emma."

"Including the murder?"

She smiled coyly. "That, I'm afraid, we'll have to leave unsolved. Although we will report the finding of the body in the lighthouse.

Maybe some folks will put it together … but I don't want to cause trouble for the family."

A shiver ran down my back at the thought of those three people hiding in that underground room, over a hundred and fifty years ago. And the man who had died there. "Did you ever find out anything else about Hatley Cove?" I asked, thinking of the name that had come up several times in the log.

"I found one reference to it being on the west side of the island," she said, "but nothing exact."

"Smuggler's Cove is on the west side of the island," John said. He was right; the small, treacherous cove was carved into the cliffs not far from the inn.

"Again, we'll probably never know," Matilda said. "But it's a good bet that's where some of the slaves hid, at least some of the time."

Another mystery that would never truly be solved, I thought. I'd never found out the source of the light that had flashed the night before Dirk died, either, I realized. Some things, I supposed, would always remain like that; half-hidden, lost in the mists of time.

At least we knew what had become of Harry and the fugitive slaves, even if we would never know for sure who had killed the slave-catcher.

I thought of Caterina, who had murdered the man who had killed her daughter. A mother's love can be an incredibly powerful force—women will often sacrifice anything for their children's sake. Had the little girl's mother killed her would-be captor rather than see her daughter returned to slavery?

Only the little doll we had found would be able to tell us, I realized. And she would be forever mute.

Matilda sighed. "It's amazing, isn't it? The stories that have happened on this island."

John looked up at the clock, then at me. "Lunch is in twenty minutes, Nat. Why don't I set the table?"

"Oh, did I come at a bad time?" she asked, looking concerned.

"It's never a bad time," I said. "You're welcome to join us for lunch, if you'd like."

"Oh, no—I couldn't. Besides I've got to get back to the lighthouse—we're meeting with a few curators who are going to help design the new exhibit." She was brimming with enthusiasm.

"Thanks so much for coming by," I said, smiling at her. "It's wonderful how much you've turned up—I figured it was a dead end, but you've found an amazing amount of stuff."

"You never know, when it comes to history. A little digging in just the right place, and it's incredible what you can come up with!"

As she marched back up the hill, her envelope tucked under her arm, John carried a stack of plates to the dining room while I finished the chicken salad and sprinkled a few fresh tarragon leaves into the bowl.

The island had a rich history, I thought as I pushed through the swinging door to the dining room a moment later and set the bowl on the buffet. As did the inn I had purchased on instinct almost two years ago. An instinct, I thought, fingering the engagement ring I still hadn't gotten used to, that had opened up a whole new world to me.

I walked over to the window, taking in the sweeping view of the dark blue water and the craggy gray humps of the mountains on the mainland. I'd only known them for eighteen months, but already I felt, somehow, that I belonged to them.

My eyes drifted to the lonely spire in the distance. Since that night before Dirk's death, I'd never seen the light flash again—except for the one evening when the new light was unveiled. What had lit the light that night? I wondered. The ghost of the murdered slave-catcher, whose body had lain so long under the floor of the lighthouse?

I would probably never know.

As eerie as the run-down lighthouse had been the night I found Harry Atherton's hidden log, the derelict interior, I knew, had had new life breathed into it by Matilda and the tireless restoration team. Gone was the spooky feel I'd encountered in the spring; now, the windows were adorned with freshly painted window boxes, lobelia and nasturtiums a bright contrast to the fresh white clapboards of the keeper's house. Just as I had imagined that night.

Coming to the island had breathed new life into me, too, I thought, glancing back at John as he laid the last of the plates on a table, then joined me at the window.

"It's a dream come true," I said, relishing the moment—the clear fall day outside, the cozy inn I'd envisioned almost two years ago and struggled to bring to life—and the handsome man beside me, with whom I would be sharing my life.

He wrapped his arms tight around me, as if he would never let me go, and his lips touched my hair. A tingle passed through me.

"It is," he said softly. "But the best is yet to come."

THE END

271

THE RECIPES

PUMPKIN PIE OATMEAL

2 c. old fashioned oats

3¼ c. fat-free milk

¼ tsp. salt

6 tbsp. brown sugar (or Splenda brown sugar blend)

1½ c. pumpkin puree

1–2 tsp. pumpkin pie spice (to taste)

Add oats, milk, and salt to pot, heating until almost boiling. Lower heat to medium and cook five minutes, stirring occasionally. When oats have thickened, stir in brown sugar, pumpkin, and pumpkin pie spice to taste; cook on low an additional two minutes, or until pumpkin is heated. Serves four.

NAT'S "SWEET NOTHING" CHOCOLATE MERINGUES

3 large egg whites
⅛ tsp. cream of tartar
¾ c. granulated sugar
3 tbsp. unsweetened cocoa powder

Preheat oven to 375 degrees and cover 2 baking sheets with parchment paper. Put the egg whites and cream of tartar in a medium bowl. Beat with an electric mixer on medium speed until soft peaks form. Gradually beat in the granulated sugar, then beat on high speed until the whites are stiff and shiny. Sift cocoa over the egg whites and fold in until just blended. Drop tablespoonfuls of batter, 1 inch apart, on the prepared baking sheets, then bake for 30 to 35 minutes, or until the cookies are dry. Peel the cookies from the paper and cool on a wire rack. Store covered at room temperature. Makes 24 meringues.

SWEET AND TANGY TERIYAKI MARINADE

½ c. cooking oil or orange juice (or a mixture of both)

1 c. soy sauce

3 tbsp. brown sugar or honey (or Splenda brown sugar blend)

3 cloves garlic, minced

1 tbsp. grated ginger root (fresh)

2 tbsp. sherry or mirin

2 tsp. sesame oil

Combine ingredients; marinate meat or fish for 4–12 hours before cooking. (This is great for summer grilling—particularly with grilled peppers, onions, and summer squash on the side!) Marinade will cover six to eight chicken breasts, small steaks, or fillets.

SHRIMP SALAD
WITH CHIPOTLE-LIME-YOGURT DRESSING

Salad

> 1 16-oz. container mixed field greens
>
> 2 salad cucumbers, peeled and sliced
>
> 1 red bell pepper, diced
>
> 2 medium tomatoes, cut into wedges
>
> 4 green onions, diced (including greens)
>
> 1 avocado, sliced (optional)
>
> 1½ lbs. peeled, cooked shrimp

Divide greens among four large salad bowls; top with chopped vegetables and arrange shrimp over vegetables. Drizzle with Chipotle-Lime-Yogurt dressing.

Chipotle-Lime-Yogurt Dressing

> 1 (8-oz.) container fat-free Greek yogurt
>
> ½ cup adobo sauce from chipotle peppers
>
> 2 tbsp. fresh lime juice
>
> 2 tsp. lime zest
>
> ¼ tsp. cumin
>
> ¼ tsp. chili powder
>
> ½ tsp. seafood seasoning
>
> Salt and pepper to taste

Combine yogurt and adobo sauce in a bowl. Stir in the lime juice, lime zest, cumin, chili powder, and seafood seasoning. Add salt and pepper in desired amounts. Drizzle over salads; store extra in refrigerator. Serves four.

GRAY WHALE INN TURKEY CHILI

2 lbs. ground turkey

1 tbsp. olive oil

1 onion, chopped (about 1 c.)

1 tsp. ground coriander

2 tbsp. ground cumin

1 tsp. oregano

1½ tsp. salt

1 bay leaf

1 28-oz. can tomatillos, drained and chopped

2 4-oz. can diced green chiles

1 small jalapeño, seeded and finely sliced

2 c. chicken broth

2 15-oz. cans white beans

Optional toppings: Cilantro, avocado, Greek yogurt or sour cream, shredded cheese, chopped tomatoes

In a large saucepan or pot, brown turkey meat over medium-high heat (use a spray of olive oil if it sticks). Drain and set aside. Heat olive oil over medium heat and saute onions until softened. Add turkey, coriander, cumin, oregano and salt, stirring to combine. Add remaining ingredients, except white beans, reduce heat and simmer, uncovered 45–50 minutes. Gently stir in beans and cook for another 30 minutes. Serve with optional toppings, and/or with cooked brown rice. Makes six to eight servings.

NAT'S MIDNIGHT MINT BARS

2 eggs, beaten

½ cup melted butter

1 cup sugar

2 oz. unsweetened or semisweet melted chocolate

½ tsp. peppermint extract

½ cup all-purpose flour

Mint Frosting

2 tbsp. softened butter or margarine

1 tbsp. cream

1 c. confectioners' sugar, sifted

1 tsp. peppermint extract

A few drops red or green food coloring (optional)

Chocolate Frosting

1 oz. semisweet chocolate, melted with 1 tbsp. butter

10 crushed peppermint starlites or 2–3 crushed candy canes

Combine eggs, ½ cup melted butter, and granulated sugar; beat well. Add the 2 ounces of melted chocolate and ½ teaspoon peppermint extract; stir until well blended. Stir in the flour and blend well.

Pour into a greased and floured 9-inch square baking pan. Bake at 350° for 25 to 30 minutes.

Blend the 2 tablespoons butter and the cream; add confectioners' sugar, 1 teaspoon peppermint extract and optional food coloring, then spread over the cooled bars. When frosting is firm, mix chocolate and melted butter; spread over the bars and sprinkle with crushed peppermints. Place in refrigerator until topping is firm, then cut into small bars. Makes 24 bars.

ABOUT THE AUTHOR

Although she currently lives in Texas with her husband and two children, Agatha-nominated author Karen MacInerney was born and bred in the Northeast, and she escapes there as often as possible. When she isn't in Maine eating lobster, she spends her time in Austin with her cookbooks, her family, her computer, and the local walking trail (not necessarily in that order).

In addition to writing the Gray Whale Inn mysteries, Karen is the author of the Tales of an Urban Werewolf series. You can visit her online at www.karenmacinerney.com.